Parsley, Sage, Rosemary, and Crime

Too Many Crooks Spoil the Broth

TAMAR MYERS

Parsley,

Sage,

Rosemary,

and Crime

DOUBLEDAY

New York London Toronto Sydney Auckland

PUBLISHED BY DOUBLEDAY
a division of Bantam Doubleday Dell Publishing Group, Inc.
1540 Broadway, New York, New York 10036

DOUBLEDAY and the portrayal of an anchor with a dolphin are
trademarks of Doubleday, a division of Bantam Doubleday Dell
Publishing Group, Inc.

Library of Congress Cataloging-in-Publication Data

Myers, Tamar.
Parsley, sage, rosemary, and crime / Tamar Myers. — 1st ed.
p.   cm.
I. Title.
PS3563.Y475P37   1995
813'.54—dc20   95-14704
CIP

ISBN 0-385-47140-8
Printed in the United States of America
October 1995
First Edition

1   3   5   7   9   10   8   6   4   2

For my parents, with love and respect

I would like to acknowledge the wise, tempering hand of my editor, Judy Kern, the sweet temper of my agent, Nancy Yost, and the temper tantrums I did *not* throw when my husband, Jeffrey, made his own astute suggestions.

Parsley, Sage, Rosemary, and Crime

One

I SHOULD HAVE KNOWN there would be trouble when a man who introduced himself as Bugsy showed up one morning and offered to buy the PennDutch Inn.

"It's not for sale," I said.

"Lady, everything's for sale. For the right price."

I thought about that for perhaps three seconds, and came up with three things that were definitely never going to be for sale: my virtue, Grandma Yoder's hand-cro- cheted lap robe, and, of course, the PennDutch Inn. Of these three, I guess I'd have to say that the inn would be the last to go. I mean, how could I ever sell the place where four generations of my family had been born, and at least a couple of generations had died?

"You couldn't name a figure that high," I said to Bugsy.

Bugsy pulled a little notepad out of his suit pocket and

scribbled down some numbers. "An offer you can't refuse," he said with a smirk.

I refused.

Bugsy got busy scribbling again. "Playing hardball,
eh?"

"I don't even play Ping-Pong with strangers." But just
to hedge my bets, I glanced at the scrap of paper. My
heart began to pound as if I'd just played five games of
Ping-Pong at the church social. I may even have swayed a
little.

"It's a great deal," said Bugsy. "I mean, this place is a
dump. It's gonna have to be totally demolished anyway.
That there's a lot of moola for a joint like this."

That did it. That hiked my hackles. The PennDutch
Inn is anything but a dump. It only barely qualifies as
rustic. Sure, it's over a hundred and fifty years old, but
the inevitable nicks and scratches garnered over that century and a half give it that certain special *patina*. That's
what that yuppie reviewer wrote in her column, the one
who made the PennDutch the most famous inn of its
kind in the eastern half of the country.

"Scram," I said sweetly. "Get lost. Take a long walk
down a one-way road."

"Do you know who the hell you're talking to?" Bugsy
had grabbed both lapels of his suit and was tugging outward at them, apparently in a vain attempt to make himself appear bigger.

"Sure, I know who I'm talking to," I said. "I'm talking
to a rather skinny young man with a large whitehead on
his left nostril who's wearing a gray polyester suit that
needs pressing badly." Honesty is my forte.

Bugsy didn't blink. "Okay, lady. If you don't want to
sell, how about leasing the joint?"

"No need," I said. "I already rent rooms. By the week.

And everything's been booked for the next two years. Now, like I said, scram."

Bugsy didn't budge. "I don't want to rent a room, lady. I want to lease the place. The entire joint."

"They give free hearing tests at the high school on the first Tuesday of every month," I informed him.

Bugsy didn't back off. "I want to lease this place for eight weeks, for half of what I was willing to buy it for."

I decided to trot on down to the high school myself. It had been a while since I'd had my ears checked. "Would you please repeat what you just said?"

Bugsy obligingly backtracked.

"Now, why would you want to do that?" I asked. I was born forty-four years ago, and while I haven't slept my way around the block like my sister, Susannah, I have been around it a couple of times.

"It's simple," said Bugsy. "We're filming a movie. Reels and Runs Productions. I'm the advance man. We want to use your inn as the location."

Okay, so that in itself excited me, but not so much that I was ready to throw all caution to the wind. Susannah has told me that there are movies in which . . . well, never mind. But if anybody did that at the PennDutch Inn, even if it were just acting, Grandma Yoder's ghost would never leave me alone. "What kind of movie will it be?" I asked.

Perhaps spotting my weakness, Bugsy began to blather. "It will be a full-length feature film, of course. We've got some first-rate Hollywood talent lined up. The producer is—"

"What is the movie about?"

Bugsy burped. "Murder, of course. You know, those two that happened here."

I should have known. He meant the double murders last year, which got written up in a book by some dilettante author who lives all the way down in South Caro-

lina. You remember, the ones that happened the week I
inadvertently rented the inn to a hunting party *and* a
group of animal rights activists on the same weekend.

"I'm assuming, then, that you are prepared to buy the
rights to the story as well," I said sagely. Just because I
don't watch much television doesn't mean I'm illiterate.

Bugsy appeared baffled. "Rights? What rights? Lady,
this isn't a docudrama. This is a feature-length Hollywood
production."

"All the same, Mr. Bunny, you need to have Susannah's
and my permission, not to mention that a whole host of
others are going to have to give their approval before
Reels and Runs can run those reels."

"The name's Bugsy," he said belligerently. He glanced
down at his notepad and pretended to scan a few pages.
"Ah, my mistake, Miss Yoder. This movie, *The Quilted
Corpse*, isn't going to be about those exact murders, it was
simply inspired by them. Actually, there are five murders
planned, and the victims are all men, so you see, it's not
at all the same."

"Nevertheless, Mr. Bugsy, if my sister and I find ourselves portrayed in that movie, we will, of course, be compelled to sue."

"Sue away," babbled Bugsy blithely, "because, like I
tried to tell you, you aren't even in this one."

My mind flicked back to the real murders, and the period since then. It was, of course, a horrible ordeal for
survivors and victims alike, but afterward, business picked
up quite a bit. You wouldn't believe the number of folks
who want to sleep in the rooms where the murders happened, or even in the very bed where Susannah found
the corpse clutching Mama's best Dresden Plate quilt.

"Even if your movie was only inspired by the real
murders, this kind of publicity could give my inn a bad
reputation," I said evenly.

"Which is why I'm willing to pay half of the buying price I quoted," said Bugsy. He looked hopeful.

"Make that two-thirds of the high figure you quoted, plus me and my sister get to remain at the inn, and we have a deal."

Bugsy didn't balk. "Deal. Now, of course, we may need to gut a few walls and raise a few ceilings, you understand. For the camera and lighting equipment and all."

"Gut one wall and die," I said, or something to that effect. I know, I am an Amish-Mennonite with a long heritage of pacifism, but I have human limitations, and Bugsy was bumping into my boundaries. If I don't stand up for myself, who will? Not my sister, Susannah, that's for sure. She hardly stands up at all anymore if she can help it.

Bugsy began to bargain. "Look, we'll make as few structural changes as possible, and whatever changes we make, we'll change back to the original before we're through. You won't even be able to tell that we've been here. And, of course, you'll have full approval and veto power over any changes in advance."

I wasn't buying Bugsy's bit. "How can you replace a one-hundred-and-fifty-year-old wall with a new one and still have it be the same?"

Bugsy was unabashed. "Easy. That's called synthomaterialistic substitution. It's just one of the many wonders of Hollywood."

"Make that three-quarters of the price you quoted and we have a deal. And, of course, I'd still have veto power."

Bugsy beamed. "Of course. And it's a pleasure doing business with you, Mrs. Yoder."

"That's Miss. Miss Magdalena Yoder."

"Name's Steve."

"Steve Bugsy. It has a certain ring to it," I said charitably.

Bugsy had been bluffing. "It's Steven Freeman, not Steven Bugsy. Bugsy is a Hollywood thing."

I tried not to frown. Susannah says she could plant corn kernels in my frown furrows. "I am not familiar with the Hollywood scene, Mr. Freeman. But here in Hernia, Pennsylvania, we tend to be straightforward."

Bugsy bellowed in apparent delight. "You're a gas, Miss Yoder. Say, do you always look like this?"

"Like what?" I glanced quickly down at my long-sleeved blue dress and my sensible shoes. Unless I had another piece of broccoli caught between my two front teeth, I was sure I looked just fine.

Bugsy belched again. "You look, uh . . . authentic, Miss Yoder. You ever do any acting?"

Being the gracious and cheery owner of a trendy and very busy inn *is* a full-time acting job. But outside of that, I'm sure my experiences didn't qualify at all. Except for the occasional rerun of *Green Acres,* which I managed to catch on Susannah's little black and white portable, I didn't even watch TV.

Bugsy barged ahead before I could answer. "Never mind. If you want it, I'm sure you'll get the part. Of course, we'll have to give you a screen test first."

"Will they be true and false questions, or multiple choice?" I asked in all sincerity. Just as long as they weren't essay questions, I stood a chance.

"It's not that kind of a test, Miss Yoder. It's a test to see how you come across on the screen. The movie screen. We just shoot some film and have you say a few words."

I should have said "Get behind me, Satan." Instead, I said, "Come on in, Bugsy, and I'll get you a cup of brew." I meant coffee, of course.

"Vanity of vanities, all is vanity," said the author of Ecclesiastes, and he was right. If I hadn't been so vain the day I met Steven Freeman, alias Bugsy, there wouldn't have been a third murder to add to the PennDutch's growing list. And this third murder was to be the most gruesome of them all. What follows is exactly what happened.

Two

HERNIA, PENNSYLVANIA, is a nice place to live, but you wouldn't want to visit there. Unless you have family, or get your kicks out of being comatose, there isn't much to do. Yoder's Corner Market and Miller's Feed Store are the only two commercial establishments in town worth noting, at least since Bob's Gas Station stopped selling Ho-Hos and bottles of Yoohoo. Most of Hernia's workforce spend their weekdays in nearby Bedford or Somerset. Their summer evenings are spent on their front porches, their winter evenings in front of a fire. They are, by and large, a conservative, religious lot who are either very happy or too ignorant to know better.

Norah Hall, the town's most accomplished gossip, and therefore statistician, informs me that there are only fifty-three television antennas scattered about town. There just happen to be three hundred and eleven residences in Hernia, a mountain town that doesn't get cable. According to Norah, then, only a fourth of Hernia's fifteen hundred and twenty-eight residents watch TV on a regular basis. That figure does include Anna Guildersleeve, who at last count was said to harbor thirty-seven different personalities in her one rather diminutive person. So much for statistics.

My point is that when the news that Runs and Reels Productions was going to be filming a movie at the PennDutch Inn reached the ears of Hernia's inhabitants, which it somehow did within a matter of hours, the town was sharply divided in its reaction. Some people saw the impending event as their one big opportunity at stardom. Others felt very strongly that the moral fiber of Hernia was at stake, and that my soul, in particular, hung by a slender thread above the eternal flames of hell. A townwide prayer meeting was called at the First Mennonite Church on North Elm Street the very evening of Bugsy's first visit. I would have attended that meeting myself except that Norah Hall and her daughter Sherri got in the way.

I was, in fact, just reaching for my front doorknob, when the door opened, and the pair of them burst in.

"Is he here?" asked Norah breathlessly.

"What's he like?" wheezed Sherri. She was a fat little girl, not a day over twelve, and was dressed in something like a belly dancer's costume. A Viking belly dancer, that is. She had a pair of gold foil cones positioned over her undeveloped breasts, and another pair fastened to her head like horns.

"Well, where is he?" demanded Norah.

"He's in the kitchen. What do you want with him?" I asked calmly.

"Mama wants me to perform for him," said Sherri.

"Then perform away," I advised. "He can hear you in there, and besides, he'll be out in a second."

"Hit it, then," barked Norah.

Sherri put her hands on her hips and began gyrating, right then and there, in the middle of my lobby. "Like a virgin!" she sang out.

"Not hardly," I said.

Sherri performed a few more bars and then stopped in mid-gyre. "Where is he?" she whined. "Why isn't he coming out?"

"Go get him," said Norah crossly to me.

I decided to humor her. Mose Hostetler is my seventy-four-year-old Amish friend and neighbor. He and his wife, Freni, both work for me at the PennDutch, she as my cook, he as my handyman and milker of cows. Both Mose and Freni are related to me in more ways than Julia Child can prepare chicken. They are, of course, related to each other. The bloodlines of most Amish, and those Mennonites descended from them, are so tangled and intertwined that most of us are our own cousins. This enables me to attend a family reunion when I am, in fact, the only one present.

"Mose, you have a couple of visitors," I said, trying to keep a straight face. "They want to see you in the lobby."

"English?" asked Mose innocently. He meant anyone who was not Amish.

"Very," I said. "Two female visitors."

Freni, who had been scrubbing grease off the back of the stove, straightened and stared our way. Mose is about as likely to have an affair as he is to run for president, but Freni keeps a close eye on him anyway.

"What do the English want?" asked Mose. He is as shy as his wife is not.

"Just hurry up and go out there," I urged. "They're demanding to see you."

Mose tucked his thumbs nervously under his suspenders and, with me leading the way and Freni bringing up a very ample rear, we plodded out into the lobby.

"Hit it!" cried Norah again.

Obediently Sherri began to gyrate and wail. I'd once seen a cat go through the exact same motions and make pretty much the same sounds. Of course, it had been hit in the midsection by our barn door.

"God in heaven!" cried Mose, who turned and fled before the blush could spread across his cheeks.

"Sodom and Gomorrah!" gasped Freni. She started to follow her husband back to the kitchen, but just like Lot's wife, turned to take another look.

"That wasn't the director!" screamed Norah. "That was just an Amishman!"

"And he's my man," Freni screamed back.

Fondly, I shoved Freni back into the kitchen. "What director are you talking about, Norah? You said you wanted to see the man in the kitchen."

"Don't give me that, Magdalena!" she snapped. "The one who was here this morning. Where is he? Where have you hidden him?"

I smiled patiently. "That wasn't a director, dear. That was an advance man."

"A what?"

"An advance man. Like a scout. He was just leasing the inn in advance. They're not going to start shooting the movie for another six weeks."

"Are you sure?" Although it was a question, there was a hint of a threat woven in there somewhere. As Hernia's premier gossip, Norah Hall wields a great deal of local power.

"Of course I'm sure," I said smoothly. "And when the producer does show up, you'll be the first on my list to call. Although, why, I can't for the life of me figure out. The movie is going to be about the murders that happened here last year, and nobody involved was under twenty-one.''

"Sherri is quite advanced for her age,'' said Norah hotly. "Sherri, stick out your chest for Miss Yoder.''

Sherri stuck out her pudgy but otherwise undeveloped chest, and the gold foil cones bobbled in response.

"Nobody involved in those murders dressed even remotely like that,'' I felt compelled to point out. "And as far as I know, none of us sang either.''

"Ha! Just like I thought. You are so naive,'' said Norah. "When you go to auditions, you have to maximize your opportunities.''

"Uh-huh.''

Norah shook her head in disgust. "You still don't get it, do you? Maybe the director won't want Sherri to act in this dumb movie, but if he sees what she's capable of, he could keep her in mind for future possibilities.''

"Why, you should be ashamed, Norah Hall,'' I said with genuine concern.

Norah stared at me. I once saw that look on one of our cow's faces, when Mose forgot to turn off the milking machine. "You idiot, Yoder! Come on, Sherri, let's get out of here!''

"Bundle up, dear,'' I urged the ingenue. Summer chest colds are no picnic.

The two English left amid a slamming of doors and a muttering of words I wouldn't even contemplate repeating. As for me, I simply settled in my favorite rocking chair, across from the check-in desk, and put my mind to work on how to tell some of the country's richest and most influential people that their reservations were being canceled, beginning four weeks from now.

I had just decided to be shy with Sly and a bit of a grump with Trump, when my sister, Susannah, came billowing into the lobby. Susannah always billows when she moves. She wears enough fabric to clothe a small third-world country, and she wears it tossed and draped about her in no apparent design. On a windy day Susannah takes two steps backward for every step forward.

When she spotted me sitting there, minding my own business, Susannah swirled to a sudden stop. "How dare you ruin my life, Mags?" she accused.

I looked up calmly from my reservations list. "What did I do this time?"

Susannah stomped one of her slender but rather long feet. This act was accompanied by the emission of a sharp, high-pitched bark. Of course, it wasn't Susannah who barked, but her pitiful excuse for a pooch, Shnookums. I love dogs, but Susannah's dog doesn't deserve the name. For one thing, it is smaller than a teacup. Ninety percent of it is bulging, nervous eyes, and the other ten percent is voice box. And somewhere in those figures you have to allow room for the world's most active sphincter muscle. Susannah carries this yipping, shivering, twelve-ounce creature everywhere she goes, and conceals it in those swirling, billowing clothes. Of course, that isn't hard—Susannah could conceal a Great Dane in her outfits. Shnookums generally gets to ride in one of Susannah's half-empty bra cups, however. That is something a Great Dane could never do. Susannah has often threatened to get a second little rat dog to ride in her other cup, to balance the load. Personally, I think an apple or an orange would make a lot more sense.

Susannah stamped her foot a second time, and Shnookums yelped again. "It isn't fair!" my sister cried. "The whole town found out about this movie deal before I did. And I'm your flesh and blood!"

"Don't remind me," I said sweetly. "And just where were you when the whole town was finding out?"

"I had to go to Pittsburgh, Mags. For a job interview."

That was certainly news to me. Susannah doesn't have her own car, and we don't subscribe to the Pittsburgh papers. "What job? And how did you get there?"

"It's a modeling job. A *real* modeling job."

Mama would have been proud of me. I didn't laugh. Never mind that Susannah has a body like a punctured air mattress, and is on the shady side of thirty—so shady that even mushrooms don't grow there. "Well, did you get the job?" I asked charitably.

Susannah rolled her eyes so far back into her head that if she had a brain she could have seen it. "You're so provincial, Mags. These things take time. They have to study my portfolio. And then there are callbacks and things."

I nodded sympathetically. I knew she hadn't gotten the job. "Who took you into Pittsburgh?" I asked dangerously.

"Melvin Stoltzfus," Susannah said. She said it as a challenge, and I accepted it as such.

Melvin Stoltzfus has been Susannah's boyfriend for almost a year now. Rumor has it that Melvin was kicked in the head as a teenager while trying to milk a bull. Of course both Melvin and Susannah deny this, but the truth remains that Melvin is so stupid, he once mailed a gallon of ice cream, by parcel post, to his favorite aunt, who lives in Harrisburg.

Mama and Papa would never have approved of Melvin Stoltzfus, but they're dead now. They died needlessly in a mishmash of sneakers and pasteurized milk when the car they were driving was squashed between two trucks in the Allegheny Tunnel on the Pennsylvania Turnpike.

At least my parents, in their wisdom, had seen to it that the farm was left in my name until such time as I deemed Susannah responsible. This, in effect, made me Susannah's caretaker. It is a position that I hate almost as much as Susannah does. But my sister is a long way from being a responsible adult, and I will not capitulate and throw away my inheritance just to get her off my back. I do recognize, however, that there is very little I can do to speed up her maturation. And in all honesty, I must say that as much as I disapprove of Melvin, I have to admit that Susannah seems faithful to him, which in this day of AIDS is a step in the right direction.

"Well, at least Melvin found his way back to Hernia," I said. It wasn't meant as a criticism. Melvin once took a wrong turn in Bedford and ended up in Albany, New York. I know that none of us is perfect, but you would expect more from the man who is Hernia's chief of police.

"Forget Melvin!" snapped Susannah.

"Gladly."

"I mean, why didn't you tell me a famous Hollywood director was going to be here holding auditions?"

"You must have talked to Norah *before* she dragged little Sherri down here. Susannah dear, there was no big Hollywood director here today. The only man from Hollywood here today was an advance man, a location scout. The rest of the team won't even arrive for another four weeks."

"You told Norah six!"

You see what I mean about Norah Hall? Even after she'd been here, and found only an Amishman, she persisted in spreading rumors about some big-shot director. Now, rumors can often be good for business, but the kind of phone calls this rumor generated didn't add as much as a penny to my pocket. Even as Susannah was standing there, the most annoying of the calls came in.

"Hello, PennDutch," I said somewhat irritably.

"Magdalena, is that you?"

It sounded a little like Bette Midler, but then again, I couldn't be sure. "That depends. Who are you?"

"This is Martha. You know, Martha Sims, Pastor Sims's wife."

"Then this isn't Magdalena," I said, and hung up. Martha Sims has the intelligence of a goldfish, and the personality to match. Since Hernia is such a small town, I know virtually everyone in it, but I would know Martha under any circumstance, because it was her husband, Orlando Sims, who tied the knot between Susannah and her ex-husband. The Simses are Presbyterian, and I have nothing against that, except that it was Susannah marrying a Presbyterian, and then divorcing one, that started my sister on a long and twisted road away from the traditions of her forefathers. Of course, there may have been other factors involved.

The phone rang again almost the second I hung it up. "This is the PennDutch," I said as mechanically as I could. "I cannot take your call now because I'm on the—"

"Magdalena, that is you. Don't hang up now, Magdalena. It wasn't Orlando's fault that your sister's marriage broke up. Listen, dear, about that producer you've got out there, may I speak to him?"

"It's the director you want to speak to, not the producer," I said, "only this one is not a director, but a location scout, and besides which, he isn't even here."

Now, that should have made sense to your average human being, but like I told you, Martha Sims can only look forward to being average. "When will the producer be back?" she asked.

"A week from Monday, at two forty-five P.M.," I said helpfully.

"Thanks," said Martha sincerely. "Please tell him that I called, and that I'll be back in touch with him then."

"Will do." I hung up the phone.

Fifteen phone calls later I unplugged the thing and staggered off to bed. If I'd had any sense at all, I'd have used the phone one more time and called Bugsy to cancel our arrangement. But it was from Melvin Stoltzfus's paper I had copied that one time I cheated in grammar school. What more can I say?

Three

FOUR WEEKS LATER to the day, Bugsy showed back up on my doorstep.

"Yes? What is it?" I inquired.

"It's me, Yoder, Bugsy. You know, Steven Freeman."

I stared hard at the man. Actually, there were three men: one who could possibly have been Bugsy; one who was very tall despite a pronounced stoop; and a short one who was so hairy that he undoubtedly plugged the shower drain with one usage. The guy who vaguely resembled Bugsy did have a whitehead on his nose, but it was now on the other side. None of the men was wearing a gray, shiny suit.

"Do you have any ID?"

Steven smiled. He whipped out a driver's license with a photo that looked more like him than real life. And in that picture he was wearing a gray, shiny suit.

"Come in," I said graciously.

"Yoder, this is Arthur Lapata, the director. *The* Arthur Lapata."

"Is there more than one?" I asked innocently.

Steven still smiled. "And this is the assistant director, Donald Manley."

"That's Don, darling," said the short, hairy man. He reached out to press the flesh, but I refrained, fearing that my fingers would become hopelessly entangled in his knuckles.

Steven smirked knowingly. "Well, today's the big day. Our equipment trucks will be pulling in at any moment, and we'll start to set up shop. What do you think, Arthur?"

The Arthur Lapata had been glancing around the lobby, and he looked pretty satisfied to me. The lobby of the PennDutch, along with all its rooms, is decorated with genuine Amish furniture and tools. Grandma Yoder would have laughed at the concept of a ceramic goose with a bow around its neck, and she would have viewed as absolutely idolatrous the little Amish boy and girl figurines that are so popular in gift shops.

"I don't know, Art," said Don, shaking his hoary head, "it looks a little too plain to me."

"We are called the 'plain people,' " I pointed out quickly.

Don ignored me. "I think we should have our people kitsch it up a bit. Maybe hang some corn cobs and grape bunches from the ceiling. That kind of thing."

"It's not supposed to be a sukkah," sniffed Steven.

Hairy Don ignored him as well. "That's it, Art, we'll kitsch up the joint a bit. Give it that kind of Lancaster look. Make it obvious that it's Amish we're dealing with here."

He pronounced it *AYE*-mish, which grates on my

nerves something awful. "That's *AH*-mish," I said crossly, "and the only kitsch around here is the kitchen."

Hairy Don laughed but said nothing. Neither did *the* Arthur, although I thought I saw him nod at Steven. Whatever their communication, Steven grabbed me roughly by the arm and pulled me rudely aside.

"Look, Yoder, you've got to straighten up your act. These are the big boys you're playing with. They know their jobs."

"But Amish don't hang corn cobs and grape bunches from their ceilings," I protested.

Steven snickered. "They do if Arthur Lapata says so. We'll put in pink plastic flamingoes, and they'll be Amish ones, if that's what Arthur wants."

"But you said that I have the power to veto any changes," I reminded him.

Steven smirked. "Those were structural changes we agreed to, not decorative changes. Did you read the contract you signed?"

I confessed that I had not. I had looked at it but not actually read it. The hen prints in my chicken yard would be easier to read.

"There you have it, then. I suggest you go and read your contract like a good girl." Steven smiled.

Boy, did that put a bee in my bonnet! Steven Freeman was half my age, and he had the nerve to call me "girl." Why, I was a full-grown woman before he was even a gleam in his father's eye. "Look, buddy-boy," I said without being too rude, "I am not a girl. I am a woman. I am a woman old enough to be your mother. Is that clear?"

Steven's smile soured. "I was hoping you wouldn't be a problem, Yoder. But if you persist in getting in the way, we'll simply have to ban you from the set."

It was my turn to smirk. "That will be a little hard to

do, since part of the deal was that Susannah and I keep our rooms."

"Then stay in your rooms. Just stay off the set."

I felt myself losing ground. Literally. "What about the screen test you promised me?"

Steven shrugged. "What about it? It may well be that our casting needs have changed since last time we spoke."

I will not be backed into a corner in my own home, especially not by a pipsqueak like Steven Freeman. Instead of tugging on my lapels like Steve had done, I thrust out my certifiably scrawny bosom and drew myself up to my full five feet ten inches. "And you, Mr. Freeman, may find that your transportation needs have changed by tomorrow morning."

Steven scoffed. "Like you really scare me, Yoder. We have our own trucks and equipment."

It was my turn to smirk. "That road out there is Hertzler Lane. It is not a public road. It was paid for and is maintained by the families that live along it. Eleven families in all."

"So? How hard do you think it would be for me to convince just one of those families to cooperate?" Steven began rubbing his thumb and forefinger together.

I smiled. "Well, let's see. Five of the families are Hertzlers. They're related to me three times on Papa's side of the family and one on Mama's. Two of the families are Speichers. They're related to me four times on Mama's side, and twice on Papa's. Then there're the Yoders—"

"There will be an open casting call for extras and minor supporting roles at ten A.M. in the lobby, the day after tomorrow. I hope you can make it."

"See you then," I said brightly.

Steven strode off without another word.

I sinned then. It wasn't lustful thoughts that filled my heart, but thoughts of murder.

By nine A.M. of casting day there were more than three hundred people lined up in my driveway. A row of cars snaked out to the road and then split like a two-headed serpent down Hertzler Lane in both directions for as far as I could see. That there weren't any cars actually parked on the lawn was only due to the fact that Susannah and I had chased them off with our pitchfork. Apparently no one in Hernia or Bedford wanted a role in the movie badly enough to get their car scratched for it.

As for the Big Boys, as I had come to call them, they were probably still sacked out in their motel rooms in Bedford.

"Undoubtedly they have harlots in their rooms doing unspeakable things," I said crossly to Susannah.

"Those are starlets, Mags, not harlots. And don't knock it until you've tried it."

"Mama would turn over in her grave if she heard you talk like that," I said reproachfully.

"Mama was a sexual being herself," said Susannah.

I clamped my hands over my ears. Partly it was to shut out Susannah's wicked insinuations, and partly it was to shut out Norah Hall's complaining voice.

Norah and little Sherri must have arrived while it was still dark, or perhaps they had even spent the night in my driveway. At any rate, Mose says he saw their car parked there when he came by to do the milking at a quarter to six.

The second car to show up belonged to Pastor Sims and his wife, Martha. Thankfully, only Martha was in the car. I still owed the pastor a piece of my mind for having married Susannah to that creep of an ex-husband in the first place. Seeing as how it was a mixed marriage—her being a Mennonite and him a Presbyterian—the pastor should have insisted they get counseling. Or at least wait a month or two. Why is it that folks can get married at the drop of a ring, but buying a house takes weeks? Somebody should have done both a credit and a title check on Susannah's ex. It wasn't until they were in divorce court that Susannah learned her true love had a former wife and six kids. Not to mention that he owed over a hundred thousand dollars in back alimony and child support. That news upset Susannah so badly that she didn't date again for at least a week.

Even with my hands over my ears, I could hear some of the things Norah and Martha were saying.

"Magdalena lied," said Martha self-righteously. "She told me the producer wasn't coming back for six weeks. Why, if I hadn't seen the audition notice down at Sam Yoder's Corner Market, I might have missed out on it entirely."

Norah threw an accusing look my way. "I didn't know you had an interest in the performing arts, Martha dear. I mean, aren't you just a trifle over the hill to be starting out?" She patted her daughter Sherri lovingly on the head, taking care not to mess up the gold foil horns.

"I am *not* just getting started," hissed Martha. "I had the lead role in my senior class play."

"Gracious," said Norah. "How can one remember that far back?"

"At least I lead my own life, Norah Hall. I don't have to live vicariously through my children."

"That's because you don't have any children," snapped Norah.

I must admit, I had taken my hands off my ears by that point. A good fight, if it doesn't involve you directly, can definitely help the circulation. But unfortunately, just at that point a pair of black limos pulled up, and finding no

place to park in the driveway, settled on the lawn. I saw
these limos for about ten seconds before my view of them
was obliterated by the crowd that had surged around
them.

"Call the police," I directed Susannah. I wasn't so
much concerned for the occupants of the limo as for the
damage to my grass caused by the stampede. A good lawn
is like a priceless heirloom, and it must be handled with
the greatest of care.

Susannah obediently did what she was told, undoubtedly hoping to get Melvin Stoltzfus on the line. That left
me alone at the front door with the Halls and Martha.
Perhaps it was the look in the chubby Hall child's eyes
that made me lose my judgment, but I found myself inviting the three of them in. Despite their intense desire to
be cast in the movie, they at least hadn't swarmed after
the limos like the rest of the crowd, but had sensibly
maintained their places in line. Orderliness, if not intelligence, must not go unrewarded.

"Come on in," I invited them. "But don't touch anything that doesn't belong to you," I said pointedly to
little Sherri. Children, even the best-behaved of them,
tend to massage things with their sticky fingers the way a
cow placidly chews her cud.

We had to wait only ten minutes before a beleaguered
Bugsy burst into the lobby, followed closely by his superi-
ors.

"What the hell is going on out there?" shouted Don,
the hairy one. "I've never seen such a bunch of losers in
my life."

"Look, buster, I'll thank you not to swear in my home.
And as for those people out there, I think they all want a
part in your movie," I said.

Don ignored my gentle admonition. "And who the hell

are these pathetic people?'' he shouted, gesturing wildly at Martha and the Halls.

Neither Norah nor Martha are my friends, but they are hometown folk, which puts me squarely on their side when squaring off with strangers. "These are my friends, Martha Sims and Norah and Sherri Hall. They are not pathetic. They are here for the casting tryouts. The ones you posted notice to all over town."

Don waved his hairy arms while he ranted some more. "I wanted lookers. Good-looking babes. You know, Hollywood material."

"Except that this isn't Hollywood," I pointed out. "The only lookers you're going to find out here are hookers, and you're going to have to go all the way to Pittsburgh for that."

"Thanks a lot, both of you!" cried Martha. "At the risk of sounding conceited, I consider myself to be a good-looking woman in her prime."

"Prime rib, maybe," snipped Susannah as she came into the room from making her call. "I think he's looking for something a little more like this." She began to prance and pirouette like a Lipizzan stallion. Her voluminous outfit trailed behind in her dramatic swirls. It was like watching Lawrence of Arabia in drag.

"That's more like it," grunted Don.

Susannah smiled seductively.

Bugsy beamed.

Arthur remained aloof.

For a few precious seconds there was silence in the room. Then Norah shouted, "Hit it!"

"Like a virgin," wailed the dumpling-shaped Sherri. She began twisting and bobbing like she had the time before.

"I think I might have a laxative in the medicine cabinet," I said loud enough for everyone to hear.

I thought I saw Arthur smile. At any rate, he nodded to Don, and perhaps even whispered something. Don in turn mumbled something to Steven, alias Bugsy, who nodded in agreement.

"Okay, ladies," said Don, turning to us, "this is what's happening. "You," he said, pointing to Susannah, "have the part of Rambling Rhonda."

Susannah shrieked with sheer joy.

"And you," said Don, pointing this time to Martha, "have the part of the lady in the bathtub."

Martha didn't shriek. Instead, her eyes shot daggers at Susannah. "Doesn't this lady at least have a name?"

Don looked right past her and at little Sherri. "And you will be Terrible Tina, the teenager from hell."

"I told you not to swear, buster," I reminded him.

Meanwhile Norah and her offspring were dancing up and down in ecstasy, like a pair of Watusis.

"And you, Miss Yoder," began Don, and then he stopped and looked at Arthur. Arthur smiled and nodded again. "You," Don continued reluctantly, "will be Mama Miller, the matriarch of the clan."

Steven sidled suddenly over and seized my hand. "Congratulations, Yoder!" he said. "That's a speaking part. You'll get paid extra for that."

"Don't the others have speaking parts?"

Steven held up a thumb and forefinger with about a millimeter of space between them. "One slip of the splicing equipment and their parts will end up on the cutting room floor."

Before I could respond with my own little shriek of joy, Don turned to Steven. "Get outside and survey the scum. See if you can find a couple of good-looking bimbo types for dressing."

Steven was good at his job, and in no time at all he returned, trailing two Hernia high school girls whom I recognized. They were the Biddle sisters, who definitely hail from the wrong side of the tracks, even though Hernia doesn't have any. But you know what I mean. The Biddle sisters are so made up and lacquered with hair spray that it would take a hurricane to strip away enough layers to reveal anything natural. Both girls were wearing jeans so tight, they undoubtedly cut off their circulation. That could be the only explanation for the way the girls walked. As for their bazooms, if Sam's Corner Market runs out of facial tissues during the next cold season, we'll know where to go.

"Howdy, Mrs. Yoder," said Cindy Biddle. To say she chewed gum like a cow would be to insult my two Holsteins.

"That's *Miss* Yoder, Cindy. I'm not married."

"Figures," said the simpering little strumpet, and she strolled across the room to meet Don and Arthur.

Nadine Biddle wasn't any better. She ignored me altogether and headed straight for *the* Arthur. Clearly, she'd been clued.

"My jeans are made of memory-stretch denim," she cooed. "Feel them. They'll remember your touch."

"Oh, my God, it's the whore of Babylon," said Martha, who was pretty close to me in age.

Arthur Lapata, much to his credit, merely smiled at Nadine. He declined to nod.

Don sprang into action. "You," he said, pointing to Cindy, "stay. You," he said to Nadine, "wait outside with the others."

"But that's no fair!" protested Nadine, at the same time wiggling her bottom like a dog in heat.

An anguished look came to Don's eyes. Instead of insisting that Nadine leave, he loped back over to Arthur and whispered something I couldn't hear. Arthur nodded then, but I for one could tell that it was a reluctant nod.

"You can stay," Don said unabashedly when he returned. "I'll give you that memory test later."

Nadine giggled and bobbled her bottom some more. It was the most disgusting carnality I'd ever witnessed, and right there in the front room of Mama's house. Mama had undoubtedly begun to turn over in her grave with the regularity of a roast on a rotisserie.

"Does your mama know where you are?" I asked.

The child didn't even have the decency to answer. She sashayed over to the side of the room and plopped herself down in my favorite rocker. Then she dumped the contents of her scruffy little purse into her lap and began applying new layers of paint to her face. Martha was right, this was the whore of Babylon.

"What have I wrought?" I cried to deaf ears. Then I remembered that I'd been given an actual speaking part in the movie, and my mood picked up considerably. I, Magdalena Yoder, not known for having been the prettiest girl in high school, was going to be on the big screen. Imagine that. And I had yet to see my first movie in a real movie house. Gloria Swinehart, with your bouffant hairdo and panda-bear mascara, eat your heart out. You were the meanest to me in eleventh grade, and now where are you?

"Vanity of vanities, all is vanity," said the author of Ecclesiastes, and he was as right as rain.

Four

THE FIRST DAY of filming, we had shoofly pie for break-fast. We don't normally eat pie for breakfast, but the film crew was expected to arrive at six, and anyway, we were all too excited to care what we ate.

"Save a piece of that for Arthur," admonished Freni. She meant *the* Arthur Lapata. For some strange reason, my Amish cousin and the Hollywood whiz kid had hit it off. Not that Freni approved of the movie being made, or of any movie, for that matter. If I had to guess, I'd say it was because Arthur Lapata bore an uncanny resemblance to Freni and Mose's only son, John.

"Well, of course I won't eat any more," said Susannah with a meaningful glance in my direction. "My role in the movie calls for a svelte, trim body. My character's name is Rambling Rhonda, not Big Mama Miller."

"It's just Mama Miller," I said for the umpteenth time. "There's no 'big' in front of it."

"You're both as thin as sticks," said Mose. There was concern in his voice. Ever since Papa was killed in that mishmash of sneakers and milk, Mose has been a surrogate father to Susannah and me.

"Are you sure you have everything under control here?" I asked Freni.

Reels and Runs Productions had hired Freni, independently of the inn, to cater for them. Of course Freni would use the inn as her base, but still, it was an enormous task for a seventy-three-year-old woman, even one with as much spunk as Freni. Mose would help out, but I still needed him to take care of our two dairy cows and the flock of chickens.

"Don't you worry about me, Magdalena. I've already checked, and there aren't any vegetarians this time."

"Good." I said a silent prayer of thanksgiving. Freni has a hard time classifying foods, and assigns the less obvious ones (for her these include eggs, grains, and dairy products) to the category of the food with which they are commonly served. Don't ask me to explain how, but over the years cheese has become a fruit, and eggs a vegetable.

"Of course the English do have some funny ideas."

"What do you mean this time?" To Freni, everything about the outside world was an enigma. Even Susannah was beyond comprehension now that she wore sleeveless dresses and makeup.

"Well, Magdalena, this Arthur is a very nice boy, but he wants me to boil his ties for him."

I mentally scratched my head. Granted, I don't have both feet out into the world like Susannah, but I do read a lot. "Did you tell him there's a dry cleaner in Bedford?"

Freni frowned. "This is about more than just cleaning the ties, Magdalena. I think he eats them afterward."

"Come on!"

Suddenly Susannah began to howl with laughter, and that really is the only word to use in this case. Of course that rat-size pooch of hers was activated by Susannah's yowls and began contributing some pitiful pips of its own. Together they sounded just like the dog pound in Somerset at hose-down time.

"Get a grip on it, Rambling Rhonda," I said. "It wasn't that funny."

"But it is!" screeched Susannah. "Arthur Lapata doesn't eat *ties*. He eats *Thai!*"

"I hate riddles," grumped Freni.

I explained to Freni that Thai cooking, the cuisine of Thailand, was quite popular in the outside world. "I ate it myself once in Pittsburgh, when I went to visit the Mystery Lovers Bookshop in nearby Oakmont."

"Your mother would have had a fit," said Freni. To Freni, even a quick stop at McDonald's is enough to jeopardize one's soul.

"Leave Mama out of it, you—" I started to say pleasantly, but was interrupted by the arrival of the film crew.

By seven o'clock that morning all the day's extras, the "window dressing," as Steven Freeman called them, had been assembled at the inn to see makeup and wardrobe. There were about twenty of them altogether, but Steven quickly split them into two groups, the "Executive Extras" and the "Regulars." Supposedly the Executive Extras, which included the Biddle sisters, little Sherri Hall, and Martha Sims, were to be used in more scenes than the Regulars. This, of course, flattered all the Executive Extras, but angered the Regulars.

The Regulars mumbled and grumbled while the Executive Extras primped and preened. Susannah mumbled and grumbled the loudest because she hadn't been included in either group.

"But I'm Rambling Rhonda," I heard her remind Steven. "My character even has a name. Why haven't I been included with the Executive Extras?"

Steven smiled. "Because you're not an extra, that's why. You're a stand-in."

"What's that? What do you mean?"

Steven smirked. "Arthur seems to think you look like Darla Strutt. They're going to use you to block in the scenes for the lighting crew before they do the actual shooting."

I could tell that Susannah was torn between ecstasy and agony. She was undoubtedly ecstatic that the director thought she looked like the star, but in agony because as a stand-in she wouldn't be on film at all. Even the most Regular of the Regulars would imprint more celluloid than she would.

"Why do I have to be *only* a stand-in?" she whined. "I mean, couldn't I be a stand-in *and* an Executive Extra? Even a Regular Extra?"

Steven shrugged. "That all depends on how much you're willing to put out."

"What?"

"Effort, I mean."

"Sounds like sexual harassment," I said. "I don't watch TV talk shows, but I know harassment when I hear it."

"Then your hearing definitely needs to be checked," scoffed Steven.

"Magdalena, stay out of this," snapped Susannah. She turned to Steven. "Who is Rambling Rhonda? I mean, why does a stand-in get that name?"

Steven snickered. "Rambling Rhonda is the industry's code name for Darla Strutt. Her heels are so round, she needs to wear orthopedic shoes just to stand up."

"You mean she's loose?" I asked.

Steven sucked his lower lip. "Let's just say that there's a sign above her bed saying 'Two Billion Served.' "

Susannah flapped several yards of fabric in annoyance. "Well, I may look like her, but I don't act like her. I'm still saving myself for that one special man."

"So is Michael Jackson," I couldn't help saying. I may not watch TV, but I'm not above sneaking a quick peek at the tabloids when I'm in the checkout line. After all, one can't properly fight evil if one is uninformed.

But Susannah had business on her mind. "I want to speak to Arthur about this. I'm really very talented, you know. There's no reason I couldn't be a stand-in *and* an extra. You wouldn't even have to pay me more."

Steven scowled. "Arthur is a busy man. You don't go disturbing the top director about little things like this. Tell you what, I'll arrange for you to speak to Don when we break for lunch. But of course I'll expect a little extra cooperation in return."

"My middle name is cooperation!"

"It's Sister Cooperation," I said quickly. "That's the name they gave her at the convent."

Steven stalked off without another word.

For the next half hour, the makeup and wardrobe departments did their job on us. The results were mixed. The Biddle bimbos had been made to look even bimboier, which I wouldn't have believed possible if I hadn't seen it with my own eyes. Little Sherri Hall had been made to shed her gold foil cones for a junior, bimbette version of the above. Martha Sims, the minister's wife, had been transformed into a senior bimbo—a senior bimbo in a bathrobe, no less—a style that plainly does not suit most women over forty. As for Susannah and me, we came out looking virtually the same as our former selves.

"That's because they typecast us," explained Susannah. "I already look like Darla Strutt, and you, well, you look sort of like a Mennonite."

I patted my sister lovingly on the back for having said such a sweet thing. I am proud of who I am, but not so proud, mind you, that it's a sin. Susannah, on the other hand, has totally rejected her roots. Not only has her apple fallen far from the tree, it has rolled into a different orchard altogether. Mama would be mortified if she were alive. So, out of loyalty to Mama, I patted Susannah hard enough to make Shnookums yelp. Then the three of us set off to search for the movie stars.

By eight o'clock that morning, there were three big trucks and seven trailers parked on the lawn. At least two of the trailers served as dressing rooms for the film's real stars, Darla Strutt and Rip Oilman.

"Isn't he just to die for?" moaned Susannah when Rip emerged from his metal cocoon for the first time.

I grunted something vague. Rip was good-looking, if you like that sort of slick type whose best friend is his comb, and who undoubtedly smells like that new cologne department they put in next to menswear at the Somerset Sears.

We were standing at the parlor window, which had the best view of Rip's trailer, but even so, our glimpse of him was fleeting. A crowd of groupies, most of them Bedford girls, mind you, had closed around the man like the waters of the Red Sea. When Rip finally did make it to the house, his mood was in need of improvement.

"What the hell is going on?" he shouted at Arthur. "My contract clearly states that I'm to be shielded from the civilians. Either you get some security out there, or I'm walking."

Arthur merely nodded, first at Rip, then at Don.

Don, the hairy one, took Rip aside, but Susannah and I were unable to hear what they said. Whatever it was, it didn't calm Rip down any. If anything, he became more agitated, and a few swear words, which I shall not repeat, polluted the air.

Arthur then nodded at Steven. Steven shrugged and seemed to approach the two men warily. Again we couldn't hear the conversation, but whatever Steven said was effective. In no time at all, the three men were slapping each other's backs in what is apparently some sort of male-bonding ritual. Peace had been restored.

At least until Darla Strutt made her entrance. I don't watch movies, but Susannah does, and suddenly it was crystal-clear who Susannah was patterning her life after. At five foot four, Darla Strutt was five inches shorter than Susannah, and a good ten years older, but otherwise they might have been twins. Like Susannah, Darla Strutt flowed into the room trailing yards of fabric. Unlike Susannah, Darla Strutt carried her little pooch, Fifi, out in the open. In her arms, the way God intended.

"Mommy, it's her!" shrieked little Sherri Hall, who had been sitting quietly in a corner with her mother despite Rip's somewhat dramatic entrance. The pudgy prepubescent girl jumped off her chair and rushed the swirling star.

Like Susannah, Darla Strutt rolled her eyes in annoyance and stamped an unseen foot. "Arthur, must we have a child on the set? Children can be so tedious, you know."

Norah Hall sprang into action like a tigress who had seen her cub threatened. "Sherri is not tedious! And she's not a child! She's a very talented young lady who's going places."

"Off this set, if I have my way," snapped Darla Strutt.

"Hit it!" cried Norah reflexively.

"Like a virgin," crooned Sherri, but without the bobbing foil cones, it just wasn't the same.

"Arthur! I demand that they be banned from the set!"

But Arthur Lapata was so engrossed in conversation with a sound technician that he couldn't hear Darla Strutt's demands. Don did, however. Like a big hairy dog, he was all over her, except instead of barking, he was muttering things. And salivating. It was a disgusting thing to watch.

Even Darla Strutt seemed to be disgusted by the assistant director. "Give me some space, Don!" she gasped.

Don managed to step back without looking taken aback. "Sure thing, hon."

"Now tell her what you told me," coached Darla Strutt. She was pointing to Norah Hall.

Don grinned and made a slicing motion across his throat. "We won't be needing your daughter anymore, doll. There's been a script change. Fill in those forms that you were given when you checked in this morning, and make sure Steven gets the white copy. The kid will get paid for today at least."

Norah's mouth began to open and close like a baby bird begging to be fed, but no sound came out. Mercifully Steven appeared out of nowhere and rather forcibly began to usher the pair outside.

"You'll pay for this!" screamed Norah at Don.

Meanwhile, in a last-ditch effort to be discovered, little Sherri began to wail her tune again. There must have been a universal, if not canine, angst in her voice, because Darla Strutt's Fifi suddenly joined in. When Susannah's precious Shnookums began adding to the din, I put my hands over my ears to shut out the noise, but I could not shut out the sound of Mama turning over, rhythmically, in her grave.

They shot one brief scene that morning. It took almost an hour to shoot, even though the scene itself was less than a minute long. Susannah and I were not in that scene, and I'm more than grateful for that.

"Go on upstairs and get in the tub," I heard Steven say to Martha Sims. "They're ready for you now."

I scooted over. "What tub? And why?"

"Stay out of this, Miss Yoder," Steven snarled.

"This is my inn, and the tubs belong to me. So what's this about Martha getting into one of them?"

Steven swatted Martha on the behind with a sort of ledger he was holding. "Go on, they're waiting for you. This is your big scene."

Martha flung me a proud look and pranced obediently up the impossibly steep stairs for which my inn is so famous.

Steven started to slip away, but I nabbed him in time. "Hold it, Bugsy!"

"Make it snappy, Miss Yoder. Time is money in this game."

"Then I'm a millionaire," I said. "Now, what's this about a bathtub scene?"

Bugsy balked at answering. "Take it up with Art, or Don. I don't write or direct the scenes. My only responsibility is to get the actors to their marks on time."

I glanced around for *the* Arthur Lapata, but he was nowhere in sight. Not that it would have made any difference—I'm not all that good at interpreting nods. I did, however, see the hirsute Don leaving the downstairs commode just in time for me to intercept him.

"Yes, Miss Yoder? Make it quick, I have to direct this scene."

I stared with fascination at his hairy visage for a second or two. "Mr. Manley, it's about this scene. Bugsy, I mean Steven, said it has something to do with a bathtub. What's with the bathtub?"

Don tried to rest a woolly limb across my shoulders, but

I shrugged it off. "Look, darling, it's a real cute scene that's going to play very well. The Amishman Freddy—that's Rip—comes into the bathroom and discovers one of the guests taking a bath."

"Naked?"

"Of course, darling. What else? Anyway, Freddy the Amishman gets all embarrassed at first, but then he plays it cool and takes off his clothes and climbs into the tub with the lady. A lot of big laughs, guaranteed."

My face felt as hot as if I'd been baking bread. Undoubtedly this was just a foretaste of where we'd all end up if I didn't put a stop to the evil scene. "Over my dead body, mister!"

Don laughed and gave me a noogie with his shaggy knuckles. "Naw, the dead body comes later, when Freddy discovers that the lady in the tub won't play."

"It'll be your dead body!" I screamed loud enough for everyone in the inn to hear. Then I stomped off to find Arthur Lapata.

He was in the kitchen, chowing down on Freni's shoofly pie. Freni was hovering over him like a mother bird. I wouldn't have been surprised if she suddenly leaned over and dropped food in his mouth.

"Mr. Lapata! Are you in charge here, or is Don?"

"Calm down, Magdalena," said Freni sharply. "Mr. Lapata is just having a midmorning snack."

"In the meantime, Donald Manley is turning the PennDutch into a den of iniquity."

"Nonsense," scoffed Freni. "Arthur would never permit such a thing. Would you?"

Arthur shook his head. He might have mumbled something too, but his mouth was too full of shoofly pie for any of it to be intelligible.

"He says that Mr. Manley is very good at what he does, and that he's already given him the go-ahead to direct a number of scenes in this movie," said Freni. "Arthur says that Mr. Manley has impeccable instincts. He also says that—"

"Does the man actually speak?" I asked.

"Don't be so rude, Magdalena." Freni cut me a thin sliver of shoofly pie, and then another huge slice, which she put on Arthur's plate.

Foolishly, I decided that the few seconds it would take to consume such a thin slice were not all that important in the grand scheme of things. I sat down and began to eat. As usual, the pie was superb.

$$\boxed{Five}$$

FRENI HOSTETLER'S RECIPE
FOR SHOOFLY PIE

Makes 8 servings

1 nine-inch unbaked pie crust
$1^1/_2$ cups flour
$^1/_2$ cup dark brown sugar
1 teaspoon cinnamon
$^1/_2$ teaspoon nutmeg
Pinch of ground cloves
$^1/_4$ teaspoon salt
1 stick cold butter ($^1/_2$ cup)
$^3/_4$ cup water
$^3/_4$ cup unsulphured molasses
$^1/_2$ teaspoon baking soda

COMBINE the flour, brown sugar, cinnamon, nutmeg, cloves and salt. Cut the butter into pats and add it to the flour mixture. Using a fork, mash the butter into the flour mixture until you get a texture like coarse crumbs. Combine the water, molasses, and baking soda. Pour into the unbaked pie crust. Then spoon the crumb mixture onto the liquid. Bake at 375 degrees for thirty-five to forty minutes. Best if served at room temperature.

Six

FRENI QUIT HER JOB twice during lunch. The first time was when Darla Strutt lit up a cigarette and then put it out in one of Freni's casseroles, claiming to have improved it. The second time was when it was discovered that the blackened Hawaiian mahimahi, which everyone raved about, was really a box of fish sticks that Freni had left in the oven too long. Both times Arthur Lapata came to the rescue, and by nodding, and presumably muttering, managed to smooth Freni's ruffled feathers.

Personally, I enjoyed lunch. Don Manley was not there, and neither was Susannah, nor Martha Sims, for that matter. With the exception of Darla Strutt, who stayed only long enough to put out her cigarette, the only obnoxious person present was Bugsy Freeman. Of course Rip Oilman was there, but as long as we civilians didn't get in his way, he left us alone.

I was just reaching for a piece of Freni's green-tomato

pie when Susannah came bursting into the dining room in an explosion of fabric. "Help! Help! Mr. Manley's been forked," she shouted.

Of course, that didn't make any sense to me. Then again, Susannah seldom makes sense. "Have a seat and dig in," I said, "but don't touch that casserole over there."

Susannah ignored my kindness. "No! He's been forked, I tell you. Forked!"

It was becoming clear that Susannah's histrionics were not staged. She wasn't even glancing over at Arthur Lapata. I swallowed the lump in my throat that is invariably the precursor of doom. "What do you mean by *forked?*"

Susannah made some stabbing motions with her arms.

"You don't mean knifed, do you?"

"Forked!" screamed Susannah.

"Where?"

Susannah patted her stomach gingerly, as if she too had been forked.

"No, where is he?"

"In the barn!"

I was not the youngest person in the room, and I was wearing a dress, so there was already a crowd gathered around Don Manley when I got there. I pushed through just far enough to see what Susannah had been talking about. Sure enough, the man had a pitchfork in his belly.

Unfortunately, I have seen corpses before. But those had been poisoned, although one had the added distinction of having been thrown down the stairs. At any rate, Don Manley, forked, was not a pleasant sight. He was still standing, as a matter of fact, because the tines of the fork were pinning him against an upright beam, like a giant moth on a specimen board. Except that moths have very little blood. This specimen seemed to have had gallons of blood. I was going to have to hire Clyde Maynard from the Meat Locker over in Bedford to help me clean it all up. Of course Runs and Reels Productions would pay for it. I'd see to that.

"Call the police," I said to Steven. "The number is above the phone."

Steven, along with everyone else, simply stood and stared at Don.

I sprinted back to the house myself and dialed the police. In Hernia, that puts you in touch with the paramedics as well, not that Don Manley would need them.

"Hernia police and emergency services," a woman responded.

I recognized the voice as belonging to Zelda Root, Hernia's assistant police chief, and breathed a sigh of relief. Because of its small size, Hernia has only two people on its police force: Zelda and the chief himself, Melvin Stoltzfus.

"Zelda, there's been a murder out at my place," I panted into the phone.

"I know," said Zelda complacently. "And they're filming it now, right?"

"Wrong! You've been working with Melvin too long, Zelda. This is a real murder. The assistant director's been forked. Right through the gut."

"Is that movie lingo, Magdalena?"

"It's farm talk, Zelda. Somebody speared him with a pitchfork."

"Is he still alive?"

I hadn't thought of that. I didn't think a person could be alive if he'd been forked to a barn beam, but people have a way of surprising you. Leah Brockmeyer managed to survive for three weeks after she slipped down her cellar stairs and broke both legs, and all she had for sustenance was a bushel of apples and a one-pint bottle of imitation vanilla.

"He might be alive," I conceded, "but I wouldn't bet the farm on it."

"I'll call the Bedford paramedics anyway, and give Melvin a call. It's his day off, but he's probably at home, washing the squad car."

"Give the poor guy a break and let him have his day off," I hastened to say, but I was too late. Zelda had already hung up.

In fact, I hadn't even made it back out the door when the phone rang. "Lou Ann's House of Perms and Magical Makeovers," I said as convincingly as I could. "How may we help you?"

"Yoder, is that you?"

"Guilty, Melvin."

"So it *was* you who stabbed the actor with the pitchfork?"

"He isn't an actor, Melvin. He's the assistant director. And I didn't stab him."

"Then you shot him? Magdalena, did you just lie to Zelda?"

"Yes, I told her I adored you. Look, Melvin, somebody by the name of Don Manley has a pitchfork through his gut. Are you going to sit there and talk about it all day, or what?"

"You're toying with me again, Magdalena, aren't you? Did you or did you not stab this man with a pitchfork?"

"I did not stab him!" I clamped a hand over my own mouth, which hopefully muffled the sound a little. In my case it is risky business, shouting loud enough to wake the dead.

"You said you were guilty a minute ago."

"Of answering the phone, Melvin, not murder."

"Yeah, sure. How do you know it was murder, then? Maybe the guy fell on the fork."

"He's standing up, Melvin. Pinned to a beam like a butterfly. You know, like the ones on display in our biology room in high school."

"I didn't take biology in high school, Magdalena. My folks got a special exemption for me, on account of I'm allergic to the smell of formaldehyde."

"That figures." I mean, if Melvin had taken biology, perhaps he would have known enough not to try to milk a bull.

"What does that mean, Magdalena?"

I ignored his hostile tone. "The point is, Melvin, that there's a man in my barn with a pitchfork through his middle, and it wasn't an accident, and he didn't put it there himself."

"The first rule in police work is not to rule out anything until you have concrete evidence to the contrary," said Melvin pompously.

"So?"

"So, maybe the guy did do it to himself. Suicide by impalement is not as uncommon as you think. The Japanese—"

"Would you care to give me a demonstration?" I asked hopefully. I hung up the phone. Experience has taught me that this was the fastest way to get Melvin out here. As long as it was going to be Melvin, and not Zelda, I wanted to get it all over with as soon as possible.

I walked, rather than ran, back to the barn. I wasn't in a hurry to see some Hollywood honcho, even an arrogant one like Don Manley, nailed to a beam. On the way, I passed the old outhouse, which, of course, is no longer in use. The door had somehow come open, so I closed it, and not without pride. It is a six-seater, after all, the only six-seater outhouse in the county, according to old Doc

Shafer, our local historian. It was built back in Great-
Grandpa Yoder's time, but even Doc Shafer can't figure
out why so many seats were needed.

Between the outhouse and the barn lies the chicken
coop. Really, it is a large, fenced-in hen yard with a
wooden structure housing the laying boxes. At any given
moment there are likely to be as many as six to eight hens
sitting on the boxes doing their thing. At least that can be
explained.

I know all my chickens by name, but my favorite is
Pertelote, a Rhode Island Red of great dignity. Pertelote
is too old to lay anymore, but the nesting instinct still
beats strong within her feathered breast. From time to
time she usurps the nests of lesser hens, and if left undis-
turbed, hatches the adopted eggs herself. Despite the fact
that Pertelote has gotten a bit cranky with advancing age,
she is an excellent mother to her foster chicks, whatever
their race. In fact, Pertelote had recently raised a brood
of Leghorns, and I was experimenting with her on a small
clutch of duck eggs, of which she seemed rather fond.
Therefore, I was a bit surprised to find Pertelote out in
the hen yard.

"Go back to your eggs," I admonished her, "or Freni
will fricassee you." It wasn't an idle threat either, because
Freni has had her eye on Pertelote's plump rump for a
year or two, even though shoe leather would be more
tender than a chicken Pertelote's age.

Of course Pertelote ignored my warning, and I made a
mental note to check on her surrogate eggs when I had
time. Duck eggs are, after all, larger than chicken eggs,
and an old thing like Pertelote might find the task of
straddling them day in and day out a bit wearing.

Anyway, it took me a couple of minutes to get back to
the barn, so I guess I'm responsible for what happened
while I was gone. Steven, alias Bugsy, had managed to

pull the pitchfork out of the beam, and in doing so, out of Don. It hadn't been Steven's intent to pull the fork out of Don, it had simply been an accident, one of which no one seemed to disapprove. The sight of Don impaled like a shish kebab concerned folks more than did the damage they might cause him by removing the fork. Don now lay prone at the base of the beam, although the pitchfork was nowhere to be seen. Almost as startling to me as Don's new position was the fact that his face had gone from white to gray.

"What on earth happened?" I demanded, elbowing my way through the crowd.

"We had to get him off the post," said a cameraman who I think was named Al. "He was still alive, you know."

"He couldn't have been!"

"But he was," said one of the makeup girls. Her name I knew. It was Heather, one of those ubiquitous plant names so popular in the seventies. Although just a child herself, this Heather looked like she was about to give birth to a whole field of Heatherettes.

I just shook my head. He was definitely dead now. I'm no expert, but I've seen pot roasts with more life in them than Don had at that moment.

"He spoke," said Al. "We all heard him say something."

"What?"

"I don't know," said Heather. "Something." She started to cry.

"I think it started with 'M,' " said Al.

"He was probably calling for his mother," I explained, although it was hard to imagine Don Manley ever having had a mother. Even if she were still alive, the San Diego Zoo would probably not release her without a lot of red tape.

Steven spat on his hands, and then rubbed them on his

pants. Apparently he had gotten blood on them while unpinning Don. "Did you make the call?"

The sounding siren of Hernia's one squad car answered for me. A few seconds later, the Bedford paramedics pulled up as well.

Seven

"BUT YOU'VE KNOWN ME my whole life!" I protested.

Police Chief Melvin Stoltzfus rotated his head slowly in my direction. For some reason, he'd been looking at Zelda, who, I think, was supposed to be taking notes. It was not inconceivable that he had a crush on her. "Familiarity is not a legal defense, Yoder."

"But I'm a Mennonite! A pacifist. I don't go around stabbing people with pitchforks."

"There's a first time for everything. And Mennonites do commit crimes of violence. Remember Leyland Neubrander? He ran over his mother-in-law with a combine in November of eighty-three."

"You weren't even a policeman then," I reminded him. The three of us were standing alone in the barn with the door shut. Outside I could hear the crowd milling and murmuring.

Melvin's huge head bobbled momentarily on his long,

thin neck, as if it were trying to steady itself. There is something about Melvin, perhaps his bulging eyes, that always reminds me of a praying mantis. "I may not have been on the force then, Magdalena, but I know the case. Leyland Neubrander is my cousin."

That didn't surprise me. Melvin Stoltzfus is my cousin too, if you go back far enough. That's something I try to refrain from doing in his case.

"Forget Leyland Neubrander and his being a Mennonite. The point is that I'm not a killer."

"You threatened him in public, Magdalena."

"I did not!"

"Yes, you did. I have depositions from at least five witnesses who say they heard you threaten to kill him."

My heart began to pound. "I said something to the effect that he could shoot that lurid scene only over my dead body. I certainly didn't threaten to kill him."

"You said over *his* dead body," said Melvin pompously.

"I don't see what difference that makes. You know I didn't mean it."

Melvin's left eye swiveled ever so slightly, but independently, in its socket. "The difference is that his body, not yours, was found nailed to the center beam in your barn."

"Forked," I corrected him.

I don't think Melvin heard me. *"And,* Magdalena, what makes this even more interesting is that it was your sister, Susannah, who found the victim first."

"Why, Melvin Stoltzfus!" I said loud enough to make Zelda jump. "You leave Susannah out of this. How can you even imply such a thing? She is your girlfriend, after all."

Melvin's right eye began to swivel now, away from his left. Perhaps he did have hindsight, a trait undoubtedly useful to a detective. "Can you account for your time up until Susannah discovered the body?"

I felt suddenly relaxed. "Of course I can. I was in the inn all morning. Either in the public rooms with the others, or in the kitchen with Freni and Mose."

"And they'll swear to it?"

I couldn't help laughing. "Freni and Mose won't swear to anything. It's against their beliefs. You know that."

Melvin's eyes swiveled back into alignment. "The others, I mean. Are you sure you have alibis?"

"Then I am a suspect?" I glanced quickly at Zelda, but as usual she was inscrutable. I've seen hens with more facial expression than Zelda Root.

"Let's just say that at this point everyone out here is a suspect." Melvin began to rub his hands together briskly. "And you, Magdalena Yoder, are what we might call *suspecto numero uno.*"

"Speak English, Melvin," I said crisply, although it's possible it may have sounded like snapping.

"He means you're our number one suspect," said Zelda dispassionately. I am one hundred percent sure that the woman's family tree and mine have never intertwined their branches. We are at polar ends of the nervous spectrum.

I held out my wrists. "I demand to see my lawyer."

Melvin's eyes swiveled away from center for a second, then locked back into place in a prolonged stare. "You aren't under arrest, Magdalena. Not yet, at any rate. But I am going to have to ask you not to leave the area."

"Shucks. My flight to Paris was nonrefundable."

Either Melvin smiled slightly, or his mandibles twitched. "I'll solve this case before you know it, Magdalena. It's simply a matter of gathering the facts and arranging them in the proper order. Yessiree, it's all a matter of facts."

"What about gathering evidence, Melvin?"

Melvin's mandibles mangled themselves into what approximated a self-satisfied grin. "The body is halfway to Bedford by now, Yoder."

"And the murder weapon? Have you collected that yet?"

It was like an entire marquee of light bulbs had flicked on in Melvin's head. "I was getting to that, Yoder. First things first. Now, let me see this pitchfork."

"Can't."

"Withholding evidence will land you in the hoosegow immediately, Yoder, without even a chance to pass go."

"Go fish, Melvin. I don't have the pitchfork, or I'd let you have it." I then proceeded to explain to Melvin a million times that the pitchfork was missing. You wouldn't think that would be such a hard concept to grasp. I mean, by the time Melvin and Zelda arrived, there had been the body, surrounded by a crowd of people, but there had been no pitchfork. There was only a thin line of blood, along with some other horrible ooze, where Steven had tossed the pitchfork. There was no sign of the fork itself.

For the next two hours Melvin and Zelda ransacked my barn, but of course they didn't turn up any pitchfork. It was gone, just like I'd said. You can bet your bippy I made them put everything back in its place. A barn should be kept just as tidy as a house. After all, the good Lord was born in a barn, wasn't he?

"If it shows up, call me at once, Yoder," said Melvin needlessly. Of course I wouldn't call him—not until after I'd had a good long turn at examining the thing. Even then I might forget to call him, or even accidentally lose the pitchfork again, depending on what I discovered.

"Will do," I said, and smiled. When you have to lie, it is wise to smile. Smiling helps keep one from blinking, the

sure giveaway of a liar. Now, don't get me wrong: lying is
a sin, but it is one of the more necessary sins. And since I
don't indulge much in the other sins, having never com-
mitted adultery or coveted my neighbor's ass, I don't feel
too bad when I have to lie. And when it comes to dealing
with Melvin, having to lie is a given.

After Melvin and Zelda drove off in Melvin's restored
Studebaker which doubles as his squad car, I went to
check on Pertelote. To my relief, nothing was amiss. She
had settled back on the duck eggs, and although she had
to spread out as thin as a crepe suzette to cover the
things, she seemed as happy as a clam, or whatever it is
happy hens resemble. She seemed much happier, at any
rate, than an old hen had a right to be. Clearly, whatever
had disturbed her earlier was a thing of the past.

"Good girl, Perty," I said reassuringly. "Keep up the
good work." The duck eggs were scheduled to hatch in
just one more week, and I had been looking forward to
the event for three weeks already. Normally, a hen has to
sit for only three weeks altogether, provided they are
chicken eggs she is brooding. Fortunately, Pertelote, like
most of my other hens, couldn't count.

Pertelote acknowledged my encouragement with an angry cluck, warning me to keep my distance. One would
think she would welcome distractions, but that is not the
case.

"You're looking at an extra week, dear," I said charitably, and turned to leave.

It was then that I noticed a grocery slip lying on the
floor on top of the straw. It was from Sam Yoder's Corner
Market, and came from one of those cash registers that
prints the name of the item along with the price. Although a cousin of mine, Sam had married a Methodist,
and then become one himself, which might explain his
modern ways.

Anyway, I picked up the slip and was about to crumple it and put it in my pocket to be thrown away later, when something printed on it caught my eye. "Parsley," I read aloud in disbelief.

I wadded the paper but kept it in my fist. That did it. Freni Hostetler was going to get a piece of mind. Spending good money on parsley, when we had some growing out by the back door, was a sin. A sin worse than lying, if you ask me. Undoubtedly, it had to do with her fascination with *the* Arthur Lapata. Apparently our parsley wasn't good enough for him and the Hollywood crowd. As if Sam's parsley were any better! I stomped out of the henhouse louder than I should have, much to Pertelote's displeasure.

I found Freni in the kitchen, humming to herself. The nerve of that woman! Although I love her dearly, sometimes Freni Hostetler has all the sensitivity of a stone.

"Freni! How dare you?" I know, perhaps my tone was harsh, but I was having a bad day.

Freni blinked a couple of times, and then comprehension spread slowly over her broad, plain face. "Ach, yes. You are right, Magdalena. The hairy man might have been English, but he was one of God's children, after all. I should not have been humming."

"Humming, shmumming. I'm not talking about that. I'm talking about parsley."

Freni blinked again. "Perhaps you should take a nap, Magdalena. Although it is a sin to be idle, surely these are special circumstances."

"Parsley!" I almost screamed. "Why did you waste good money buying parsley at Sam's, when there's enough of that stuff out by the back door to stuff a mattress?"

"That does it," said Freni, untying her apron. "I quit,

Magdalena. I'm not going to be accused again of something I didn't do."

"You can't quit, Freni. Your agreement is with Reels and Runs Productions, not with me. But since I'm backing your little operation, I have a right to see that my investment isn't wasted."

"But you have no right to speak to me that way, Magdalena. Buying such a thing as parsley! Imagine that!"

"So you didn't buy it?" I got out the crumpled grocery slip and smoothed it out. I'd let the evidence speak for itself.

Freni snatched the slip from my hand and scanned it. Her already wrinkled brow began to crease further, first with concentration, and then with horror. She dropped the list like a hot potato. "Your mother would be ashamed of you, Magdalena. Showing such a filthy thing to me."

I scooped the list from the floor and began to read aloud. "Parsley, 59 cents. Creamed corn, 75 cents. Plastic wrap, $2.25, ketchup, $1.45, feminine deodorant spray—"

"Stop!" cried Freni. She sounded like a desperate woman about to be executed.

I stopped. Clearly, this was not Freni's list. Frankly, I was surprised the woman even knew what such a thing was.

"I'm sorry, Freni. Really, I am. I hadn't read the entire list before. Is there anything I can do to make it up to you?" I stepped forward in an act of reconciliation. I wasn't going to hug her or anything. Just maybe pat her on the arm.

Freni backed up a couple of steps. Perhaps she feared the fire and brimstone were still forthcoming. "Take that nap, Magdalena. That's what your mother would tell you to do if she were here."

"But she isn't here!" I wailed. Mama had no business dying while I was still alive.

I took that darn nap anyway. If it's true that joy cometh in the morning, then at least a little cheer can be expected from a sound nap. I slept like a log.

I woke up with a pounding head. After washing my face with cold water and downing three aspirin, I drove straight out to see old Doc Shafer. Like most people in Hernia, Zelda excepted, Doc is a distant cousin and a lifelong friend. Doc claims to be eighty-three years old, although sometimes I think he pads his age a little, just for the added respect. At any rate, Doc used to be sweet on my mother, and now he's sweet on me. At least I'm pretty sure old Doc is sweet on me: he tries to kiss me, and he once patted me on the behind. But to me Doc is just a friend—a sympathetic ear and a source of usually good, sound advice.

Doc is a veterinarian with a now-limited practice. He lives on the opposite side of Hernia from me in a rambling old white frame structure that houses both him and his resident patients. The four-legged kind, I mean. Perhaps I shouldn't mention this, but Doc does treat humans from time to time.

Because Hernia's one medical doctor, Alvin Hostetler, is a little on the arrogant side, many of our old-timers seek Doc out when they suffer from minor ailments. Of course Doc knows that treating humans is, for him, against the law. But the way Doc figures it, at his age, what does he have to lose? Anyway, Doc's human patients never pay him directly. Suffice it to say, Doc's lawn is never in need of mowing, and the fruits and vegetables that pile up on his front porch are top-notch.

Any description of Doc would be woefully incomplete if one were not to mention that he is a superb cook. The

old coot lives to eat, not the other way around. Doc Shafer firmly believes that there is a direct correlation between a hearty appetite and passion. I'm beginning to
think so too. Whenever I visit, I can be assured of a large
meal and a not-so-subtle advance. So far the food has
been worth it.

It was a warm, late August afternoon, and despite the
traumatic events of the day, I enjoyed the ride out to
Doc's. August has its detractors, those who say that it is
too hot and dry, and that it is the faded end of summer.
The dog days, they call it. I love August. I love driving
down the shimmering asphalt of the narrow county roads
when the corn is tall. For some reason, it makes me think
of the ocean, which I've never seen. I love the high, shrill
sounds of the summer insects, the closest I'll ever come
to a night in a tropical forest. The cottony cumulus
clouds of an August day are unsurpassed. The warm August nights are soft, like brushed velvet. August is magic
to me, and if I have to be accused of a murder, I'd rather
it be then than in any other month.

I was in a fairly good mood when I drove into Doc's
long, circular driveway. During the drive from town I had
managed to shed the entire murder business, Melvin and
all. In fact, I had no intention of even bringing up the
subject to Doc then. And, as if he'd been cued, old Doc
showed up at the door with a spatula in hand. Doc's food
will take your mind off everything but your taste buds.

"It's potato pancakes with apple sauce, fried pork
chops, and fresh green beans," he said.

"Do you have enough for two?" I asked foolishly. Doc
normally cooks enough for four, and if no surprise visitors show up, eats it all himself. The endocrinologist who
discovers the secret to Doc's metabolism is going to end
up a rich woman.

"There's green-tomato pie for dessert, and homemade ice cream, if you'll crank it yourself."

"Cranking is my specialty."

Doc and I settled down to a long dinner that began very pleasantly. He told me about Esther Millhouse's pet Labrador who had somehow managed to swallow a waterproof watch with an alarm, and who now, every morning at five, barked when it felt the alarm go off. Esther much preferred the barking to the sound of the alarm, and had simply wanted to know if leaving it in the dog would be harmful.

"And would it?" I asked with a mouth full of pork chop.

"The point is that Esther was concerned about it being harmful to the watch, not the dog. She didn't want me operating as long as the watch continued to work and the alarm went off on schedule. So I took a little magnet off one of those little refrigerator doohickies, wrapped it up in some dog food, and fed it to Rover. The next day Esther called me up and said the watch had stopped."

"You didn't!"

Doc grinned. "Then Esther brought the dog back in and I removed both the watch and the magnet. Rover's back in the kennel there now, doing just fine."

"You're quite something, Doc." I think that was a mistake.

"So are you, Magdalena." Doc pretended to reach for another potato pancake, but he had something else on his mind.

I dodged, nearly spilling the apple sauce. "Watch it, Doc."

Old Doc frowned. "You still dating that guy down in Baltimore?"

"We aren't dating, Doc. I haven't even met him yet. We just talk on the phone. We're good friends."

"He isn't right for you, Magdalena. That Maryland crowd is a wild bunch anyway, but hooking up with someone over the phone is asking for trouble. It's like answering one of those personal ads in the back of a magazine. They're all weirdos, you know."

I ignored Doc's comments. It was clear that he was jealous of my deepening relationship with Jim Fortuna of Baltimore. True, I had met Jim on the phone, but it was purely accidental. A federal drug enforcement agent working under cover had been murdered at the PennDutch, and when I was calling the work number listed on her registration, Jim had answered the phone. It was Jim's number all right—the number for Jumbo Jim's Fried Chicken and Seafood Palace, and the federal agent had simply usurped it. Ever since then, Jim and I have been planning to get together—just to chat face-to-face, mind you, but it has never quite worked out.

"What kind of a man calls himself Jumbo Jim?" Doc persisted in asking. "Isn't that a little arrogant?"

I could feel myself blushing. "The jumbo part stands for the size of the portions he serves, and you are a dirty old man."

Doc grinned happily in acknowledgment. "Just as long as he stays south of the Mason-Dixon line, I don't mind too much. But like I said, those Marylanders are a tough bunch, so you'd be wise to keep it a long-distance relationship."

"I'm afraid it's a little too late for that," I said dangerously.

Doc's eyes narrowed. "How so?"

I swallowed hard. I hate hurting Doc, but I do have my own life to live. "Jumbo—I mean Jim—is coming up this weekend. At least he was planning to before what happened this morning."

"You mean the murder out at your place?"

I don't know why it surprised me that Doc already knew about it. When Roy Beiler died of a heart attack in Emma Rumple's bed, Doc knew about it even before Mrs. Beiler did. I have long suspected that Doc has strategically placed spies. "You seeing Zelda?" I asked boldly.

"What?" said Doc. He seemed genuinely astonished.

"Never mind. Doc, you know I didn't do it, right?"

"Right."

"So, how do I prove to Melvin that I didn't?"

"That's not your job, Magdalena. In this country, at least last time I checked, you are considered innocent until proven guilty. Not the other way around. It's Melvin's job to come up with the evidence against you."

"Yeah, I know, but this is Melvin Stoltzfus we're talking about. It wouldn't surprise me one bit if he produced Elvis as his eyewitness."

"Guess I shouldn't have treated him when that horse kicked him in the head."

"Bull."

"Whatever. From what I gather, the most damning piece of evidence is missing. At least that's in your favor."

I must have stared at Doc with my mouth wide open, because the next thing I knew he had shoved a piece of pork chop in. I spit it out. "Doc! What do you mean by damning evidence? You know I didn't do it."

"Of course you didn't. But your fingerprints are all over that pitchfork, aren't they?"

"Yes, but so are Mose's, and, come to think of it, Steven Freeman's. And that's all in addition to the killer's."

"Right, but like you said, you are dealing with Melvin, and . . . uh . . . and—"

I did the mature thing and decided to save Doc a little embarrassment. "You mean I opened my big fat mouth and shouted out something that might have sounded like a threat."

"Close enough."

"Oh, Doc," I wailed, "what will I do?"

Doc reached out to pat me, but instinctively I pulled away. Fortunately he didn't seem to mind. "Look, Magdalena, if I were you, I'd keep my eyes open for clues leading to whoever really did it, and point Melvin in that direction. He might not stay with the scent long, but it will at least give you a breather. In the meantime, you might be able to piece together a few things yourself."

"In other words, I should solve the crime myself, just to keep Melvin off my back?"

Doc looked genuinely sorry for me. "Considering the alternative, I'd have to say yes."

"Life isn't fair!" I wailed.

"Of course not," said Doc. He looked around, as if trying to spot spies, and lowered his voice to an almost inaudible whisper. "So cheat a little bit."

Eight

SOMETIME during my brief absence from the inn, a plague of reporters had descended on my front lawn. Although they weren't eating my grass as locusts might have, they were damaging it all the same.

"Get off my grass," I said not unpleasantly at first.

But reporters, like locusts, are not known for their acute hearing. Locusts don't even have ears, and as for reporters, the appendages they sport are for show. A reporter's ears might as well be made of latex.

"Get off my grass before I pitch you off," I said perhaps carelessly.

"Would that be with a *pitch*fork?" asked a particularly obnoxious-looking young woman. I hate pert and perky little women who are color-coordinated and flawlessly coiffed. And it's worse if they're young.

"No comment," I said, still living dangerously.

"Then perhaps you might care to comment on the deceased's mob connections."

"His what?"

"Oh, come now, you're not going to pretend you don't know anything about Don Manley's ties with the syndicate? He was scheduled to go before a New Jersey grand jury at the end of the month on money-laundering charges, something he presumably did to help pay off a huge debt that—"

"Arnold Hetrick from *Far-Out Magazine*," interrupted a rather seedy-looking man. "Is it true, Miss Yoder, that you and Don Manley were lovers, and that you killed him because he was having an affair with Darla Strutt on the side?"

"That's absolutely not true, Arnie," I said. I grabbed the unsuspecting pert reporter and put my arm around her shoulders. "It's we who are lovers." Then I gave her a quick smooch on the forehead and fled inside while the two of them were still in shock.

Susannah was furious when I got back to the inn. She got right in my face, as they say. "Some dude named Jumbo called for you four times! What do you think I am, Mags, your damned answering service?"

I smiled sweetly. "Swear at me again, Susannah, and it will be your last time."

"What is this, another murder threat?" my sister asked meanly, but she backed off.

"So, what did Jim want?"

"How should I know? Call him and talk to him yourself."

I did.

"Jumbo Jim's Fried Chicken and Seafood Palace," said the cheery voice.

"Hi, Jim, it's me, Magdalena."

"Doll!"

"Susannah said you called. Sorry I was out."

"No prob. We still on for this weekend?"

"That depends, Jim. There's been another murder out at my place, and our police chief thinks I'm a suspect."

"You guilty?"

"Not of murder, Jim."

"Then no prob, doll. Be at your place at six sharp on Saturday."

"Things are a little bit hectic here, Jim, what with the movie and the murder. Can we meet at Ed's Steak House in Bedford? It's right off the turnpike, on old U.S. 220."

"Can do, doll. See you then." Jim hung up.

Okay, so Jim isn't big on words. Anyway, talk is cheap, as Grandma Yoder used to say. At least I had the makings of a man in my life, which was more than I could say for a long time. All right, so it was the first time, but we all have a first time. It's nothing to get proud about.

In Hernia, when someone dies, people take notice. Men shine their shoes and get out their ties, and the women bake a couple of pies for the postfuneral meal. Things must be different in Hollywood. Once Don's body was removed from my barn to the county morgue, Reels and Runs Productions proceeded with their business as if nothing had happened. The very morning after the murder, shooting resumed.

"There have been a few script revisions, folks," Steven stated as he passed around new copies to those of us with speaking parts.

I glanced anxiously at my copy. After a couple of seconds, I gave up glancing and sat down to read, as had virtually everyone else. The script fairies, or whoever they were, had been very busy overnight. Whereas the old script had been primarily about a berserk Amishman who strangled and then did unspeakable things to women in a bathtub, the new script called for the movie to be filmed almost exclusively in a barn. My barn. And instead of a mad Amishman drowning women, there was now a mad but grossly deformed Amishman living among the hay bales who was terrified of anyone entering his secret domain. A sort of *The Hunchback of Yoder's Barn*. Only this was no sweet, passive hunchback, but a mean-tempered fellow with a deadly aim when it came to throwing pitchforks. Of course, there might have been other elements to the story as well, but it was hard for me to see them. Although this new version lacked exploitive sex, it was still packed with violence—a distinctly *un*-Amish or Mennonite trait.

I wasn't the only one who was dissatisfied with the revision. "I won't do it, Art," said Rip Oilman through clenched teeth.

Art mumbled something that presumably Rip heard, but Rip still wasn't placated. "I won't play a grossly deformed hunchback. My fans want to see me as I am." He patted his chest. "You're going to have to get someone else for the part."

"Try Melvin Stoltzfus," I couldn't help saying. "He's a natural."

Art ignored me and mumbled something else to Rip. I couldn't hear everything, but it had something to do with a contract.

"Then I'll buy myself out," said Rip. "I didn't want to come to this backwater location to begin with. The set is a dump, the food stinks, and you call that a motel we're staying in?"

"Right on," said Darla rudely.

Art broke character and shuffled over to Rip. Grabbing him by the arm, he steered him over to the far corner of the room. Then both men mumbled for an interminable length of time. When they broke huddle, Rip was smiling, and Art, at least, looked pleased.

"Then I want more money too," whined Darla. "I've been a star longer than Rip."

"Far longer," agreed Rip.

Darla flashed him daggers. I'm sure she would have flashed him pitchforks if she could have done so.

Steven swiftly translated Art's latest mumbling. "Okay, folks, we're going to break now for an early lunch, and then afterward, we meet at the barn for a rehearsal of Scene Thirty-two, on page one hundred and forty. There's no dialogue in that scene, so it shouldn't give us any problems. Miss Strutt, Mr. Oilman, Miss Yoder, and the Biddle sisters, we'll be needing all of you."

"And not me?" asked Susannah on the verge of tears.

Steven smiled. "Of course you. We can't shoot any of Miss Strutt's scenes without you to block them in. You're a very important person."

Susannah elbowed me on the way to lunch. "Did you hear that, Mags? Steven said I'm a very important person."

Fortunately, before I could think of a suitable response, Freni ambushed me. "Psst! Magdalena!"

I stepped gratefully into the kitchen, which smelled wonderful, as it always does when Freni cooks. "What is it?"

There was panic in Freni's voice when she spoke. "This early lunch. They can't do that. It's not ready yet!"

"Just do the best you can, Freni. It's they who called an early lunch. It's not your fault."

My temperamental little kinswoman untied her apron and pulled it over her head, nearly knocking off her white prayer bonnet in the process. "I quit, Magdalena. These English are too unpredictable. A meal is ready when it is done cooking, not before."

"What are you cooking?"

"Roast beef and barbecued chicken. But the roast beef is still raw and Mose just now put the chicken on the grill."

I patted Freni reassuringly. "You don't have a problem after all. The English love their beef raw. They call it 'rare.' And as for the chicken, stick it close up under the broiler for a few minutes until it turns nice and black. Then tell them it's Cajun style."

Freni reluctantly did what I suggested and got her highest reviews ever. Even the rude Rip Oilman, who had previously criticized her cooking, said that it was the best meal he'd had in recent memory. Allowing for the fact that Rip's memory probably goes back only a matter of days, it was still a nice thing to say.

Of course, Freni really only cared what Art thought about the meal. She was, after all, more fond of him than ever. If Art had grown a beard, shaved off his mustache, and worn plain clothes, Freni would have undoubtedly adopted him. Meanwhile, Freni's real son, John, toiled meaningfully away on the family farm, less than a mile away as the crow flies, all but forgotten by his mother. And just because he had married Barbara Zook, a six-foot-tall, sturdy gal from one of the western Amish communities, who had the bad habit of speaking her own mind from time to time. Apparently, two unfettered tongues in the same family do not tranquillity make.

I was the first of the cast to report to the barn. Although I am normally very conscientious and punctual, those were not my motives. I simply wanted to see the individual looks on the other cast members' faces when they entered the scene of the crime. My own, I'm sure, was a bit unusual.

Melvin had roped off the immediate area surrounding the post against which Don Manley had been forked, but it was visible from virtually any point on the lower level of the barn. The vast amount of blood the assistant director had spilled had, for the most part, soaked through the cracks of the barn floor, but there was one warped floor-board that had caught some of the blood and held it, as if it were a shallow wooden bowl. The blood had congealed and evaporated to the point that the residue resembled something very close to good old-fashioned German blood-pudding sausage. The entire bloodstained area was swarming with flies. In the midday August heat, my once clean and tidy barn smelled like a slaughterhouse, which, of course, it was.

Anyway, I climbed up to the first level of the hayloft, where most of the mad-Amishman scenes were to be filmed. Already the crew had positioned cameras and huge lights mounted on rolling pedestals. What seemed like miles and miles of cable spread in all directions. It was as if a giant spider had spun her web throughout my barn. Fortunately it was August, and Bessie and Matilda, my two Holstein cows, could spend their days outside. Mose had even volunteered to milk them outside, which would probably work in Bessie's case, because she was a wanton, shameless bovine anyway. Matilda, however, was very shy about giving her milk, as befits a Mennonite cow.

I sat there on the edge of the loft with my feet dangling over, and contemplated what my greed had wrought. There I was, dressed in traditional Amish garb, about to play the mother of a mad, pitchfork-pitching Amishman, in the same barn that had been built by my own Amish ancestors—peaceful ones, all of them. Back in the French and Indian War days, my ancestors, the Jacob Hochstetler family, had submitted to massacre by the Delaware Indians rather than lift a finger in their own defense. Historically we were a peace-loving, plain people, and now here was I, desecrating everyone's memory, and for what?

Money and a very slim chance at fame, or at least recognition. But it was a lot of money, enough to see Susannah
and me well into our dotage, even if the PennDutch
failed. And as for the fame, it is indeed a two-edged sword
that only the best of us can resist plunging willfully into
our own breasts. Clearly I did not number among the best
of us.

But of course I didn't stop there. Like just about everyone else, I made up excuses to justify my choices. The
movie would be made anyway, I reasoned. At least by allowing it to be filmed at the PennDutch, I could keep an
eye on it and try to exercise my control. We were to be in
the world, but not of it, Scripture told us, and I was simply
making sure that I was in it. I can admit now that I was in
it way over my head, but at the time my ability to rational-
ize was my most practiced skill. And anyway, the new
script, while it called for violence and other behavior un-
characteristic of the Amish, was at least devoid of exploitive sex. You'll give me that much, won't you?

The first people to return from lunch were some of the
crew members. I could tell they were unhappy that I was
up in the loft, sitting among their equipment, but I was
much older than they and dressed quite a bit differently,
so they were too intimidated to say anything. At any rate,
besides looking irritated when they saw me, none of them
showed much of a reaction when they trooped into the
barn. I certainly didn't see guilt written on their faces.
And I know what guilt looks like—I do use a mirror, you
know.

Of all the people that showed up on the set that day,
only Susannah averted her eyes from the beam to which
Don Manley had been pegged. But despite the fact that
Susannah is my sister, I very much doubted that she was
the killer. To stab someone, even through the abdomen,
with a pitchfork as blunted as mine would take consider-

able strength—something Susannah just does not have. She may be tall like me, but she is rail-thin. And besides which, with all her swirling yardage, Susannah would most certainly have gotten blood on her, and she hadn't. Even Melvin Stoltzfus hadn't been so stupid as to not check Susannah for blood. And she had come up clean. Anyway, it seemed to me that the killer was not on the set that afternoon, or else was an expert at masking emotions.

"What else would you expect?" asked Doc that evening over another piece of green-tomato pie. The pie, incidentally, came on the heels of two bowls each of Grandma Yoder's Secret Corn Chowder, which I had cooked.

"I don't get you, Doc."

"Well, they're actors, aren't they, Magdalena? Even Art, the producer, used to be an actor, and I bet that Bugsy fellow has had a few drama classes too. Anyway, my point is, they're trained to wear masks. To show emotions on their faces that they're not actually feeling."

"It's hopeless, then, I guess."

Doc laughed and shoved the pie dish toward me. "Have another piece, and don't be so quick to give up. Look, you can't prove anything anyway by the look on somebody's face. You need concrete evidence."

"How do I look for evidence, and how do I know it when I see it?"

"Well, for starters, quit looking on the outside of people, and start looking on the inside. Look for motive. Ask yourself who has the strongest motive, and then, once you've got motive, you can start looking for physical clues."

"I believe they call that method acting."

"Hunh. Whatever. The thing is, Magdalena, most people don't go around killing unless they feel they have a good reason." Doc paused and played with his pie for a few seconds. "Well, at least that's the way it used to be. Nowadays, if you can believe what you hear on the news, people kill each other for the damnedest reasons. None that makes any sense to me."

"Or me."

"But that's exactly my point, isn't it? It has to make sense only to them, not us. You and I probably wouldn't kill for any reason, but there are a lot of reasons out there why people kill, and you need to come up with the most likely one in this case."

"How about the mob, Doc? A reporter told me Don Manley owed a lot to the mob."

"Maybe," said Doc, but he didn't sound interested in that theory. "If I were you, I'd look closer to home. Find someone this Manley guy stepped on in an unforgivable sort of way. That type of thing. It's just a thought, Magdalena, but that's what I'd look for."

"Thanks, Doc."

"Say, you still planning to meet that chicken fryer from Baltimore on Saturday?"

"Jim? Yeah, Doc. We're going to have dinner at Ed's Steak House. What of it?"

Doc looked away, but not before I caught the look in his eyes. "Just you be careful, Magdalena. Those Maryland folks are a tough lot, and the ones from Baltimore in particular. You want me to go along? Just in case, I mean."

I patted old Doc's hand. I was genuinely warmed inside by his consideration. Or was it his jealousy? It didn't matter. As long as it didn't get out of hand, whatever Doc was feeling flattered me. "That's okay, Doc, I'm sure I can handle Jim just fine." At least I was looking forward to trying.

That night I dreamed about my upcoming date with

Jim. In my dream, Jim was a tall, broad-shouldered man in his mid-forties. I suppose he had a handsome face, but all I remember were his cold blue eyes.

"Hi, I'm Magdalena," I said in my dream.

"My name is Parsley," said the man with the cold blue eyes. "Elvis Parsley." He laughed, the kind of laugh that sends shivers down your spine.

"But I thought you were Jim," I said. We had been standing outside Ed's Steak House, but suddenly it had become my henhouse. Neither of us seemed to care about the change of setting.

"My name was Jim," said the man, "but now it's Parsley. Can't you ever get anything right, Magdalena?"

"Yes, of course," I started to protest. Then the man with the cold blue eyes, who I had thought was Jim, turned into my mother. Mercifully I woke up at that point.

Nine

ABOUT FOUR in the morning, I woke up with a full bladder. Mama used to call that hour of the morning the deathwatch. She claimed that more people died at four in the morning than at any other time. When Grandma Yoder died, it was precisely 4:03. I know, because I was awakened by what I thought was Grandma's voice saying good-bye. I remember glancing at my bedside clock, and telling myself that it was all a dream and I should go back to sleep. But then, before I could as much as close my eyes, I heard Mama crying because, as I learned later, Grandma had just died. Mama had been holding her hand when it happened.

Anyway, after I used the toilet, I couldn't go back to sleep again. It wasn't that I sensed someone had just died, but because my mind was racing with thoughts about who had killed Don Manley. It might even have been the spirit of Don Manley who was putting those thoughts in my mind, but of course I would never suggest such a thing to anyone. We Amish-Mennonites firmly do not believe in ghosts, even if they stare us sometimes in the face.

About five o'clock I gave up on going back to sleep and got dressed. In the summertime that's just when the first birds began to twitter, and it's almost impossible to go back to sleep then under the best of circumstances. When I got outside, the sky had lightened enough so that I could see the corn tassels in the field behind the six-seater and the chicken coop. Without exactly meaning to, I found myself skirting these two buildings and heading for the barn.

Just before the main entrance to the barn is the Dutch door that leads to the cowshed. The top half was open and I poked my head in. Matilda, ever the shy one, mooed softly in the corner, but Bessie ambled over to me and snuffled my hair. "Be good girls and give Mose a lot of milk this morning," I urged them.

I walked over to the main door. It was open about eighteen inches, which surprised me. Normally, either Mose or I close it at night. But with the camera, light, and sound equipment it now contained, we did more than close it. I specifically remembered Mose telling me that he had locked the door with a padlock at Art's request. The padlock was missing.

I have always been a confronter, rushing headlong into difficult situations. I hate being held hostage by my own fear, preferring to act rashly than wait in agony. So, acting rashly, I slipped into the barn and felt for the light switch. Back in the days when my people were Amish, there had been no light in the barn, but my grandparents had joined the Mennonite church and were allowed electricity. It was Grandpa Yoder who had wired the barn, and he'd done a bang-up job. Then Papa improved on it by replacing Grandpa's incandescent bulbs with fluorescent fixtures. When I flipped the switch just inside the door, the barn was flooded in light, from the pigeon-filled rafters to the bloodstained floor.

It was at that instant of revelation that I caught my glimpse of someone, or something, slipping out through the small side door that locks only from the inside. Foolishly, I called out and ran to investigate. But there was nothing revealing for me to see. On that side of the barn the woods creeps up close, and who or whatever I'd seen, had presumably been swallowed up by them.

"You should have called me first," said Melvin both before and after a futile hike in the woods to look for clues.

"I'm sorry, Melvin. I acted without thinking. I bet you'd have done the same thing if you were me." I meant it as a sort of compliment.

Melvin's left eye began to wander in its orbit. "I hardly think so. What you did was to interfere with police business. And it could have gotten you killed, Yoder."

I looked away from Melvin so as to avoid the temptation to be critical. He can't help it if he looks like a praying mantis and has the intelligence of a moth. It is unchristian of me to dislike him so.

"Melvin, isn't there any way you can get fingerprints from the doors?"

"Ever hear of gloves, Yoder?"

"There's a pair I keep for milking in the cowshed," I said cruelly.

"Very funny, Yoder. I don't suppose it occurred to you that the trespasser was wearing gloves when he handled the doors."

"Or she."

"What?"

"I mean that the trespasser, as you call it, might well have been a woman."

Melvin laughed, either that or a cicada sounded its mating call. "A woman! You're a barrel of laughs, Yoder. Not that it's occurred to you, but the trespasser and the perpetrator may well be one and the same. And no woman, Yoder, despite your fancy women's lib, could pin a man to a beam with a pitchfork."

It was my turn to laugh, and this time with relief. "I guess that leaves me out of it. I'm no longer your *suspecto numero uno,* then, am I?"

Melvin's left eye scanned my face, while his right one seemed to be studying my shoes. "Have you gone mad, Yoder?"

"I've been close, but so far not nearly as close as you. Why?"

"Because you most certainly are still my *suspecto numero uno.* But with an accomplice, of course."

"A what?"

"An accomplice. Come on, Yoder. Even Lee Harvey Oswald didn't assassinate Kennedy by himself. The question is, who is your co-conspirator?"

Had I been handed a pitchfork just then, I might well have made a gelding out of Melvin. "For your information, Melvin Stoltzfus, there is a word for people who see plots and conspiracies everywhere. The word is paranoid. Read my lips, Melvin, I do not have a co-conspirator."

"Ah-ha! So you admit that you killed Don Manley by yourself."

"I admit no such thing. I couldn't have killed him by myself, remember? I'm just a woman."

"Exactly," Melvin agreed. "I've been trying to tell you that all along. No woman, even you, Magdalena, is strong enough to drive a pitchfork through a man's gut and pin him to a beam."

"Would that we were," I said dangerously.

"What?"

"Nothing. Except that you're barking up the wrong tree, Melvin. In fact, you're not even in the right woods. And as for your statement that the murderer could not possibly have been a woman, you're full of—" I didn't finish my sentence, but kicked discreetly at a pile of pigeon droppings.

"And anyway," said Melvin as if he hadn't heard a thing I'd just said, "it's a fact that most women murder their victims through less violent means. You know, poison and such."

"Lizzie Borden took an ax," I reminded him.

"That theory has been challenged," he said smugly.

I started to rack my brain for another example of female brutality, and then, realizing how absurd it all was, stifled a laugh of my own. There was nothing to gain by convincing Melvin that the trespasser had been a woman, and there was quite possibly something to lose from it. In the convoluted paths of Melvin's mind, such a suggestion might well come home to rest at my feet. That the trespasser had been a woman I was becoming increasingly sure, although I could not pinpoint anything specific I had seen to back up my hunch. A hunch was all it was at the time, but a woman's hunch, as Grandma used to say, is worth two facts from a man.

I was in one scene that morning. It was the one where Darla Strutt, having first fallen in love with the mad Amishman, Yost Yoder, and then been betrayed by that love, is tied to a beam and forked through the middle. I played Yost Yoder's mother, Anna, who lives in a world of denial and cannot admit her son's condition. So, you see, it wasn't as bad as the original script, where Freddy the mad Amishman rapes women in the bathtub and then cuts their throats, but still, it was enough to keep Mama turning in her grave.

I had exactly eighteen words to say: "Ah, my darling son, what have you done now? But perhaps it isn't as bad as it seems." I practiced saying them over and over, making them come out slightly different each time.

"Imagine Meryl Streep saying them," Susannah suggested.

Unfortunately I have never been to a movie. However, I had played the part of Pocahontas in the eighth grade, so that's what I based my delivery on for the camera.

"Cut!" snapped Steven. We were still in rehearsal, and the cameras weren't even rolling.

"Shall I start over fresh?" I asked cooperatively.

Steven smirked. "Two sticks of dynamite and a bulldozer couldn't give you a fresh enough start, Yoder."

I prayed for patience. "I mean, do you want me to start over at the beginning of my lines."

Steven stared at me.

"Well, should I start over again, or not?"

Steven steadfastly refused to answer. I think he was willing me to shrink to near nothing in size and fall between the cracks in the barn floor. Clearly it was time for me to take my destiny in my own two hands, which are, after all, quite lovely. So I repeated my lines one more time, but this time I said them as I, Magdalena Yoder, would say them—*if* I were the mother of a mad Amishman who had just pinned his paramour to a barn beam.

"Brava!" someone shouted. "Brava!" I nearly fainted when I discovered it was Art Lapata.

"So you do have a voice," I said when he took me aside.

Art smiled. "Yes, but I hate to waste it on riffraff."

"Ah, so I've been suddenly elevated from riffraff to something else. What might that be? Scum?"

Art chuckled warmly. "I've had my eye on you the

whole time, Miss Yoder. I immediately noticed a certain presence."

"It's all right to say tall. Five ten, as a matter of fact. And if you're asking, the weather up here is just fine. Maybe even a degree or two cooler than down there, where you are."

"And fire too," said Art.

"You can't fire me—I quit!" If Freni could say that— which she did with some regularity—then so could I.

Art laughed openly. "Simmer down, Miss Yoder. I have no intention of firing you. To the contrary, I'm more interested in hiring you."

It was my turn to stare. "But I'm already hired. I work for you. I mean, I have a part in this movie."

Art lowered his voice just a smidgen. Not that he was becoming a recluse again. I think he just didn't want the others to hear. "This isn't a movie, Miss Yoder, this is a grade-B fiasco. I mean, I want you in a real movie."

Staring too long, especially in a barn, can make your eyes water. "Then why are you here, filming this, if it's nothing but a fiasco."

Art spread his hands in a gesture of resignation. "It's a matter of a contract. You see, Miss Yoder, I'm under obligation to do one more picture with Reels and Runs Productions. Unfortunately for both parties concerned, the executive producer has abominable taste, and strong nepotistic tendencies."

I put my hands over my ears. "I don't listen to dirty talk, Mr. Lapata."

Art gently pulled my hands away. "Nepotism is when people give preferential treatment to their relatives. In this case, the executive producer, who is also our main financier, had his nephew write the script. The original script, at any rate. The one with all the bathtub scenes."

"That was pure trash."

"Exactly. And although I couldn't absent myself completely from the project, I tried to distance myself as much as I could."

"You did a good job. I was beginning to think you were a mute."

"If only I'd been deaf and blind as well. You see, not only did this nephew write the script, he was hired as my assistant director."

I stared again. I'm convinced that I suffer from a genetic tendency to have the eyes remain fixedly open when shocked. "You mean that Don Manley is, or was, the executive producer's nephew?"

Art nodded sorrowfully. "I should have fought it more. Even sued to get out of my contract if necessary. I guess I thought I was taking the easy way out."

"The straight-and-narrow path is often the hardest, but it is the right one," I said, quoting Mama. I don't think you can undo grave spins, but it can't hurt to try.

"Of course, I made a huge mistake. I see that now. And even after it was too late to back out, I should have stayed in charge. If I hadn't let Don take over so much, he might not have been killed."

"Maybe not here," I said without much pity, "but sooner or later."

"He was totally obnoxious," Art agreed.

We talked more at supper, much to Freni's dismay. She glowered at me every chance she got, and if she'd been one of those hexy Dutch instead of a God-fearing Amishwoman, I'm sure she'd have put a spell on me. Of course she need not have worried. I wasn't about to adopt Art Lapata, even though he was maybe a year or two younger, and I definitely wasn't in search of a boyfriend. After all, Saturday was only two days away, and Jumbo Jim had first dibs on my heart.

"Who wrote the revised script, then?" I asked. I was

careful not to talk with fried potatoes or pork chop in my mouth.

"I did. What do you think? Honestly."

"Honestly?"

Art nodded.

"I like *Green Acres* better."

"I don't blame you. *My Mother the Car* had a better premise."

"Why don't you just tell the real story of the PennDutch murders?"

Art sighed. "Truth is, we couldn't get all the necessary releases. The congressman who was involved threatened to sue—"

"You mean ex-congressman, by now."

"Yeah, anyway, you get the drift."

Then something occurred to me. "Look, Art, I know you put a lot of work into the new script, but it isn't too late to change it, is it?"

"What's on your mind?"

"Well, you could tell a more realistic story. Instead of a mad Amishman and his out-of-touch mother, why don't you do a story about an Amishwoman whose son marries a girl she doesn't like, and all the problems that stem from that?" I glanced furtively at Freni. Her broad back was turned in my direction, which undoubtedly meant she had tuned me out. Her hearing would kick in only at the sound of her beloved Arthur's voice.

Art's eyes seemed to bore right through me. At first I thought I'd said something dreadfully wrong. Perhaps he had married a girl his mother didn't approve of. Oh, Lord, I thought, when will I ever learn to keep my big mouth shut?

Then Art pounded the table so hard that even Shnookums, safe within Susannah's bra, felt the tremor. I assume that Darla's mutt was similarly affected, because both dogs yipped. "That's it!" shouted Arthur. "That's a wonderful idea!" Then, conscious that everyone was staring at us, he lowered his voice considerably. "You will, of course, help me with the script? I mean, as a technical adviser."

Needless to say, I was immensely flattered. But something else was nagging at my mind, and with enough persistence to give me the needed dose of perspective. "I'd love to help out," I said honestly, "but I don't have a lot of time right now."

Art smiled reassuringly. "Don't worry about having to memorize all your dialogue. I prefer my actors to ad-lib. Up until this fiasco, it's always been my trademark."

"I'm not worried about that. What I'm worried about is finding Don Manley's killer. That's what I need the time for."

He looked surprised. "Why you? Why can't the police handle it?"

I said a quick prayer that God would guard my tongue. "Because our police department here in Hernia is not exactly on the ball," I said with relative charity. "And because at the moment I am their number one suspect."

Art blinked a couple of times, but didn't faint or anything. "I see. Well, I meant what I said, Miss Yoder—"

"You may call me Magdalena."

"Magdalena, then. I still want you to help me out on the script. As much as you can."

"Thanks," I said softly. Then I turned and pretended to look at a quilt hanging on the dining room wall. Nobody, but nobody, gets to see me cry.

Ten

GRANDMA YODER'S SECRET CORN CHOWDER

Makes 8 servings

1 pound bacon
1 large onion, chopped
1 can cream of chicken soup
1 pint half-and-half
2 cans creamed corn
Salt and pepper to taste

START by cooking up the bacon. Grandma fried her bacon in a cast iron skillet, as does Freni, but when it's my turn to cook, I zap it in a microwave. Crumble the cooked bacon and set it aside, saving two or three tablespoons of the grease.

In a large pot, sauté the onion in the bacon grease

until it softens and begins to brown. Stir in the cream of chicken soup and the half-and-half. Dump in the creamed corn and season to taste with salt and pepper.

Serve with the crumbled bacon sprinkled on top. This soup tastes even better when made the day before and allowed to sit in the refrigerator overnight. Just remember to heat it up very slowly the next day so it doesn't scorch, as it is rather thick.

Eleven

ART AND I stayed up until the wee hours rewriting the script, but by the time we knocked off work, we had enough pages to resume shooting the next day. While it certainly wasn't Academy Award–winning material, it was pretty darn good if I say so myself.

Since none of that morning's scenes involved me, I decided to follow up on some people who seemed, at least to me, to have a motive for doing Don in. The first person I picked, only because she lived on my way into town, was Norah Hall.

The Halls live in one of those split-level ranch houses that combine pastel-colored aluminum siding and fake brick on the exterior. Incongruously, there are a couple of fiberglass pillars stuck here and there—a sort of Tara designed by Picasso. Their home is fairly new, and the maple trees planted in the front yard are hardly more than bushes. Their neighbors on both sides and across the road live in houses that are variations on the same theme. In Hernia, at least, homes like these scream out that their owners have bought into the upper-middle-class cliché. Heavy debts, multiple marriages, a penchant for electronic gadgets, status cars, and an obsession with health and exercise are all common denominators. And, of course, large eat-in kitchens with islands set adrift here and there. It is a dictum among these folks that there are few things in life more important than the exact shade of avocado for one's refrigerator, unless it's the size of one's CD collection. Life for these people, or so I imagine, is one long nightmare. Living in abject fear of a power failure has got to take its toll.

There was one late-model car in the Halls' driveway and naturally, given that I too think in clichés, I just assumed it was Norah's. Ed Hall worked at a bank in Bedford, and as far as I knew, it was not a banking holiday. I made my way somewhat timorously up the impeccably clean walk, which was lined with precisely edged grass of a disgustingly uniform length. It wasn't until I was right at the front door that I noticed the wooden painted goose with the bow around its neck half-hidden in the shrubbery. I rang the doorbell, hoping that someone would answer it before I puked.

Norah took forever to answer, and when she did, she was wearing a sort of orange kimono thing. Perhaps she thought of it as a bathrobe, but whatever it was, Susannah would have loved it. "Yes?"

"Norah, it's me, Magdalena. May I come in?"

"I know who you are, Magdalena. Frankly, I'm a bit busy right now. Can you come back later?"

How busy can you be in a bathrobe, I wanted to ask. "When later?" I asked pleasantly.

"People with manners always ring first, before they call on you," said Norah coolly, not answering my question.

"I'll remember that next time they shoot a movie out at my place and you and Sherri pop up."

Norah's mouth began to twitch, but before she could sputter out any words, a man's shape loomed up behind her. He too was wearing a kimono, a blue one, but he most certainly was not Ed Hall.

"Hi there," I said in my friendliest voice.

He grunted a greeting.

"Magdalena, this really isn't what you think it is," said Norah predictably.

I didn't stifle my laugh. Susannah has used that phrase on me a million times, and invariably she's right. Whatever is going on isn't what I initially think it is, it's much worse. "I'm not here to pass judgment, Norah. I simply need to ask you a few questions."

"He's not married, if that's what you think, and no, Sherri isn't here, she spent the night at a friend's."

"Uh-huh. But that's not what I wanted to know. It has to do with the movie they're making out at my place."

Norah's face had the look of a little girl being forced to choose between her favorite ice cream and her favorite candy. "All right, Magdalena, come in, but just for a second. You don't mind excusing us, do you, Garth?"

Garth? But of course, what other name would an adulterer have? I followed Norah into the perfectly decorated living room, perfect in that its furnishings were identical to the ones in the surrounding houses, with, perhaps, slight variations in color schemes. Garth, after having grunted a few more words, retreated docilely into another room.

"Please, have a seat," said Norah.

I sat down on a puffy, cream-colored sofa, and Nora settled her kimono in a puffy, cream-colored chair.

"Arthur Lapata sends his greetings," I lied. It is all right to lie, you know, if your life is at stake.

Norah beamed. "Such a dear, talented man. I've seen every one of his movies and loved them all. Have you seen *Seven Little Nerds and How They Grew?*"

I waved a hand noncommittally. "Oh, yes, Art is very special. Not like Don Manley was."

Norah frowned. "Manley was a rude, arrogant boor. He couldn't see talent if it bit him. Whoever did him in was doing the world a favor."

"Do tell."

"Of course, I knew there would be other opportunities. I just didn't think they'd come so soon."

"God works in mysterious ways. I suppose you went straight home that morning? I mean, after Manley so cruelly and wrongly dismissed your daughter."

Norah's brow puckered even more. "Of course I didn't go straight home. What kind of a mother do you think I am? My daughter was destroyed by that man, Magdalena, absolutely destroyed."

The angrier Norah got, the happier I became. It's when Susannah is the angriest that she's the most likely to spill the beans. "So then, after that scumball of a man destroyed your daughter, what did you do?"

Norah's cackle would have made my hen Pertelote proud. "Why, I took her into Somerset to do some serious shopping! What else do you think one does at a time like that?"

"You mean you didn't hang around my place for a while? Maybe take a walk out to the barn?"

The orange kimono popped up off the cream-colored chair. "And just what are you trying to get at, Magdalena? You don't for a second think I might have had something to do with that creep's death, do you?"

Lying to save oneself embarrassment is only marginally acceptable, but I did it anyway. "Ha, that's a good one!

Of course not. I was only hoping that you might have seen something suspicious."

"The only suspicious thing I can think of is your motive for coming here. Arthur Lapata didn't send you out here to give Sherri another chance, did he?"

I must admit, that one took me by surprise. "No, but I'm sure he'll keep her in mind for his next picture."

"Anything else you wanted to know, Magdalena?"

I thought of asking how much she had paid for the slime-green wing chair no one had chosen to sit in, but prudently decided to stick to business. "You weren't by any chance roaming about my henhouse, were you, dear?"

It may have been just my imagination, but I thought I saw the woman blush. "Most certainly not! This is a cholesterol-free family. Now, is there anything else you wanted?"

"Actually, some tea would be nice. With cream and sugar."

Norah didn't even smile. She didn't exactly drag me to the door, but she did put her hands on me. I left without resistance. Four hundred years of pacifism is a hard thing to shake.

Hernia is a fairly homogeneous town, but there are two small streets on the south side that are frequently, and uncharitably, referred to as Ragsdale. When Susannah and I were girls (at separate times, of course), our school bus used to stop in this part of town to take on students. It was common knowledge among us children that the Ragsdale kids were a breed apart. Some of them wore tattoos, many of them smoked, and on at least three occasions Miss Proschel, our bus driver, had to confiscate knives. Like many other stereotypes in this world, Ragsdale's bad reputation was based on both fact and fancy.

I will admit that I was nervous when, after leaving Norah's bland burb, I headed toward Ragsdale. At the first sign of a broken-down sofa on a front porch, my pulse began to race. When I spotted the first washing machine beside one of these broken-down sofas, my heart began to pound. Call me prejudiced, but I just can't help it. I know that the depth of my feelings is irrational, but ever since Billy Scott sat on the bus beside me and demonstrated without a shadow of a doubt that he was too poor to wear underwear, I have been devoid of middle-class guilt.

The Biddle house fit the Ragsdale profile perfectly. It was long and narrow with a gray, tar-shingled exterior. The front porch sagged under the weight of *two* broken-down sofas, plaid, of course, and a washing machine. The screen in the front door was slashed in at least three places, and through it I could see the light emitted by a huge TV set. Some silly game show was in progress. I think the woman who spun the wheel was called Vanity White.

Since there was only the loose end of a wire where the doorbell should have been, I knocked. Even that was tricky. The screen door had neither a spring nor a hook, and when I knocked, it swung open in front of me, bidding me to fall in after it. I grabbed the much-gouged lintel. "Hello?" I called.

Nobody answered.

I didn't exactly just walk in then, but, still holding on to the lintel, I leaned in as far as I could. "Hello? Anybody home?"

Slowly, like Lazarus might have risen from the dead, somebody sat up on the inside sofa. In the dim light and cigarette haze, it was hard to make out any details. "Whatcha want?" said a gravelly voice.

"I'd like to speak to Mr. or Mrs. Biddle, please."

"Who're you?"

"My name is Magdalena Yoder. I own the PennDutch Inn, where the movie is being filmed."

The figure on the couch stood up and shuffled to the door. It was only when it was about ten feet from me that I realized it was a woman. She was wearing purple stirrup pants, pink bunny slippers, and a black and yellow striped polyester tank top. Her hair was set in huge, lethal-looking rollers the size of orange juice cans. If the loose door-bell wire ever came in contact with one of those, the wearer would have a permanent that was indeed permanent.

"What's it about? My daughters okay?"

I had no way of knowing. The Biddle sisters weren't even scheduled that day, and they certainly hadn't shown up at the PennDutch to my knowledge. "As far as I know, they're just fine. It's not them I wanted to see, but you and your husband."

"Red's in the tank, down in Bedford."

"Does he clean aquariums?"

She looked at me like Susannah does when I say something dumb. "Red's sleeping off a drunk. Speaking of which, you wanna drink?"

I am ashamed to confess this, but I was sorely tempted. Except for the snakebite remedy Papa used to hide in the basement, these lips have never tasted alcohol. Just once I'd like to take a swig—make that several swigs—of the real stuff and see what all the hoopla's about. Of course, I would really never do such a thing, because my body is the living temple of the Lord. That's what I teach to my students in Sunday school. And besides, Mama said that if you drink alcohol, it shows up in your veins somehow, and people in the know can take one look at you and see that you're a sinner. Mama also said that people could tell if you'd lost your virginity or not, but I never did notice when Susannah lost hers.

"No thanks," I said ruefully.

"Well, you wanna come in and sit down at least? You're letting the flies in."

I glanced at the ripped and flapping screen, but curbed my tongue. "Sure, that'd be fine."

I was fascinated by her decor. I wouldn't have thought it possible to dent, scratch, or otherwise mar the furniture and walls so thoroughly. As for the floor, the bits of this and that that had accumulated on it through the years made it look like a ticker-tape parade had passed through.

"Here, you can sit here," she said. She swiped a couple of pounds of crushed chips, stray rollers, and used cotton balls onto the floor. There might have been a couple of used emery boards in there too.

I sat down, but didn't put all my weight on my buttocks until my knees finally gave out.

"So, what's this all about? What do you wanna see me and Red for?"

This necessary lie had been well prepared, and I was able to spit it out quickly and smoothly. "Well, I've been hired as chief personal liaison between Reels and Runs Productions and its short-term employees. My job is to ascertain whether or not a harmonious and mutually beneficial atmosphere exists between said parties."

Mrs. Biddle was cooler than a snake in a bucket of ice water. She sucked on her cigarette a full minute before responding. "Come again?"

"What I meant to convey is that I am now acting as a mediator between management and its temporary employees in order to nip in the bud, so to speak, any festering grievances that might later lead to a full-blown labor dispute."

The woman finished sucking the life out of that cigarette and reached for a new one. "You're full of excrement, Miss Yoder. Odious, odoriferous offal."

"I beg your pardon!"

"Okay, to put it more simply, you're full of—"

"I know what you said! What I want to know is, where did you learn such, ah—"

"Big words, Miss Yoder?"

"Uh-huh."

"I'm bilingual, Miss Yoder. I can speak hifalutinese like you, or plain old everyday Ragsdalese."

"Well, you don't have to be so rude about it" was all I could think to say.

She lit up the new cigarette. "Remember Rissa Armbruster from your high school days?"

"Sure. She was in my class. She was valedictorian."

"Have you ever wondered what happened to her?"

Of course I had. Many times, especially in the years immediately following graduation, I'd secretly hoped that Rissa Armbruster would meet with some terrible calamity. If not a maiming automobile accident, then at least a severe case of disfiguring postadolescent acne. Not only was Rissa the prettiest girl in my grade, but she beat me out for valedictorian by one-tenth of a grade point. "I guess I've thought about her now and then," I admitted. "Why?"

"Because I was also voted most likely to succeed, that's why. And here I am!"

"You!"

"*C'est moi.* Now, when your mouth can close far enough for you to regain the power of speech, tell me why you're really here."

"To see how you and your husband feel about your two young daughters playing bimbo parts in some grade-B movie," I finally managed to say.

Rissa lackadaisically blew a trio of beautifully formed

smoke rings. "We support them all the way. They might be bimbos to you, Miss Yoder, but then again, anyone would be, wouldn't they?" She didn't wait for an answer, which is a shame, because I had one ready. "You come from a different world, Miss Yoder. No, make that a different universe. But what the hell difference does it make to you what my children do, or how I feel about it?"

"Because I'm about to be accused of murder," I blurted out stupidly.

"And you think we Biddles might have had something to do with it?"

Rissa put the cigarette back in her mouth, to free up her hands. I didn't resist this time either, but frankly, she was a lot rougher than Norah had been.

Twelve

THE PRESBYTERIAN PARSONAGE on Grove Street is a two-story white frame house that was built around the turn of the century. It is Victorian in style, with ginger-bread trim here and there, and boasts a couple of interesting stained glass and lead windows. Grove Street is not pretentious, but it is pleasant, with ancient spreading trees and tidy but not fussy, lawns separated by wrought iron fences. The classy people who don't have to prove it live on Grove Street, and on neighboring Elm, Maple, and Hickory streets. Susannah claims that the Cleavers, the Andersons, and the Stones all retired there, whoever they might be.

The Martha Sims who answered the door did not look at all like the Martha Sims I had seen on the movie set, or the Martha Sims I had seen at community church affairs. Presbyterians, at least those of Martha's ilk, are permitted to wear makeup, and the Martha Sims I knew, always did.

She also had a reputation for being a natty dresser who not only knew her color chart, but yours as well, and was quick to point out when she thought you had deviated from your appropriate hues. Susannah much admired Martha Sims, despite their differences in taste. But then again, why wouldn't she? It was the Presbyterians who got Susannah started on the wide and winding road to moral decay and spiritual degradation to begin with.

While I personally would not refer to Martha Sims as the whore of Babylon, as Freni has been known to do, I do think she sets a bad example for the wives of clergymen everywhere. A minister's wife is supposed to be dowdy. After all, when you're on the right track—that straight and narrow road—if you don't look at least a little bit frumpy and grumpy, how are people supposed to know you are sincere? Anyway, the Martha Sims who opened the door to me that morning was wearing blue jeans, of all things, a Bart Simpson T-shirt, and not a hint of makeup.

"Is your mommy home?" I asked before remembering that Martha and Orlando Sims had no children.

"Very funny, Magdalena. Incidentally, that shade of blue just isn't right for you. You're a spring, not a winter."

"It's summer, Martha. August. Remember?"

The woman didn't even have the courtesy to invite me inside. "We honor God by doing the best with what he gave us, Magdalena. And you could do so much with yourself."

I tried to smile pleasantly. After all, a little pain makes one feel more alive. "Martha dear, I didn't come here to talk about fashion."

Martha did not return my smile. "As I've told you before, I'm not responsible for whom your sister married. She tried to push the door closed in my face, but I've had a lot of practice pushing back against salespeople, and, in some cases, Susannah's boyfriends.

"I'm not here to see you about my sister."

"Then what do you want?"

"It's about the movie. Arthur Lapata sent me." Although it isn't any easier, it is definitely more fun to lie to a minister's wife. I know it sounds awful to hear me say that, but I'm only being truthful.

Martha stopped pushing. *"He* sent you?"

I tried the same sort of smile that Buick Bob uses when he so rudely interrupts *Green Acres* with his four-minute commercials. "Art is now in the process of writing a new script, and he wants some directional feedback from people in the community who are both knowledgeable and influential." How Bob manages to hold that smile for four minutes, while talking the entire time, is beyond me.

"Come in, Magdalena, please," said Martha quickly. She didn't exactly pull me in, but she might well have had I not been so quick on my feet.

Martha bade me sit on a walnut burl Victorian love seat upholstered in antique-blue cut velvet. It was really quite attractive. While Martha trotted off to the kitchen to fetch us both some tea and pound cake with strawberries and whipped cream—her idea, not mine—I glanced appreciatively around the room.

The love seat was only part of a well-preserved matched set. In addition to the Victorian furniture, the Sims house contained many other treasures that piqued my interest. I was in the process of examining a bronze statuette of a nude but not unattractive man riding a fish, when Martha returned with her tray.

"That's a copy of Antonio Berretta's *The Dolphin Hunter.*" There was obvious pride in her voice. "We found that in a flea market over by Cannonsburg. Only fifteen dollars, I think it cost us. It's signed, you know.

There are only three signed copies in existence, and this is one of them."

I tried not to look or sound too impressed. "Where is the original again? I forget."

"Florence, of course."

"Ah, yes, of course. Where else?"

"Cream, or lemon?" asked Martha. I could tell she was quite used to pouring tea for the ladies of her church.

"Both."

Martha made a face. "Won't that curdle?"

I smiled patiently. "I won't be having both at the same time, of course. First I thought I'd have a cup of tea with lemon, and then a cup with cream." I rather liked my surroundings and planned to dawdle as much as possible. If when I did leave I was a Presbyterian, it was Martha who was going to have to answer to her Maker.

"So, tell me about this new script, Magdalena. Is it very different from the old one?"

"Very," I said quite honestly. "There are no nude bathtub scenes."

Martha blushed. Without her makeup it was a dramatic sight. "I'm glad to hear that. That first script was pure trash."

"An abomination," I agreed.

"More than that. Even allowing for some prurient sexual interest, from a structural point of view it simply had no plot."

I sipped rather than commented. Matters of prurient sexual interest were beyond my ken.

"Of course I didn't believe for a minute that it was a genuine Arthur Lapata script. Even the most provincial ignoramus could tell that."

"Of course."

"I suppose Mr. Lapata had some stupid contractual arrangement whereby he was forced to direct that piece of illiterate garbage, and that Mr. Manley's death somehow has changed all that, and he is now free to write and direct what he wants?''

I hope I didn't stare too long, although I did read somewhere that staring is a good way to counteract wrinkles. "Yeah, something like that. You seem to know something about the business, Martha.''

Martha smiled appreciatively and slopped another spoon of whipped cream over my slice of pound cake, which, incidentally, was store-bought. "I was a theater major in college. I had plans, you know.''

"No. What kind of plans?''

Martha pointed to a large gilt frame hanging on the wall behind me. "See that?''

I turned and saw that the frame contained an enlarged black and white photograph of a young woman of about twenty. The woman was draped in feathers and standing between what looked like two cardboard, cut-out palm trees. The disparity between the regality of the gilt frame and the frivolity of the photo was perhaps Martha's only lapse in taste. "It's very interesting," I said tactfully.

Martha chuckled knowingly. "Oh, I know it's a mismatch, but it's my favorite photo and my favorite frame, so what the heck!''

"It's a beautiful frame.''

"Thanks, but it's the photo I want you to see. That's my paternal grandmother, Cassandra Hicks. *The* Cassandra Hicks.''

"My paternal grandmother was *the* Elizabeth Yoder.''

Martha looked at me with what seemed like renewed interest. "Silent or talkies?''

"Definitely the talkies.'' Honest to goodness, Grandma Yoder could gab up a storm.

Martha looked at me intently. "How very interesting,

Magdalena. It must have been quite a shock to the family."

"Not really. It runs in the family."

"Exactly! That's my point. It does run in the family. I always knew I was going to be an actress when I grew up, just like Grandma. People used to say I had the same eyes, the same sort of—well"—she spread her hands to indicate humility—"well, I guess you'd have to call it charisma."

"I know what you mean. Susannah has always said that I'm a carbon copy of Grandma Yoder. I used to hate it when she said that, but more and more I take it as a compliment."

"Imagine that! I never knew you wanted to be an actress, Magdalena."

Maybe I chuckled just a little. "But I don't. Not really. I said I wanted to be like Grandma Yoder, not that I wanted to be an actress, Martha."

"But your grandma was an actress, wasn't she?"

Even Grandma would have laughed at that. Grandma Yoder never saw a movie in her life, much less acted in one. Unlike her, I plan to see at least one movie before I die. Come to think of it, I may as well start with the one I'm in.

"Grandma raised chickens, Martha, when she wasn't too busy raising children. She never was west of Somerset, or east of Breezewood. But Grandma had moxie, and that's what I think Susannah means."

Martha didn't offer to refill my teacup when she refilled her own. "Well, Grandma Hicks was an actress, and one of the most famous ones of her day. She was one of only a handful to make the transition from silent to talking pictures. They say—"

"Is there more cream in the kitchen, Martha?"

Martha put down her cup and regarded me coldly. "For some of us this isn't a game, Magdalena."

"Well, if you're out of cream, I suppose a spoonful of whipped cream would do just fine. Cream is cream, isn't it? Unless this is that nondairy stuff."

"It's real whipped cream, Magdalena." So saying, she snatched it away before I could reach it, and stood up. "Now, tell me again why you're here."

"Ah, because of the new script," I remembered to say. "Art is writing a new script, and he is interested in community reaction."

"Ah, yes. What is it you want from me? Did you bring a copy of the new script with you?"

"No, I don't have a copy with me. But Art wanted me to assure you that this new script is very mainstream— that it reflects family values." I went on to tell her the basics of the story line.

"Sounds good," she said, "but didn't they already make a move about the Amish? Something with Harrison Ford in it?"

I confessed that I didn't go to movies.

Martha sighed sympathetically. "All of this hullabaloo about the Amish just seems a little strange to me. I don't suppose Hollywood considers us Presbyterians quaint enough."

"Well, I'll definitely put in a good word with Art," I lied. If I didn't pacify her soon, the whipped cream was going to sour.

"I keep forgetting why you're here, Magdalena." Either Martha was a better liar than I, or she had Alzheimer's. She definitely sounded sincere.

"I'm here because Art is especially interested in your opinions on the direction the new script is taking."

"And why is that?"

I looked longingly at the whipped cream, which

Martha was still holding. "Well, your opinions are especially valid because you've read the old script and know what Art was up against."

"Sick, vile trash."

"Exactly, and of course it was tragic that Don Manley was killed the way he was, but in a way it would have been almost as tragic had he lived. Think what a movie like that would have done to the community." I meant the Amish-Mennonite community, even if I didn't say it.

"You are so right, Magdalena."

"So anyway, it's important to Art that the new script be acceptable to the mainstream elements in this community. If there is anything overtly offensive in it, he is willing to reconsider its inclusion."

"So this is still very much a work in progress?"

"Most definitely."

"Which means, of course, that he will have to recast it, since there will be new roles?" The whipped cream bobbed seductively just out of my reach.

"Yes, and no."

"Is that like taking both lemon and cream in your tea?"

"What I mean is, the changes called for recasting, but it has already been done."

The whipped cream danced a hasty retreat. "What do you mean, it's already been cast?"

I swallowed hard. "Well, the new script has fewer roles than the old one, and Art was able to recast it with the actors the studio already had under contract."

"I see. But what about the extras? Are the Biddle sisters still being used?"

"Well, yes, at least I think so. But they'll be on screen for only a second or so, and that's only in a few scenes."

The corners of Martha's mouth began to twitch. "I see.

And how about you, Magdalena? Will you be working as an extra as well?"

"I hardly think so."

"And why is that?" I thought I saw a triumphant gleam in Martha's eyes. At least the whipped cream bobbed at last into reach.

"Because I've been cast as the lead," I said carelessly.

Martha didn't lay a hand on me, I'll grant her that, but nonetheless I left shortly afterward. I waited until I got back to the privacy of my own car before I licked the whipped cream off my dress. It had not begun to go sour.

Thirteen

SHOOTING A MOVIE is incredibly boring. It seemed like we spent half our time sitting around and waiting while Art talked to the camera, light, and sound crews. Then, ninety-nine percent of our remaining time was spent sitting around and waiting while minor adjustments were made to the equipment. About one percent of the time was actually spent filming, and no matter what scene was being shot, it had to be filmed over and over again. If it hadn't been for thoughts of Jim's impending visit, which teased about at the edges of my mind, I might have died of boredom.

It has happened, you know—people dying from boredom. I once overheard Mama telling Aunt Pearl that it was during "those times" that she planned all her menus for the week. Aunt Pearl agreed that "those times" were "deathly boring." And so they must have been, because Aunt Pearl died during one of "those times." That's what

I overheard Mama telling Aunt Lizzie at the funeral, although neither of them would explain what "those times" were, or even why they refused to talk about them.

Anyway, I can't say it was a light bulb that lit up in my mind, because it really was just a plain old dollar sign. But I did manage to come up with a way to alleviate the boredom for some of the others, as well as to create a tidy little income for yours truly. I'm talking about quilts, of course.

Quilting is as synonymous with the Amish as cricket is with the English, but it was the English (in our broader sense of the term) that introduced the fancy designs to my ancestors. Historically, my people used quilts to keep warm, and they were functional, if not attractive. But we had creative and artistic people as well, who were generally forbidden to express themselves in such idolatrous media as painting and sculpting. Then some of our women got it into their heads to incorporate the more innovative and colorful English designs into their otherwise functional quilts. And when the bishops, bless their souls, did not strenuously object, a new and religiously acceptable art form was begun. Today, an expertly crafted, authentic Amish quilt will fetch hundreds of dollars on the tourist market. Even a badly done one is worth a couple of hundred. Trust me, I know.

Since the inception of the PennDutch Inn, I have kept a quilting frame up in the dining room, with a quilt in progress constantly on display. Guests are welcome, even urged, to try their hand at adding a few stitches. Only rarely do Freni or I have to rip out these efforts. Usually the stitch work is passable, sometimes even very good. As soon as a quilt is completed, I replace it with another one "in progress." I sell the finished quilts, of course, in gift shops up and down the East Coast. Some of my quilts even end up in Lancaster County shops, but I have promised not to divulge which ones.

Anyway, nobody complained when I set up a second quilt frame in the barn. In the so-called "down times," everyone from Rip Oilman to the makeup girls sat down to it and contributed their stitches. I was very pleasantly surprised to discover that a quilt that would normally take me six weeks to hand-stitch, this bunch could do in one long day. Caught off guard, I didn't have another quilt in progress. So, unbeknownst to Freni, I sneaked over to her place and asked her daughter-in-law, Barbara, to keep me regularly supplied. Barbara was happy to comply; I think less for the money than because she knew Freni would bust a gut if she ever found out. Like any Amish wife, Barbara is one hard-working gal, but up until my quilt proposition, she had never earned any outside money. Freni has, of course, having worked for me for eleven years now. There is more competition between Freni and her daughter-in-law than there is between Honda and Ford, and frankly, I love adding fuel to that fire.

But around the quilting frame there was never any competition, just gentle gossip in an atmosphere of total relaxation. I know, because I spent some time there getting the neophytes started.

"You better straighten up those stitches, dear. They look like the tracks of a drunken chicken on a moonless night," I said gently to Roger, one of the sound technicians.

"Yes, ma'am."

"And you, hon"—I nodded kindly to Andrea, the prop manager—"by any chance, did you happen to be Dr. Frankenstein in a previous life? I have varicose veins that are straighter than that."

"Sorry, ma'am. I'll try and do better."

"How's this, Miss Yoder?" asked that arrogant Rip, shoving his impeccable needlework practically into my face. "Does this pass inspection?"

I prayed for a charitable tongue, and the Lord heard
me. "We think rather highly of ourselves, don't we? Just
remember, pride cometh before the fall." Mama had
used that line on me a number of times, so it had to be
acceptable. Still, I wish she had said something different
when I won first place in the countywide spelling bee.

Rip only smiled and looked for his reflection on the
head of a straight pin.

Of course that made me angry. What did he have to be
proud of that I didn't? Perhaps it was because I was an-
noyed, but the next stitch I took bound a thin layer of my
thumb to the quilt. Thanks to Susannah's influence, I let
out a very unmennonite expression.

Nobody seemed to care much. Perhaps yelps of pain
are commonplace in Hollywood. To test my theory, I
yelped again.

Only one person so much as looked my way. "I know
how you feel," said Heather, the pregnant makeup girl.

"Stick your thumb too, dear?" I asked gratefully.

"I meant the pain of losing Don."

I looked closely at Heather for the first time. It was
suddenly obvious that she'd been crying.

"How's that, dear?"

"Don Manley was the sweetest, kindest, gentlest man
who ever lived!" She burst into sobs.

I tugged on the quilt frame and managed to pull it just
out of tear range. Even pseudo-authentic Amish quilts
don't generally come with mascara stains.

"There, there, dear," I said kindly. "There's no need
to pretend with us. You're among friends."

Despite her size, Heather recoiled with the rapidity of a
black snake. "I wasn't pretending! I loved Don Manley.
I'm carrying his baby."

"Are you sure?" Andrea asked.

Heather glared at her through bleary eyes. "*I* don't sleep around."

"A pity," Rip said. "You could have done better."

Heather wiped her cheeks and looked at me. "Miss Yoder, I know a lot of people had it in for Don, but they misunderstood him. Don was really a very sensitive, caring man."

"Did you know that the Ayatollah writes self-help books," Rip asked. "The one titled *I'm Okay, You're an Infidel* was actually very good."

But now that Heather had publicly declared her love for the dead Don, nothing could ruffle her feathers. "Say what you want, but Don was always very nice to me. He always made me feel like a lady," she said serenely.

"You too?" Andrea didn't seem to be joking.

Heather's brown-eyed gaze locked in on Andrea. "Don said you would say that. Well, something like that. He said you would be jealous when you found out about our love."

"Even sixth-graders don't call it that anymore. Sorry to be the one to break the news to you, Heather, but Don loved only himself. That's all he was capable of loving."

Heather stroked her belly blatantly. "The proof is in the pudding," she said.

Andrea's eyes flashed. "Then expect to give birth to eight pounds of Jell-O."

"Ladies, ladies," I interjected. "All this talk of food is making me hungry, and it's at least another hour until supper. What say we change the subject?"

"Hear, hear," said Roger.

A few minutes later Heather excused herself to go to the bathroom. Almost immediately after that, Andrea left our cozy little group.

"You don't suppose they've simply taken their fight elsewhere?" I asked out of genuine concern. I had recently had all the bathrooms remodeled. Do you know how much good quality wallpaper costs these days?

"Chill," said Rip. "Those two might not like each other very much, but they aren't about to waste any more energy on each other as long as the true object of their hatred is alive and well, and swaggering about."

"Who's that?"

Rip pointed with his chin to the other side of the barn, where Art and Steven appeared to be deeply engaged in conversation.

"You mean Art? But he really is a pussycat when you get to know him."

Rip chuckled. "If only you knew. But I don't mean Art, Miss Yoder. I mean Bugsy. Or Steven, or *who*ever."

"Well, Steven can be a bit much," I conceded, "but one gets used to him after a while, and then he's easier to take. Sort of like getting used to the taste of coffee, I guess."

"Unless that cup of coffee ran a pitchfork through the man you love," said Rip evenly.

"Why would he do that?" I asked.

"You really are as naive as you look, aren't you, Miss Yoder?"

"Why, thank you." I patted my hair. One must accept compliments where one finds them.

"Steven's last name is not really Freeman, you know. It's Figaretti. He changed it when he went out to the coast."

"Smart cookie. Figaretti sounds too much like a car."

"That's Ferrari. And that's not my point."

"What is, dear?"

Rip leaned over close to whisper, and I held my breath. He was wearing enough aftershave to asphyxiate a horse. "Haven't you heard that Don owed money to the mob?"

"Yes," I whispered back. "A nosy reporter mentioned something about that the other day."

"Well?"

I turned my head long enough to gulp some fresh air. "Well, what?"

"Well, hasn't it ever occurred to you that Steven Figaretti might be a hit man for the mob?"

I would have reached out instinctively and given him a reassuring pat, but my instincts don't work that way. "You really should try getting a good night's sleep, dear. From what I hear, you film guys party all night long."

Rip withdrew the cloud of fragrant fumes. "You don't believe it's possible, do you. But I'm telling you, Miss Yoder, anything is possible in Hollywood."

I would have to speak to the night manager at the Holiday Inn. "This isn't Hollywood, Rip. This is Hernia."

"Hernia, Hollywood, what difference does that make? Anyway, they're both a pain in the butt, if you ask me."

"*Touché.*"

"*Touché*—isn't that Yiddish for butt?"

I looked up and slipped my stitch when I saw that the voice belonged to Melvin Stoltzfus.

Fourteen

"FORGET Slick's theories," Melvin reminded me for the third time. He had practically dragged me out of the barn and was making me walk with him back to the house. For privacy, he said, but I think it was for a piece of Freni's pie.

"I don't know, Melvin. They make sense to me. Steven Freeman had a lot to gain by Don's death. Like his job, for instance."

I didn't look at him, but I'm sure at least one of Melvin's eyes began to roll slowly in its socket. "People don't kill each other just because they want a better job, Yoder."

"Sometimes they kill for a lot less," I said despite my better judgment. We were passing the six-seater then, and I was trying to figure out if the openings were big enough for me to stuff Melvin through. The pit, I already knew, was deep enough so that the body wouldn't be detected by the casual user.

"Is that a threat?" It doesn't say much for my intelligence if Melvin can read my mind.

I strained several of my facial muscles working up a smile. "Of course not, dear. What do you think of Rip's theory that Steven Freeman is a hit man for the mob?"

I believe Melvin laughed then; it is always so hard to tell for sure. "As usual, I'm one step ahead of you, Yoder. I've already been on the horn to Washington. There were no charges against Don Manley. That reporter must have been pulling your leg."

"In his dreams."

"Slick's just doing a number on you too, Magdalena. For your information—"

"For your information, his name is Oilman, not Slick. And since you think I'm guilty, and since you're so fond of conspiracy theories, what makes you rule out the possibility that Steven Freeman is my co-conspirator?"

Perhaps quite by coincidence, both of Melvin's eyes focused on my face. "Because he's not your type, Yoder."

"Well, who is my type, then, and what's he have to do with Don Manley's death?"

Melvin's eyes cooperated with each other for an unnerving length of time. They must have liked what they saw. "Rumor has it," he drawled ever so slowly, "that you've been seeing this guy from Baltimore."

"Jim? But I haven't even met Jim yet! Melvin, this is crazy!"

"This Jim guy could be anybody, Magdalena. For all I know—"

"Which isn't anything at all, Melvin. Jim is none of your business, and I'll see him if I want to. As a matter of fact, I plan to meet him tomorrow night. How do you like them apples, Melvin? Now, this conversation is over. Unless you want to arrest me, get off my property!''

I think Melvin laughed again, but I'm not sure. We were outside, after all, and it was summertime. Those cicadas are liable to start singing any old time. "Look, Yoder, I may not have enough to pull you in on the murder charge just now, but if I wanted to, I could haul you in on two counts of breaking and entering and one count of assault and battery.''

"Susannah had no right to lock her door, and I didn't hit her. I merely raised my voice.''

Melvin had whipped out a notepad and was scribbling furiously. Suddenly he stopped. "That's not what I mean, Yoder. I'm talking about Norah Hall and Clarissa Biddle. They both claim you forcibly broke into their homes, and Norah Hall claims you pushed and shoved her when she asked you to leave. She even claims to have a witness.''

"Tell her I'll plead guilty to the charges if she'll produce the witness.''

Melvin wrote that down. "So what they said is true?''

I accidentally stepped on his toe while we jockeyed for position to climb the back stairs. "Were they the *only* ones to complain, Melvin?''

"Maybe. Well, so far, at least. What is it you're up to, Yoder? I can smell a scheme a mile away.''

"Those are Freni's pies, Melvin.''

But they weren't. Not even close. Freni had persuaded one of the crew members to drive all the way into Somerset and check out a book on Thai cooking from the public library. What I had smelled were the results of her first efforts.

"It's Arthur's favorite food,'' said Freni fiercely. "If the others don't like it, they can just lump it.''

"I'm sure it will be just fine,'' I heard myself say. I knew I was bushed when I lacked the energy to spar with Freni.

"Do you know how much straw mushrooms cost a can?"

I shrugged. "More than they used to?"

"Well, if there's no pie, I'm outta here. For now, at any rate," said Melvin loudly, but he didn't budge.

"And lemongrass . . . whoever heard of such a thing?"

"Beats me. Who?"

"Perhaps you've got some leftover pie lying around that you wouldn't mind parting with. After all, it wouldn't go very well with Thai food, would it?" Melvin was so bold as to peek into the pie saver Freni had out on the counter. It was empty.

"It doesn't *have* to be spicy, you know, but Arthur prefers it that way."

"Some like it hot."

"Apple pie should always be served warm, with a big slab of American cheese on top." Melvin had begun to shake the empty pie saver, perhaps in an attempt to ferret out any crumbs.

"And I had to get *un*sweetened coconut milk. Can you imagine that?"

"Only if I close both eyes and try real hard."

"Apple is my favorite, but cherry will do in a pinch." Melvin licked a finger and ran it around the inside of the pie saver.

Freni and I saw him at the same time, but it was she who reacted first. "Get out of my kitchen, and stay out!" Although only five foot two, Freni had grabbed the much taller and younger Melvin by his belt and collar and was propelling him toward the door.

"Yoder, you're still my *suspecto numero uno,*" Melvin shouted.

"See ya later, Mel."

"Not in my kitchen," puffed Freni.

"I'll be watching you, Yoder. I'll be on your tail every minute." Melvin's voice trailed off as if he had fallen down a deep well, or maybe an outhouse bore, but actually it was only because Freni had thrown him down the steps.

"God will punish Elvina Stoltzfus for this, mark my words. Imagine raising a son who licks out the pie saver, and not even in his own kitchen," said Freni after she had caught her breath.

"Must I?"

"And such nerve to accuse you of murder! You are innocent, aren't you, Magdalena?"

"More so than I would care to admit."

Maybe it's because she is so short, but innuendo always flies above Freni's head. "Now, take that Arthur Lapata. There is a son any mother would be proud to call her own. Imagine a son like that."

"You already have a son, Freni. John. Remember?"

"Ach, but with that wife, Barbara! What did I do to deserve a daughter-in-law like that?"

"Barbara is a fine young woman, Freni. She loves John very much, and from what I hear, she is a very hard worker to boot. What is there to complain about?"

"Magdalena, she's six feet tall, and she—"

"Has a mind of her own?"

"That she should keep to herself, if you ask me."

"Like you do?"

"Why, Magdalena Yoder, your mother would turn over in her grave if she heard the way you talk to me."

"Leave Mama out of this, Freni." I may even have spoken crossly, but can you blame me? Mama's been dead eleven years now, and Freni still tries to manipulate me with guilt by invoking her name. And what for? I was a good daughter, much better than Susannah ever was. I did everything Mama told me to do, and didn't do any of the things she forbade me to do. Well, except for that one time, and that happened by accident. How was I to know that sitting on a washing machine during the spin cycle could lead to impure thoughts?

But even after all this time, and with the full knowledge that I was a good and obedient daughter, I feel like I somehow let Mama down. Or will let her down if I just be myself. Of course Susannah doesn't have this problem. She always let Mama down, and knew it, but Mama didn't seem to notice. Susannah got away with everything but murder, and both Mama and Papa treated her like their darling little angel. I, on the other hand, couldn't as much as frown without Mama warning me about the devil creeping into my soul and filling my head with rebellious thoughts—not that there was any room in my head for them *and* Mama's injunctions.

"Sit up, Magdalena. Don't touch your privates, Magdalena. Stand straight, Magdalena. Don't touch your privates, Magdalena. Say your prayers, Magdalena. Don't touch your privates, Magdalena. Scrub behind your ears, Magdalena. Don't touch your privates, Magdalena. Study harder, Magdalena. Don't touch your privates, Magdalena." And the list goes on and on.

"A penny for your thoughts, Magdalena," said Freni with surprising gentleness.

"These will cost you at least a dollar."

"How about a taste of Thai soup instead?"

"Sure, I'm game. What's it called?"

"It's *tom yam goonk.*" The words rolled off Freni's Amish tongue as if she'd been born to the language.

"What's in it?"

"Some very strange things, if you ask me. Like fish sauce, which is really just the stuff left over when you decompose a fish in water for a year."

"Sounds wonderful. Does it come as a perfume as well?"

"Now, this version that I made for tonight is what they eat in northern Thailand. It has coconut milk in it. Grab a spoon, Magdalena, and take a taste."

I tasted. I even tasted the fish sauce—straight. It had a slightly sweet taste despite the fact that it smelled like a potpourri of rotten eggs and roadkill. "Not bad, Freni, not bad at all," I said honestly.

Freni beamed.

Fifteen

DOC SHAFER'S RECIPE
FOR GREEN-TOMATO PIE

Makes 8 servings

6 or 7 medium-size firm green tomatoes without
blemishes (and without wrinkles if you want to peel
them), approximately 3 cups when chopped
2 tablespoons lemon juice
$1/2$ teaspoon salt
$3/4$ teaspoon cinnamon
$3/4$ cup sugar
2 tablespoons cornstarch
Top and bottom pie crusts
1 tablespoon margarine or butter

WASH THE TOMATOES. Peel them if you want, but it's
a lot of trouble and not really necessary. Cut the tomatoes

into bite-size pieces. Combine the tomato bits with the next three ingredients in a saucepan. Cook for about fifteen minutes. Mix the sugar and cornstarch together and slowly stir it into the tomato mixture. Cook for a few minutes, until the sugar and cornstarch become clear. Add margarine and allow to cool slightly. Line a nine-inch pie pan with the bottom crust and pour in the tomato mixture. Put on top crust and seal the edges. Crimp narrow strips of aluminum foil around the edge to prevent it from getting too brown. Poke numerous holes with a fork across the top to allow steam to escape. Bake for 40 to 50 minutes at 425 degrees. Some people like to eat the pie warm, but Doc much prefers it cold.

Sixteen

WE SHOT ONE SCENE early Saturday morning, and then Arthur declared a holiday for the rest of the weekend. Susannah went back to bed, of course, but I had far too much on my mind. I had a date that night, after all. My first date in . . . oh, well, it really doesn't matter, does it?

Anyway, Heather, the pregnant girl from the makeup crew, had ever so kindly volunteered to do my hair and makeup—for free.

"What's the catch?" I had asked.

But according to Heather, there was no catch. "You see," she said that Saturday as she washed my hair, "you're kind of like the mother I never had."

"She must have been a child bride," I said, and got shampoo bubbles in my mouth.

Heather had wonderfully strong fingers. "Actually, she never was a bride. Mom never married, as far as I know, but I heard she slept around a lot. When I was just two years old, a New Zealand soccer team visited our town, and that's the last I ever saw of her. So, you might say I didn't even know my mother. But if I had, I would have wanted her to be just like you."

I garbled something unspecific.

"Now, I know it might not seem like it to you, Miss Yoder, but I'm trying to follow more in your footsteps than my mother's."

"Whan?"

"Of course I'm not married or anything, I know that, but then, neither are you, are you, Miss Yoder?"

"Whi—haunh."

"But anyway, Miss Yoder, you're like the mother I never had, and so I'd like to ask you just one teensy, weensy favor."

"I don't coach Lamaze" is what I tried to say, but I'm sure it sounded a lot different.

"Of course I would understand if you said no."

Here it comes, I thought, and braced myself on the rim of the basin.

"Would you mind awfully being godmother to my little Tina when she's born?"

I was really very touched, and sputtered something to that effect. Later on, while Heather was rolling my hair and I could talk properly, I pursued the subject. "You know, of course, Heather, that it is a godmother's responsibility to see to it that her godchild is raised according to the faith."

"Is it? Hand me one of the blue rods, please, Miss Yoder. You have a particularly limp spot back here."

"Oh, yes, a godmother sees to it that her godchild goes to Sunday school regularly. And that's just for starters."

"Now hand me a yellow rod, please."

"What faith do you belong to, Heather? You do go to

church, don't you?'' Then again, given the track record
of her family, it seemed doubtful.

But Heather seemed delighted I had asked. "I belong
to the Congregation of Inner Inclination, in North Hollywood. I've got some brochures on it, if you'd like to see
them.''

"Thanks, but no thanks. We all worship the same God
anyway, I always say.''

Heather dropped the comb she was using. "We of the
Congregation of Inner Inclination most certainly do not
worship God, Miss Yoder!''

"Then whom do you worship?''

"Ourselves, of course. And the Archangel Lucifer.''

I opened my mouth three or four times to respond, but
in the end decided that it was simply no use. If I was
going to be godmother to the devil's own spawn, so be it.
I already had the sister from hell. I decided to change the
subject. "So why is it that you and Andrea think Steven
might have somehow been involved in Don's murder?'' I
asked.

Heather dropped the comb again. "I never said I
thought that, did I?''

"But you do, don't you? It's easy to see that the two of
you hate his guts.''

"Steven Freeman is a sh—''

"Shhh,'' I admonished softly, "this is still a Mennonite
home.''

"Steven has always wanted Don's job. He's always been
jealous as hell. I know that Don came on a little strong for
most people—''

"Like Limburger cheese on a hot day?''

"Whatever. But deep inside he was a good, honest, and
caring man.''

"A clone of Khadafi.''

Heather jerked on a clump of hair hard enough to

make my bottom leave the chair seat. "People are always jealous of the people in power. And Don was definitely totally in charge."

"I thought Art was."

"Ha! That's because you're not in the business. Otherwise you would know that Don Manley was the nephew of George P. Manley, the executive producer. It was Don who wrote the script."

I decided not to reveal what I knew. "If you can call that a script," I said carelessly.

I temporarily left the chair again. "Don was a damn good writer. Maybe a little ahead of his time, but damn good."

I took my scalp in my hands. "Okay, so given that everything you say is the gospel truth, I still don't understand what motive Steven would have for killing Don. I'm sure that Susannah would like to be manager of the PennDutch, but I can't see her killing me for the job."

"I'd watch my back, Miss Yoder."

"Come on, people just don't go around killing other people because they want a job, or their feelings are hurt, or they're jealous, or—"

"Why do people kill, Miss Yoder? Why would you kill, Miss Yoder?"

"I don't know," I said quite truthfully. "I can't think of a single reason why I would kill anyone."

"There are those who think it might even have been you who killed Don."

"'Et tu, Brute?'"

"What?"

"Never mind."

"It isn't all that hard to get yourself worked up to the point where you would kill someone." Heather sounded like she was talking from experience. "Our society has

been desensitized to death. I mean, we see many exam-
ples of murder every day on TV."

"Not on *Green Acres,* you don't."

"It isn't hard at all for me to understand why Steven
Freeman killed Don. Pardon me, Miss Yoder, but you
really should open your eyes more to the world around
you." So saying, Heather tugged on a lock of my hair so
hard that if my eyes had been any farther open, they
might well have popped out.

I got a temporary respite from Heather's fearsome fingers when my bedroom phone rang. That's my private
line, and usually it brings bad news. But, since I had just
seen Susannah draped across her bed, I didn't expect it
to be too bad this time. With Mama and Papa dead, and
Susannah accounted for, how bad could the news be?

"Who is it?"

"Yoder, it's me."

"There's a lot of me's in the world, Melvin. Which one
are you, and how did you get this number?"

"It's Melvin Stoltzfus, Yoder, and I've had your number
for ages. I'm Susannah's boyfriend, remember?"

"Not on my good days. What do you want?"

"If you're going to be rude, Magdalena, I just won't tell
you."

"Bye-bye, Melvin."

"Wait! You can't hang up, Magdalena. This is official
police business."

"I'm taping everything you say, Melvin, so make sure
that it is." Okay, so that wasn't a necessary lie, and it
might have given Mama a spin or two, but it's Melvin's
fault if I sinned, not mine. He's the one who constantly
leads me into temptation.

"Look, Yoder, I just thought you'd like to know that
the county coroner is shipping Don Manley's body back
to Los Angeles tonight. The cause of death has been offi-

cially ruled as manslaughter. I thought you'd like to know."

"What a shock, Melvin. I was sure it was suicide."

"If you'd quit yapping and listen, Yoder, you would have heard that I said manslaughter, *not* murder."

So he had. "Okay, Melvin, I'll bite. What's the difference?"

If Melvin's pause had been pregnant, it could have populated at least two third-world countries. "Well, you know what murder is, don't you, Yoder?"

"It's what would happen if you were here in person, Melvin."

"Manslaughter, on the other hand, is sort of halfway between murder and accidental death. That is to say, there is no malice intended. No prior deliberation." There was another pause during which the population of China doubled. "Yoder, have you heard a word I've said?"

It finally sank in. "Do you mean to say that you believe Don Manley was forked in the stomach unintentionally?"

"Eureka, she's got it! My point is, Yoder, I'm giving you a break here. I'm not saying that you meant to kill Don Manley, but that maybe things got out of hand, and before you knew it, well, he was dead."

"Melvin, how does one unintentionally pin a man to a barn beam with a pitchfork?"

"Why don't you tell me? This would be a good time for you to confess, Yoder. They say that confession is good for the soul."

"But I never sat on that washing machine again!"

"You seem to forget that I'm your friend, Yoder. I've cut you some slack here. Believe me, it will go much easier on you if you confess now. And like I said, manslaughter is a lesser charge than murder. You'd only be facing ten—twelve years in the state pen, max. *If* you behaved,

Yoder, they might even let you out early on parole. So come on and fess up. Tell Cousin Mel where you hid the pitchfork.''

"Have you had any trouble sitting lately, Melvin?''

"Of course you could continue to make things hard for me, which will only make it harder on yourself.''

"Give it up, Melvin. I haven't killed anyone. *Yet.*''

"Is that a threat, Yoder?''

"Read my lips, Melvin. I did not kill Don Manley.'' It was probably easier for Melvin to read lips over a phone than in person.

I heard Melvin sigh loudly. "I want you to know, I'm keeping tabs on you, Yoder. And by the way, just exactly when and where are you planning to meet that mobster from Baltimore?''

"He's a fried-chicken monger, Melvin, not a mobster, and the details are none of your business.''

"In that case, I'll just have to sit here all night and watch your house.''

"Where are you, Melvin?''

"That's none of your business, Yoder. But for your information, I do have a car phone.''

"Well, for your information, Melvin, he's not coming here to the inn. I'm going to meet him. So you can just sit there all night.''

I hung up. After talking to Melvin, I looked forward to putting myself back into Heather's hot little hands.

I must say, despite aberrant religious leanings and her undying love for the very dead Don, Heather was a whiz at her job. My hair had never looked better. Heather even convinced me to wear a little makeup. Not a lot, mind you, but just enough to make me look like a red-blooded woman with at least one toe in the world. I knew at once that the job was a success when I ran into Susannah.

"My God, Magdalena, you look awful!''

"Thank you, dear," I said sincerely.

"Mama would kill you if she saw you."

"Heather must have been right about motives being easy to come by."

"I mean, you look like a middle-aged whore."

"Perhaps we should go into business together."

"I'm not kidding, Magdalena. This look definitely isn't you. You looked much better plain. Seriously, Sis, give it up. You look like a streetwalking clown. No man in his right mind will ask you out looking like that."

"Suits me just fine. I already have a date," I said, and walked away with my head held high.

I felt good about the new me, and that's all that counted. Of course, once the movie company and Heather vacated the premises, I would most probably revert back to my normal just plain old soap and water routine, but until then, I planned to enjoy the change. And who was Susannah to criticize me?

I was just heading for the door, purse in hand, when the lobby phone rang.

"PennDutch Inn," I said charmingly. "We're all booked up at the moment while a major Hollywood studio is filming a blockbuster movie, but we would be glad to consider your reservation two months from now."

"Magdalena, is that you?"

"Joan? Joan Lunden?"

"Magdalena, this is Martha Sims."

"Oh, it's only you."

"Magdalena, the reverend and I were thinking of inviting you to lunch on Sunday. Tomorrow, that is."

"Has it gotten past the thinking stage? Isn't it already too late to send out invitations?"

"This is the invitation, Magdalena. Will you come? Lunch will be served about twelve-thirty."

"Does this mean I have to attend your church first?"

"Frankly, I'd just as soon you didn't."

"Fair enough, Martha. But I've told you before that I'm sorry for having washed my face in the baptismal font at Susannah's wedding. It was a hot day, and we don't keep a bowl of water handy at my church. How was I supposed to know what it was for?"

"Lunch at twelve-thirty, then?"

I told Martha I would be delighted to attend, and I meant it. Why Martha and her husband would want me over for lunch was beyond me. It would be worth a case of heartburn, or another batch of whipped cream in my hair, to find out. Besides, I had yet to enter her dining room, and from what little I could see from my spot in the parlor, it promised to be very interesting indeed.

Many roads lead to the top of Mt. Fujiyama, the saying goes, but the view from the top is the same. Only one road leads from my place to Hernia, so I was stuck taking it. To get to Bedford, I have to go to Hernia first, and then turn right at Sam Yoder's Corner Market on state highway 96. Sam's is only one block away from Main, where the police station is, and I had decided to swing by there and see if Melvin's cruiser was in the parking lot. The way Melvin had been talking, I fully expected him to tail me into Bedford and arrest Jim and me on our first date. The charges would undoubtedly be nothing less than plotting to overthrow the government and pocketing a packet or two of Sweet'n Low.

However, I discovered that Melvin was out cruising the second I left my place. There's a dip to the side of the road about a quarter of a mile to the left as you come out of my driveway that's deep enough to hide a car, or even a horse and buggy. Spooning couples have concealed their vehicles in that dip for over a hundred years. Aunt Lizzie used to talk about how she and her beaus would dawdle there on their way back to the house. Sometimes she'd go on and on about it until Mama made her shut up. Susannah, I know, has dawdled in the dip on many occasions, but, of course, both Mama and Papa always turned a blind eye. The one time I dawdled in the dip was when I was eighteen and Papa's car, which he'd let me drive, slid off the road and into the creek in a snowstorm. The car wasn't hurt, and neither was I, but you would have thought I'd just returned from Sodom and Gomorrah the way Mama carried on. And I'd been alone the whole time too!

Anyway, as soon as I turned onto the highway I caught a glimpse of Melvin Stoltzfus's cruiser emerging from the dip. I suppose Melvin thought I was too stupid to look in my rearview mirror. Maybe he thought it took all my concentration just to hang on to the wheel. But whatever he thought, he hadn't thought enough.

Immediately, I pressed the pedal to the metal. I know, that's a dangerous and foolish thing to do, especially around Hernia, where there is a lot of horse and buggy traffic. But sometimes a gal has to do what a gal has to do. At any rate, the element of surprise worked in my favor, and Melvin ate my dust until I got to Stucky Street on the north edge of town, not far from Norah Hall's house. I whipped my old Chevy right on Stucky, right again on Fussenegger, right on Blough, and then right one more time, putting me back again on the highway. This time I was *behind* Melvin.

Apparently Melvin was too stupid to check his rearview mirror, because I followed him at chase speed all the way through Hernia and halfway to Bedford. Four miles outside of Bedford, Melvin gave up the chase and turned into the Hooley farm. While he was turning himself around, I simply zoomed past him and got to Bedford in record time.

Seventeen

ONCE at Ed's Steak House, I ordered a large iced tea and settled down in a booth from which I had a good view of the front door. As I sipped, I wished buckets of blessings down on Melvin's head for having gotten me there early. I much preferred to peruse the incoming traffic for Jumbo Jim than be perused myself.

A lot of good-looking men frequent Ed's Steak House, not that I'm hung up on looks, mind you. "Never judge a book by its cover," Mama used to say, and of course she was right. But the cover is often the reason we first pick up a book, and if we are truly honest, most of us will admit to applying this same method of initial selection to our relationships. Of course, Susannah never gets beyond this stage, which isn't surprising to me, since I don't think she's ever read an entire book either. Which is not to say, I hasten to add, that Melvin Stoltzfus is good-looking, just because Susannah dates him. Susannah may judge a book

by its cover, but you must remember that she has bad
judgment altogether. In Melvin's case, both the book and
the cover are trash, and Susannah is a total loser. What
else is new?

Anyway, my iced tea had gotten pretty low and I was
beginning to make loud slurping noises with my straw,
when a drop-dead gorgeous hunk of man walked through
the door. All the breath went out of me at the sight of
him, and I guess I spilled some ice too, because my lap
suddenly felt damp.

"Thank you, Lord," I prayed, hopefully not too loud,
and then waved nonchalantly at him. The man, who
really was much cuter than Eddie Albert, simply walked
past me. It wasn't until I saw him embrace a ho-hum–
looking woman across the room that I realized it might
not be Jim. When a toddler ran up to him and he
scooped it up in his arms, I turned back to the door.

The next unaccompanied man was okay looking. He
was tall, which is great for me, but he was just a little too
much on the fluffy side for my taste. By that I don't mean
that he was effeminate. I mean that he lacked muscle
tone. He wasn't exactly fat, but he had fluffy flesh—imagine six feet of whipped pâté, if you will. Just to be on the
safe side, I waved, but it was the kind of wave that could
also be interpreted as patting my hair. Fortunately for
me, this man appeared to ignore me completely and was
soon enveloped by a foursome of fluffy friends, whereupon they all trooped off to the salad bar.

The third unaccompanied man didn't even merit a
hair pat. I could see at once that he was wearing a clerical
collar, and despite what Susannah says, I would not make
a good nun. Of course I might have considered it had it
not been for Vatican II. But without the cute little cos-
tumes (it must be my Amish blood) it just wouldn't be the
same. Silently I wished the good father luck. He was far

too handsome to wander into Ed's unattended. If Susannah should spot him during one of her lapses into good taste, he wouldn't stand a prayer.

The fourth lone male to stroll in was obviously a prepubescent boy of ten or twelve, so I didn't even stop slurping for him. It was only when I had tipped my glass way up on end to tap loose an ice jam that I noticed the cherub standing next to me.

"Doll?" he asked.

"I beg your pardon!"

"Magdalena, is that you?"

I put my glass down, but not before a mound of ice came crashing out and hit me in the right eye. When I could see again, I looked at the boy more closely. Much to my escalating dismay, I could see that it wasn't a boy after all, but a very small man. "Who wants to know?" I asked not unpleasantly.

"It's Jumbo Jim, doll."

I looked him up and down again. It didn't take long. "In that case, call me Tiny," I said.

Jim jumped up and sat down boldly on the bench opposite me. "The jumbo part is for real, doll." He winked.

"Pardon me?"

Jim settled back comfortably in the booth. Fortunately, he was able to see over the table. "Wow, doll, you look even better in person than I imagined!"

I patted my hair, this time intentionally. I would have to remember to thank Heather again. "Thanks, Jim. You're quite a surprise yourself." Then to show I wasn't prejudiced against little people, I added, "Shall we go and get in line for our steaks now?"

"Sure thing," said Jim.

We got up.

"Say, doll," said Jim before I had time to even hunch over a little, "how's the weather up there?"

"What?"

"Duck, doll! There's a plane coming in at eleven o'clock."

"I beg your pardon!"

"What's the matter, doll, can't you hear me with all them clouds in your ears?"

"I can hear you just fine, thank you. I just don't like what I'm hearing."

"What's the matter? You prejudiced against short people, doll? Oops! Watch the light fixture, doll. You nearly hit your head." He laughed.

That did it. I know, Jumbo Jim could not possibly know what it was like to be a girl and wake up one morning to find yourself five foot eight and in the sixth grade, but ignorance is no excuse. Especially in his case. So I decided to give him a taste of his own medicine. "The steaks are great here," I said sincerely, "but the *shrimp* are even better."

"Watch it, doll, or I'll cut you off at the knees," Jim retorted, and he didn't sound like he was kidding either.

I simply did an about-face and left the restaurant. I think Jim may have followed me for a couple of steps, but he certainly didn't make any effort to keep up. Hopefully he was flattened by the five fluffy fellows on their way back from the salad bar.

"He was a plain old jerk," said Doc sympathetically. "They come in all sizes. There's no need to feel guilty because this one is smaller than the rest."

I was taking Jim's rudeness too much to heart. "Do you think it's the makeup, Doc? Or was it my height that threatened him?"

"Tall is good," said Doc. There was admiration in his voice. The late Mrs. Shafer had been no nymphet.

"Then it is the makeup?"

Doc reached out and patted my shoulder. "Naw, those Baltimore boys are used to a lot more than that."

"Aren't you even going to say I told you so?"

"I'd rather offer you dinner."

I wiped a couple of tears from my eyes. "What are you having?"

"Let's see. Tonight it's skillet pot roast with vegetables, freshly baked oatmeal bread, stewed tomatoes, corn relish, watermelon pickles, and for dessert, crazy cake. You do like my crazy cake, don't you, Magdalena?"

I love crazy cake. It's my favorite way to eat chocolate. I decided to repay Doc for his kindness by complimenting him the best way I could. Before I went home that night, sleepy and no longer quite as upset, I had eaten half of a nine-inch pan of cake. Doc, I assure you, ate the other half. If my dreams were less than pleasant that night, it was only partly because of Jim.

I was still full the next morning. At least, I didn't feel like eating breakfast. Of course, that might have been partly due to the fact that I was nervous about having lunch with the Simses. Clergymen make me nervous. Even Reverend Gingerich, our Mennonite pastor, makes me nervous, and I've been serving under him as a Sunday school teacher for almost twenty years.

"Be very careful about what you say and do, Magdalena," Mama often warned me. "God can see everything you do, and he writes it down in his book. At judgment day you'll have to answer to everything in that book, Magdalena. So keep those pages clean."

"You mean he grades me like my teacher does at school?" I once asked.

"That's right."

"Well, what if God is busy looking somewhere else when I do something bad, then he can't see what I'm doing and can't write it down, right?" Susannah wasn't even born yet at the time, but I knew plenty of other kids who sinned on a regular enough basis. Maybe they could act as a smoke screen for me.

Mama grabbed me by the shoulders and gave me a couple of hard shakes. "God sees *everything*. He has helpers, you know."

"You mean like spies?"

"Don't be sacrilegious, Magdalena. God isn't Khrushchev. But he has helpers, and they see things and report back to him."

"Like who? Who are his helpers, Mama? Are you one of his helpers?"

"Of course. All mothers are God's helpers. And so are pastors."

"Like our pastor at church?"

"Pastor Lantz is one of God's very special helpers," said Mama emphatically. Edmond Lantz, our pastor at the time, was a fearsome-looking man, nearing eighty, who looked just like I thought God might look. To my eight-year-old mind, not only was it possible that Pastor Lantz was God's helper, but it was conceivable that from time to time God made special in-person appearances in the pastor's body. From then on I became terribly afraid of Pastor Lantz, and breathed a huge sigh of relief when he died before I was baptized shortly after my twelfth birthday. Unfortunately, I believed that God took notice of my sigh of relief, which put a damper on the whole occasion anyway.

Of course I have since learned that Mama was no Mennonite theologian, and that many of her pronouncements were fabricated with the sole purpose of keeping me in line. This realization has been purely intellectual. My body is still held hostage by Mama's dictums, which is why I was guzzling a bottle of Pepto-Bismol when I pulled up in front of the Simses Victorian parsonage.

"Come in, come in," said Reverend Sims affably. "Martha's in the kitchen, but isn't that where Marthas usually are?" He chuckled pleasantly at his little biblical joke.

"Lunch smells delicious," I said. I didn't offer to help Martha. I believe guests should act like guests. If I had wanted to pull k.p. duty, I would have stayed home in the cozy familiarity of my own kitchen.

"Care for something to drink?" asked the reverend.

"No, thank you," I said quickly. Rumor had it that some of the Presbyterian churches allowed their members to drink alcoholic beverages, and I wasn't sure which kind Reverend Sims ran.

"Well, how is Susannah?" asked the reverend blithely. The nerve of that man.

"Susannah is the same," I said as evenly as I could. I do try not to insult my hosts.

"I hope you still don't blame me for her marriage to Maurice Entwhistle."

"He was one of your members, and you did perform the ceremony," I pointed out.

Reverend Sims spread his hands as if absolving himself of responsibility. I noticed then that he had the smallest hands I had ever seen on a man. Even Jim's hands were larger. "Maurice Entwhistle may not have been the perfect husband to your sister, but it takes two to tango, as they say."

"We Mennonites don't dance."

Just then Martha popped her head in the room and announced that lunch was ready.

I very much admired Martha's dining room decor, with its antique china hutches, and family photos on the velvet-flocked walls. As for the food she had prepared, it did

nothing to improve my stomach. The most peculiar dish
was a prune soufflé, of which neither Martha nor the
reverend partook. If it hadn't been for the parsley that
decorated it, I would never have thought it edible. The
reverend claimed that he hadn't eaten prunes in years,
which I'm sure explains the state of the ingredients in
that particular casserole. Undoubtedly they were left over
from the time when Annie Sims, the reverend's semi-in-
valid mother and a deaconess herself, had ruled over the
household in a reign of ecclesiastical terror. Anyway, the
prune dish tasted as awful as it looked, so I nibbled at the
parsley while pushing the prune mixture around my
plate.

"So what's the catch?" I asked after about forty-five
minutes of insipid small talk.

I thought I saw Martha pale, but it may have been a
burst of sunshine through the window. "What catch?
There's no catch, Magdalena. Orlando and I simply
wanted to get to know you better. Isn't that right, dear?"

Frankly, the reverend seemed at a loss for words, but a
stern look from Martha prompted a reply. "Ah, yes, we
want to get to know you better, Magdalena. Is it all right if
I call you Mags?"

"That would be fine," I said, and then, just to give
Mama a Sabbath spin in her grave, I added, "Orlando."

I saw the reverend wince, but otherwise he pretty much
kept his cool. "What did Reverend Gingerich preach his
sermon on today?"

"The Bible."

"Touché," said the reverend, "but what was the text?"

"I forget exactly, but it had to do with guilt."

"Ah, a weighty subject," he mused.

"Boy, I'll say. Reverend Gingerich talked about both
collective and individual guilt. When you—"

"I have nothing to feel guilty about," said Martha rather forcefully.

"Of course not, dear," said her husband. He reached across the table and grabbed one of his wife's hands between his small ones. "I already explained to Magdalena that we do not accept responsibility for Susannah's marriage. Isn't that right, Magdalena?"

"Yes."

By then I had a headache in addition to my stomach problems, and I wanted nothing more than to go home and take a nap. But first I had to pretend to eat dessert, which turned out to be merely a rerun of the store-bought pound cake and frozen strawberries. This time there wasn't even any whipped cream.

"Bye, dear, it was so nice to see you again," said Martha as she gave me a big good-bye hug." I hate being hugged, especially by nonrelated females. In my opinion, people who are chronic huggers are that way because they were deprived of their pillows as youngsters. Normal people don't feel a need to go around wrapping their clammy flesh around others. And what really made it uncomfortable in this case was that Martha and I didn't even like each other. It all seemed very strange to me.

"Thanks again for lunch," I said politely. "It was delicious." Even Mama would have approved of a lie like that.

"Bye now, come again," said the reverend. He didn't try to hug me, but I wouldn't have minded quite so much if he had.

"Stay in touch!" Martha called gaily as I headed down the walk.

"I will," I said stupidly out of convention. I had no intention of staying in touch with a woman whose church had corrupted my sister, and who couldn't even be bothered to bake her own pound cake.

Eighteen

SUSANNAH AND I walked over to the Hostetler farm for Sunday night supper. There are two ways to get to where Freni and Mose live. If you take the road, Hertzler Lane, to the left, and then turn left again on Miller's Run, and then left one more time on Beechy Grove Lane, it's exactly 6.3 miles from the PennDutch. But if you simply go out the back door and head straight out between the six-seater and the chicken coop, it's only eight-tenths of a mile. Even when I have the car I seldom drive it. Susannah, on the other hand, would hitch a ride from her bedroom to the bathroom if she could.

"I don't see why we have to walk there," she grumped.

"Well, we could sprint."

"Very funny, Magdalena. Just wait until I get a car. Then I'm not walking anywhere."

"That will be fine, dear."

The truth is, Susannah will never own a car, not if she

has to pay for it herself. I wouldn't say that I am a wealthy woman, but the PennDutch is successful enough to keep me quite comfortable. The same cannot be said for Susannah. Whatever money comes her way makes a big splash and then simply evaporates, like water spilled on a hot griddle. Most of the time Susannah doesn't have two nickels to rub together.

Although we'd gone only a hundred yards, I let Susannah stop and rest her poor, achy, tired feet while I made a brief detour to the outhouse. Of course I didn't plan to use it; it hasn't been used for that purpose since Grandma Yoder was alive and I was still a little girl. But for some strange reason, the door, which is supposed to be closed, had come open again. I peeked inside to see if maybe a tramp had taken up residence, but of course none had. Any tramp worth his satchel would pick the barn over the six-seater any day, although all that movie equipment and confusion could be offputting. Not that tramps stop by much anymore. But during one brief period in the seventies, we had as many as eight tramps living in the barn. I have a strong suspicion, however, that most of those guys were Vietnam War draft dodgers. As Mennonites, both Mama and Papa were staunch pacifists.

After securing the outhouse door, this time with a stick wedged tightly through the hasp, I retrieved Susannah. It is no small thing to walk between two corn fields and through a patch of woods with her. Stopping every few feet to disentangle yards of billowing fabric from the clutches of burrs and twigs is a chore I wouldn't wish on my worst enemy, but I can be just as stubborn as my sister. God had given us a beautiful, cloudless day. To have ridden to the Hostetlers in a melange of metal and rubber would have been downright sacrilegious. Besides, I wanted Susannah to see just how stupid it had been of her to buy those Italian platform shoes. Just to drive the lesson home, I led us on a few detours where I knew the walking would be rough. And, of course, I walked as fast as I could.

Not that it really mattered what time we arrived at the Hostetlers. Freni and Mose eat their big Sunday meal for lunch, as most churchgoing people in Hernia do. Sunday night supper is invariably leftovers, and in the summertime they are generally served cold. Actually, food had very little to do with the supper invitation, in my opinion. I think the whole thing was Mose's idea, and that his intent was for Susannah and me—well, me, at any rate— to mediate the dispute between Freni and her daughter-in-law, Barbara. That was a very kind and loving act on Mose's part, but to be absolutely honest about it, it was rather like asking the Irish to mediate the Israeli-Palestinian situation.

The funny thing is that Freni and Barbara are spitting images of each other, except that Barbara is a good ten inches taller. They both have the same slightly beaked nose, the same mousy brown hair (although Freni's is now streaked with gray), the same watery blue eyes half hidden behind plain-rimmed glasses, and, of course, they're both stubborn enough to make a mule seem compliant. They are, in fact, distant cousins. The Amish in and around Hernia are so interrelated that it would have been impossible for John to find a local bride who was no closer than a second cousin, which is why he went packing off to one of the western communities to find a mate. If Freni and Barbara consulted their family genealogies, which I have, and which they both stubbornly refuse to do, they would find that Barbara and John are sixth cousins—but in four different ways. If you ask me, Freni not only sees herself mirrored in Barbara, but magnified. Believe me, this is enough to scare anyone. Barbara, on the other hand, sees a diminished version of herself when she looks at Freni, and for some reason this upsets her as well. Frankly, I think she should feel grateful.

Freni met us on the front porch. "You're late," she said without preamble. Freni doesn't even own a watch, but she glanced at her wrist nonetheless.

"It's her fault," I said pointing to Susannah. Might as well let the blame fall where it's due.

"She wouldn't let us drive over," Susannah whined.

But Freni had already turned away and was headed back inside. Unlike me, who somehow feels guilty about our parents' death, and therefore somehow responsible for Susannah's moods, Freni simply won't tolerate any of my younger sister's negative behavior. "A dog whines," Freni once said to Susannah, "and that's why its place is outside." Of course, this didn't sit well with Susannah, who not only keeps her dog inside, but inside her bra. Which is not to say that the two women aren't fond of each other; I'm sure they love each other dearly. But I'm just as sure that if Freni ever found that little pooch of Susannah's unattended, she would feed it to the barn cats.

"You're late," said Barbara Hostetler, nee Zook.

I pointed at Susannah again.

"Sit," said Mose.

"Yah, sit," said John. John is a very quiet young man, and I was surprised to hear two consecutive words come out of his mouth. It was clear he was feeling anxious about the evening.

After grace, the two Hostetler women passed around platters of cold meat loaf and homemade cheese, home-made bread, and enough pickled vegetables to make a platoon pucker. We all dug in like hogs at a slop trough.

"It's a beautiful day, isn't it?" said Mose when, after a good ten minutes, no one had spoken.

"It's too hot," said Freni. She brushed back a wisp of graying hair and tucked it into her prayer cap.

"It's a lot hotter than this back home," said Barbara, even though her mouth was full.

"I think it is delightful," I said, braving Freni's glares. "I love summertime and sunny days."

"It shows," said Susannah rudely. "Sun is bad for your skin, you know. It causes wrinkles. And you don't have wrinkles, Magdalena. They're canyons. The National Park Service should offer mule trips down your face."

I was too mature to fight back. Susannah would have to wait and find her bed short-sheeted.

"Autumn is my favorite season back home. I love the cool days and crisp nights. And of course the changing leaves," said Barbara. She sounded genuinely wistful to me. Maybe even homesick.

"You mean you have trees on the prairie?" Freni asked.

"The corn looks good this year, doesn't it? I think it's going to be a good harvest," Mose said quickly.

"So do I," said John. Three consecutive words was a definite record. Any more and he'd turn into a veritable blabbermouth.

"Back home we grow wheat," Barbara said between bites. "And corn too."

Freni glared at her daughter-in-law. "Home is where your husband is."

Barbara returned Freni's glare. "Home is where you feel comfortable, if you ask me."

"Which no one did," said Freni.

"Please pass the cheese," said John desperately.

"Of course, *dear,*" Barbara said. She handed her husband the cheese plate, and as she did so, she leaned toward him so that her sleeve brushed up against his.

Even I was shocked. I had never before heard, or seen, such a public display of affection from someone sharing my genes, Susannah excluded. Perhaps Barbara's looks were coincidental. Perhaps she was really adopted—or stolen from the English as a baby.

Part of me still holds out the hope that this is the case with Susannah. It would, after all, explain a lot. Even though I was ten years old at the time of her birth, I hadn't had an inkling that Mama was pregnant. But then, why would I? Mama had always been a large woman, to put it kindly, and as for the origin of babies, I believed until my eighteenth birthday that angels brought them down from heaven, all washed and clean, and waiting to be fed. When Mama sat me down on that auspicious day and told me that Papa had given her seeds, which she had grown in her tummy, like watermelons, I wanted to barf. Anyway, I could just imagine how shocked Freni must have been at Barbara's display of wantonness.

"Why, I never!" she gasped. Her face had turned as white as her prayer cap.

"I bet you didn't," giggled Susannah.

I kicked her under the table.

"She is my wife," John said. His lips began to twitch and his eyes glazed over. "Mother, you will have to accept her, or we will go and live with her folks until we can afford a farm of our own."

We all, John included, sat in stunned silence. It was almost as bad as the time Helen Gingerich, Reverend Gingerich's wife, lost her panties on her way up to play the organ. Fortunately, on that occasion the choir soon diverted our attention with a rousing a cappella rendition of "And the Walls Came Tumbling Down." But Freni's house lacks a resident choir—she doesn't even own a radio. Being August and all, we stood a good chance of choking on flies unless someone, or something, diverted us.

I did what I could. I began to sing the theme song from

Green Acres. It is, after all, one of the few secular songs I know. Admittedly, mine is not the best voice, but it is not the worst either. Contrary to what Susannah says, I do not sound like a cat in a blender.

I think it was very rude of Susannah to laugh at my singing in front of the others. It was just as rude for John, Barbara, and Mose to join in the laughter. I would still be mad at the four of them if Freni hadn't cracked that smile. The crisis, at least for the moment, was under control.

Nineteen

AFTER SUPPER, we sat outside on the front porch and watched the August moon rise. Out in the yard the fireflies danced, crickets chirped, and in the patch of woods an owl awakened and began to hoot. On a distant farm, a dog began to howl. I love spending summer evenings outside, and would have been even more blissful if I hadn't had a sneaking suspicion that our sudden adjournment to the great outdoors was somehow related to my singing. Perhaps they figured on using the night noises as camouflage should I suddenly burst into song. Still, one must take pleasure where and how one finds it, as long as it is clean, of course.

We were all comfortable in Mose's handmade rockers, except for Susannah. My sister has never learned to enjoy times of quiet conversation, or to commune with nature. I blame it on television, mostly the commercials. If it isn't new and improved, or fifty percent off, Susannah simply can't be bothered.

Somehow the conversation meandered around to veterinarians. "Oh, by the way, Doc Shafer sends his regards to you, Mose," I remembered to say. "He says next time you need Matilda and Bertha bred, he's got a bull more than willing to do the job." For some reason, it is quite acceptable in my circle to speak of animals in the lewdest terms, while we humans only get to pass seeds around.

"Tell Doc thanks," said Mose. He seemed grateful for my efforts. "I'll keep it in mind. But speaking of Matilda, all those folks milling around out there by the barn are making her crazy. Even keeping her in the pasture doesn't help much. Her milk production is down by fifty percent. Her teats are hard as wood."

"You don't say," said Susannah.

I couldn't see her face, but I was sure she was rolling her eyes. I tried kicking her for good measure, but banged my foot on a rocker strut instead.

"Actually," said Mose as he began to stroke his beard, "Matilda started acting funny before I put her out to pasture. It was that morning before the Englishman died that she started getting real nervous." He gave Susannah what for Mose was an accusing look. "It might have been all your trips in and out of the barn."

Susannah quickly sat up straight, so quickly, in fact, her rocker almost dumped her out on the porch. I could see the bulge that was Shnookums shift in her bra. Half-empty bras must hold terrors that none of us except Shnookums can even imagine. "I went out to the barn only once," she said emphatically. "And that was when I discovered the—well, you know what."

"The body," said Mose gently. "Susannah, we are your family here, there is no need to lie. I saw you go into the barn three times that morning, not just once."

"Three times?" I piped up.

Mose nodded. "I was mending the pasture fence on the south side of the barn. The top wire has been down in one corner for some time now, and Bertha likes to step right over the bottom wire and into the corn field. That morning I decided to keep the cows penned up in the milk shed while I worked. Bertha gets kind of pushy sometimes, and if you're not looking—"

"I went out to the barn only once," repeated Susannah. She said it softly, like she didn't expect us to believe her. But of course I did believe her. It's when my sister protests loudly that my antennae go up their highest. Liars pay the highest price of all for freedom of speech.

"Go on with your story," I urged Mose.

Mose glanced at Susannah, and then quickly away. His antennae were not tuned in to her station. "Like I was saying, I was mending the fence when I saw Susannah go into the barn the first time."

"About what time was that?"

Mose doesn't wear a watch either, but he can read the sun almost as well as I can read my quartz. "About ten maybe. Anyway, Susannah goes in, but I get busy with my mending, so I don't see her go out. But I know she's in there, because I can hear Matilda bawling the whole time. Matilda's very sensitive, you know. Even though there's a wall between the milk shed and the hay barn, she can tell if someone's in there."

"Wrong!" said Susannah.

Mose looked to me for encouragement before continuing.

"Go on, Mose," I said.

"So, when I finish the job I look up and there I see Susannah again. Headed for the barn. I think to myself that this is kind of strange, because Matilda's been bawling the whole time, but Susannah's been gone for a

while. Then I notice that Susannah is carrying something."

"Double wrong."

"What kind of something?" I asked.

"I don't know, maybe a purse or something."

"Come on! Why would I carry a purse to my own
barn?" asked Susannah quite reasonably.

Mose shrugged, which was his way of saying he thought
Susannah was capable of anything—that is, short of murder. "Maybe it was a box, then."

"Right, like a coffin," snapped Susannah.

I patted my sister's arm in a motherly fashion, until she
snatched it away. "I happen to believe you, now let Mose
get on with his story."

Mose was still stroking his beard. "So, I start to wonder
why Matilda has been bawling the whole time, and then I
figure that maybe it was because I forgot to milk her."

"Ouch." Although I've never been a milk cow, I understand that if they are not milked regularly, twice a day, the
pressure on their udders can be quite painful. I suppose
it's something like the time Susannah drank a two-liter
bottle of pop while we were on a car trip, and I wouldn't
stop to let her use the bathroom.

"I do remember milking Bertha," said Mose defensively.

I smiled reassuringly. "And it was delicious. Now,
please, finish your story."

"Funny thing is that when I did milk Matilda, she was
pretty much dry. Anyway, I was just coming out of the
milk shed when I saw Susannah going into the barn for
the third time. But she was in there only about a minute,
when she ran out screaming."

"You would too if you saw what I saw!" said Susannah.

"Yah, maybe I would."

"You mean you didn't go into the barn to investigate?"

Mose spread his big wrinkled hands in a gesture of surrender. "Yah, maybe I should have. But, Susannah, well, she—"

"Tends to get hysterical over the slightest thing?" I supplied.

"Yah. I thought maybe she had seen a mouse."

"You see! Nobody ever takes me seriously!" Susannah pounded one of her not-so-dainty fists on the arm of her rocker, and in so doing she must have jarred Shnookums, because I heard him yip. Fortunately Freni didn't seem to hear it.

"I take you more seriously than you'll ever know," I said. I turned back to Mose. "Okay, so you saw Susannah enter the barn three times that morning—"

"Once! And whose side are you on, Magdalena, anyway?"

I ignored my sister. "But did you see Don Manley go into the barn?"

Mose shook his head. "I had my back turned some of the time."

"And now you're turning it on me," cried Susannah.

I felt terrible for Mose. Ever since Papa died, he has been a surrogate father to both Susannah and me. Mose and Freni never had any daughters, just the one son, John, and, well, how much comfort can a monosyllabic son be? I knew Mose cared deeply about both of us, although I've long suspected that Susannah was his favorite. When Susannah was a little girl, Mose used to let her ride on his plow horse—something he never let me do. Susannah was allowed to help him milk too, until the time she almost drowned one of the barn kittens by putting him in a half-full milk pail. But my point is that despite her wild and English ways, Susannah has always been the apple of Mose's eye, albeit a crab apple in recent years.

"Susannah, I'm only trying to gather facts," I said. "Nobody here believes you killed Don Manley."

"But they do!" wailed Susannah.

"Do you?" I asked our kin.

Mose simply looked away.

"If the shoe fits," said Freni.

"Yah," said John.

"But on the other hand, nobody actually saw her do it," said Barbara reasonably. "Back home we would have to see proof before we made up our minds."

Freni glared at Barbara, but managed to curb her tongue. The daughter-in-law she disapproved of was just going to have to take a backseat to the murdering cousin. Freni was always one for priorities.

Susannah and I started walking home in relative silence. The only sounds we produced were Susannah's sighs and an occasional puff from me. I'm not a spring chicken anymore, and the path through the woods goes up a slight incline on the return trip.

It is most probably the very same path, by the way, that our great-great-great-great-great-great-grandfather, Jacob Hochstetler, took on his westward march in 1750. This was not a voluntary walk; he had been captured by the Delaware Indians in eastern Pennsylvania and was headed for Ohio. Jacob's wife had just been stabbed and scalped, and two of his children taken captive as well, so he could not have been in such a good mood himself. But he could not have been in a worse mood than I was just then.

The way I felt, I would have been glad if a band of Delaware Indians had leapt out of the shadows and taken me captive. With any luck, they would scalp me immediately; my hair is baby fine and has always been impossible to style. Just ask Heather. With lesser luck, they would leave my locks alone and take me back to their camp and make me one of their squaws. Just as long as my brave wasn't as dumb as Melvin Stoltzfus, I would still come out ahead. A lifetime of hauling wood and water and sweeping out wigwams would certainly be preferable to the turn my life had taken recently. Having been personally accused of murder was bad enough, but uncovering evidence that my baby sister might well be the murderess was even worse. Of course, I believed there was a good explanation for the things Mose had seen. Or did I?

"Susannah, I really believe you're innocent," I said. Somewhere to my left the resident owl hooted derisively at my statement.

"Just leave me alone, Magdalena."

"No, I really mean it. I'll find out who really did it, Susannah. That's a promise."

Susannah laughed hysterically. "Sure you will, and the culprit will be me, myself, and I. The three of us, Magdalena. The three Susannahs Mose saw entering the barn that morning. At least they won't be able to put me in solitary confinement." She laughed again, but this time the harsh false laughter dissolved into whimpers, which soon became sobs. Perturbed by his mistress's distress, the ever-loyal and impossibly high-strung Shnookums began a series of high-pitched yips. Then even the owl joined in.

I hurried forward and grabbed her by the arm. "Susannah Yoder Entwhistle! You should be ashamed of yourself. It isn't like you to give up like that."

"Oh, leave me alone, Mags," Susannah wailed, and sat right down in the middle of the path.

Our ancestor, Jacob Hochstetler, would have been ashamed of her. I certainly was. He didn't quit when the going got tough, and he was only a man. "Our people don't quit when the going gets tough," I said sternly. Then I dug down into the bottom of my barrel of weapons and pulled out the meanest and dirtiest one of them all. "If Mama could see you now, she would turn over in her grave."

"Let her turn," cried Susannah. "No, I hope she spins in her grave. In fact, I hope she spins so fast that she digs her way right down to China."

I sat down beside my sister. "Susannah, how you talk!" I tried to sound disapproving, but it wasn't easy.

My sister was not deterred. "Who knows, maybe she'll wind up in one of those opium dens. Do they still have opium dens, Magdalena?"

"I don't know. But it's too bad they've outlawed foot binding. Mama's feet were enormous."

"Even bigger than yours, I think." Susannah was starting to laugh again.

I looked down at my feet, which looked huge even in the moonlight. The thought of Mama walking around China with her size-twelve feet was enough to start me laughing as well. Eventually Susannah and I put our arms around each other—an unusual occurrence, I assure you —and laughed till the tears streamed down our faces. It would have been a perfect, albeit temporary reconciliation if only that mutt Shnookums had kept his mug shut. And despite intense wishing on my part, the owl did not swoop down and carry him away.

That night I slept like a teenager. For one of the very few times in my life I remained unconscious for the entire night. Not even a brimming bladder was enough to waken me. Just before I awoke, I had the most pleasant dreams imaginable. In the best of these dreams I was sitting down to eat an entire one of Freni's meat loaves—all by myself.

Twenty

FRENI'S SUPER-DUPER COMPANY
MEAT LOAF

Makes 8 servings

1 pound ultra lean ground beef
$^3/_4$ pound ground pork
1 package onion soup mix
$^1/_2$ cup dry quick oats
2 raw eggs
2 tablespoons ketchup
$^1/_4$ teaspoon ground black pepper
3 hard-boiled eggs, peeled

THOROUGHLY MIX all ingredients except the eggs. In a nine-by-thirteen-inch glass baking dish, form an inch-high strip of mixture approximately three inches wide and eleven inches long. Space the three boiled eggs along this strip and cover them completely with remaining meat. Pat and smooth to seal in the eggs and give a nice uniform appearance. Bake at 350° F. for about 45 minutes. When slightly cool, slice with a sharp knife. Many of the resulting pieces will display a slice of hardboiled egg for a colorful and attractive presentation.

Twenty-one

YOU CAN ARGUE until you're blue in the face, but you won't convince me that Darla Strutt can act. The mumbling, fumbling, and stumbling teenage boys in my Sunday school class can act better than Darla. Maybe at one time Darla was something of a sensation, but they have yet to give out Academy Awards for that. Frankly, unless she slaps a cop, and soon, her days on the silver screen are numbered. Not that she has so many days left altogether.

Why is it that some women insist on lying about their age? Lies simply don't make you look younger. If you're going to lie about your age, then why not pretend you're older. At least people will be impressed with how young you look for that age. If you're forty, and look forty, then promote yourself as fifty. Strangers will be amazed at how well preserved you are. That is definitely the route to go if you want compliments.

Okay, I'll admit it irked me that Darla, who was supposed to play my daughter-in-law in Art's new script, was
about my age or older. Actually, I hadn't noticed that at
first, because awe had kept me at more than an arm's
length. But during one of the scenes where we had to
scream at each other with our faces just inches apart, I
noticed that Darla's face looked like plastic. Which, I
guess, explains the name of those doctors that rearrange
you. Anyway, it was suddenly obvious that in Darla's case a
lot of rearranging had gone on over the years. That Darla
never smiled was now understandable. If she ever did
smile, her boobs would undoubtedly bob up and down
like fishing corks on a well-stocked pond.

My point is that Darla Strutt is an out-and-out fake, and
she can sue me if she wants. But somehow, knowing that
she was a fake made acting with her much easier.

"Don't fluff your lines, toots, or your ass is grass," she
whispered meanly to me before our first scene together
Monday morning. Then she proceeded to blow an enormous bubble with the gum she was chewing. The woman
was more like my sister than I'd imagined.

"Chewing gum is a disgusting habit," I informed her,
"and blowing bubbles is even worse."

"Oh, yeah?" Darla blew an even bigger bubble. If her
head had been inside it, she would have looked like an
astronaut.

I smiled sweetly at her, without bobbing my boobs one
bit. Then, wielding a piece of straw, I punctured her bubble. There was a sound like a distant car backfiring, and
Darla's plastic face was covered with pink.

"Bitch!" she said.

Of course I couldn't tolerate that. I don't allow swearing in my presence, or on my premises, and Darla Strutt,
aging Hollywood slut, had just violated both those conditions. I am not a violent person, and even if I were, I

wouldn't have hit the woman for fear that something would shatter. All the gum in Hernia couldn't hold that face together.

I drew myself up to my full height. "You take that back!"

"Will not!" Darla dug into the pocket of her costume and brought out a packet of bubble gum. She proceeded to pop a few pieces into her mouth and began to chew as fast as she could. She chewed like a cow.

If you can't lick them, join them, Papa used to say. Of course, his comments were in regard to joining the top horseshoe team at the annual church picnic. Nonetheless, I took Papa's advice. I confess to snatching the gum packet from Darla's hand and cramming a few pieces into my own mouth. Despite the fact that I was a novice at the disgusting habit, in a few minutes I had a bubble going that would make a cosmonaut proud.

Suddenly Darla's entire attitude changed.

"Oh, are you from Pittsburgh?" she asked brightly.

I carefully deflated the bubble and discreetly removed the offensive gum from my mouth. "What?"

"Of course you're from Pittsburgh, or at least from the burbs! I can tell by the way you blow. I was born in the city, but we moved to Penn Hills when I was in ninth grade. I was a cheerleader for Penn Hills High School. Say, didn't you used to be Magdalena Brzezinski from Mt. Lebanon?"

"No."

"I get it now. Maggie Hobbs from Northside Catholic?"

"Not hardly."

"But you were a pom-pom girl, I know that. Gateway High?"

"Not even in my dreams."

Darla's face fell a little, and, not surprisingly, so did her bosom. "But you blow like a native Pittsburgher. Come on, you've got to at least be from Allegheny County!"

"I was born and raised on this farm, and in that house." I nodded in the direction of the inn.

Darla stared at me in amazement. "Well, I'll be," she said at last. "I was sure you were from Pittsburgh. You could always move there, you know. With a bubble that size, you'd have quite a future. The sidewalks would be yours."

"Thank you," I said.

I still think Darla is a physical fake and a lousy actress, but after that brief encounter we became friends in an odd sort of way. Bubble buddies, you might say. Between takes we sat up in the hayloft and traded early-life anecdotes. Admittedly hers were a lot more interesting than mine, but since she seemed content to do most of the talking, it really was no problem. Only once did I give in to her repeated challenges and blow another bubble. That one was so huge, it had its own gravity.

"Are you sure you're not from Pittsburgh?" she asked again, her voice full of admiration.

"Positive. But I've visited a couple of times. What about you? Ever been on a farm before?"

Darla shook her head. "Never. The first time I ever walked into a barn was when . . ." Her voice trailed off and then she sat silent, staring ahead at the space beyond the edge of the loft.

"Was when what?" I asked patiently after some minutes had passed.

Darla shivered, then sat up very straight. "What's that, dear?"

"You were about to tell me about the first time you ever walked into a barn," I reminded her.

"Was I? Oh, yes. Unfortunately that was shortly after

your sister found Don Manley's body. We all came pouring into the barn then, remember?"

"Yes, of course." But somehow I didn't think that was it. I may have been stupid enough to copy from Melvin Stoltzfus's exam paper when I was in elementary school, but I had wised up considerably since then. (If the trend holds, I just might refrain from asking Melvin's help on my tax return next year.)

"I know what you're thinking, Magdalena, but you're wrong." She sounded sincere, but not *too* sincere, if you know what I mean.

I tried to sound casual. "I was just wondering if it was possible that you wandered over to the barn before that unfortunate incident. You know, to get a closer look at the cows or something."

Don't be fooled by her glamorous image. Darla Strutt has a laugh that would put a drunken hyena to shame. "Me? Look at cows?"

"Matilda and Bertha are exceptionally cute," I said in their defense. After all, their mother, now a collection of packages in my freezer marked "roast" and "ground chuck," was unable to speak up on their behalf.

"I hate cows!" exclaimed Darla insensitively. "They're big, they're noisy, and they stink!"

"And they chew like you," I couldn't help snapping. I wasn't getting anywhere with Darla, and frankly that made me cross. More often than not, I can get people to spill the beans if there are any to spill—and Darla, by my reckoning, had enough beans in her to supply a midwestern chili fest.

But Darla didn't divulge.

Freni was also in a bit of a mood at lunch. Things had gone from bad to worse for her after Susannah and I left the night before. Apparently she had picked on Barbara one time too many, and John, for the second time, had stood up to his mother. But even John, at five foot eleven, couldn't stand up to Barbara. Not to hear Freni tell it.

"Of course there are two sides to everything," I said soothingly. "I just wonder what Barbara's side is."

Freni slammed down the institutional-size kettle of mashed potatoes with enough force to crush a rhino's skull. "And what is that supposed to mean?"

"Well, put yourself in Barbara's shoes and see how you'd feel."

"Like I was in a small boat," said Freni without cracking a smile.

I helped Freni fill the gravy boats.

"That woman is driving a wedge between me and my John," she said bitterly. She was slicing cucumbers at the time, so I prayed for her fingers.

"That woman's name is Barbara, and she loves your son very much." I ducked. It's almost as good a form of regular exercise as jumping to conclusions.

"And I don't?"

"Sure you do, Freni. You love John more than anyone could ever love him. You gave him life." It sounded clichéd, but might well be true. How was I to know of such things? "And I'm sure John loves you just as much."

"As much as her?" asked Freni. The paring knife bobbled in the air.

"More than. One's love for one's mother can never be matched." I thought of Mama walking around China in her size-twelve shoes, and suppressed a giggle.

"I'm not asking for more," said Freni. "Just as much."

"Yes, I know."

"I don't want you to think that I'm funny, like some of the English."

"I'd never think that," I hastened to assure her. Freni sharpens all her knives on a grindstone daily. "But, Freni,

you might consider being just a little bit nicer to Barbara
for a change. John will love you even more for that."

"I'll consider it," said Freni. After wiping off the cucumber knife, she resharpened it.

"And just think, it could be worse." I should have let
Susannah sew my lips shut the last time she threatened to
do so.

"Worse? How?" The knife, while not aimed at me,
pointed in my direction.

In for a penny, in for a pound. But a ton? "They could
have children. You know, little Barbaras."

Mercifully, the phone rang then. I answered it, even
though Freni was closer. A sliced phone cord is hard to
explain to the telephone company. "Hello, PennDutch
Inn, how may I help you?"

"Who is this?" the caller demanded rudely.

I despise people with bad phone manners. I am hopeful that when they die, they will go to a place where there
are only rotary phones and thirty-digit numbers. "This is
the Duchess of York," I said politely. "Randy Andy isn't
handy, but my financial adviser is. Would you care to
speak to him?"

"Magdalena, is that you?"

"Last time I checked. I don't suppose you are Martha
Sims by any chance?"

"Well, of course I'm Martha. Didn't you recognize my
voice?"

"Actually, I didn't. I identified you by the video I'm
watching, supplied by the secret camera hidden near
your phone."

Martha was silent for so long, I almost started to doze.
"Of course you're only kidding, Magdalena, aren't you?"

"Of course. That camera started malfunctioning some
time ago. Now, what is it you want, Martha?"

Martha sighed loudly into the phone. "This was only

supposed to be a brief but cheery social call. I called just
to say hi and ask how you're doing.''

"Hi back at you, Martha. I'm doing just fine, thank
you, and yourself?''

Martha sighed again, sans the drama. "I'm fine, Magdalena. By the way, did you enjoy the lunch?''

I can be quite correct if I have to. "Lunch was very
interesting, dear. Thank you again for inviting me.''

"I hope the food agreed with you. You didn't seem to
eat a whole lot. I would feel terrible if something you ate
caused indigestion.''

"Everything was just fine, Martha. I feel perfectly well.''

"Oh.'' She almost sounded disappointed. "Well, Magdalena, I really have to go now. I have a million things to
do.''

"Good-bye, then, Martha. I think I'll get back to twid-
dling my thumbs.''

"You're such a gas, Magdalena.''

"Try me after a Thai lunch, dear.'' I hung up not a
second too soon. Freni still hadn't put the knife away,
and it was beginning to wink at me seductively.

Susannah and I filled up our plates and took them outside. We weren't trying to be antisocial or anything, but
neither of us likes to eat in crowded situations, and the
dining room was packed for lunch.

"You're getting awfully chummy with her, aren't you?''
Susannah accused me as soon as we'd sat down at the
picnic table under the Siberian elm.

"She's old,'' I said sympathetically. "It's hard for her to
change.''

"She isn't that much older than you,'' said Susannah
nastily. "And you change all the time, Mags.''

"Freni is *thirty* years older than me! I think that's a
lot.''

Susannah burst out laughing. "No, I don't mean Freni. I mean Darla. It was you and Darla I saw up in the loft, giggling together like a couple of schoolgirls." I'm sure I could detect a little jealousy in her voice.

"The woman is to be pitied," I assured her. "And what do you mean, I change all the time?"

Susannah tore the crust off one of Freni's rolls and tossed it to a flock of eager sparrows. "Sometimes I think you're getting nicer, Magdalena. I mean, to me."

I hate the maudlin part of being family. "It just seems like that," I said airily. "But that's just surface stuff. I'm still the same old grouch I always was."

Susannah threw the rest of her roll on the ground, whereupon a starling materialized out of nowhere and flew off with it. I hoped she didn't see it as an omen. "Mags, you do think I'm innocent, don't you? I want you to level with me this time."

"I always level with you," I lied. "Look, Susannah, I don't think you're capable of murder. But to be perfectly honest with you, the fact that Mose saw you traipsing out to the barn three times that morning, and you claim it was only once, does need explaining."

"But you're not going to call Melvin and have him help you do the explaining, are you?" The desperation in her voice actually tugged at my heart.

"Of course not. Melvin Stoltzfus couldn't explain his way out of a revolving door. Why you date him is beyond me," I added unnecessarily, and perhaps with just a tinge of malice.

"I'm a fool," said Susannah simply. "And just so you know, I've decided to play it cool with Melvin for a while. You know—date him less, that sort of thing."

I must have stared at her for a full minute, and when I was sure her proclamation was not going to be followed by some sort of retraction, I gave my sister a big hug. It is

darned hard for me to hug, so the recipients of my hugs
would do well to think of themselves as something akin to
gold medal winners. "I love you, Sis," I surprised even
myself by saying.

"I love you too, Mags."

We finished our lunch in peace and harmony.

I was just leaving for the barn when Freni called me back
inside to take a phone call.

"Who is it?" I asked hopefully. If it was Mel Gibson, I
would find a way to break my contract and throw the
movie people out on their ears. Then Mel could stay a
spell.

"How should I know? He's English."

"Is he personal English, or business English?"

Freni shrugged and almost dropped the receiver.
"How should I know. All the English sound the same to
me."

I took the phone, prepared. When salesmen call and
try to sell me new windows, I tell them I live in an igloo. If
they try to sell me package photo deals, I tell them it's
against my religion. If they ask whether or not I have a
leaky basement, I invite them for a cruise on my indoor
yacht. Nothing quite ticks me off more than unsolicited
business calls on my private phone. I don't call those
goons at home, so why should they call me? Although
once I did suggest to the caller that I return her call that
evening, at her home, and she was more than amenable.
When she asked me to wear a garter belt and black hose
when I called, I hung up.

"Hello. Who's calling please?" I asked.

"Don't hang up, doll. It's me. It's me, Jumbo. I mean,
Jim."

"Yah, this is the Hotel Inter-Continental in Helsinki,

Finland," I said. Finnish accents have always been my forte.

"Cut the act, doll. I didn't punch in enough numbers to reach saunaland."

"No, we have no rooms available on the thirtieth. We're hosting a convention of comic book collectors from Lapland. I suggest you try a Swedish hotel."

"Look, I know you're sore, doll. And you have a right to be—"

"You're darn tooting I'm sore, Jim. You acted like a creep."

"And a scudzo, doll. I behaved like a troll."

I refrained from stating the obvious. "What is it you want, Jim?"

"A second chance, doll. I want to make it up to you."

I have my weak points. "On a ladder?"

"Very funny, doll. Look, I just want a chance to start over. Pretend like we never met before. Think you can go for it?"

"What's in it for me?"

"More than meets the eye, doll. Come on, what do you say? Give a guy a break. I was nervous, doll, that's all."

"So was I, Jim, but I didn't fillet you with my tongue."

"Sounds exciting, doll. But seriously, I guess I got this kind of complex or something. You know, on account of I'm somewhat on the short side."

"I never noticed, Jim."

"You didn't?"

"Of course I did. My point is, however, I never would have made an issue of our height difference if you hadn't."

"Yeah, well, maybe you're right. But not everyone is like you, doll. Guess I just got a little tired of all the jokes, and when I saw you, and how gorgeous and all you are, I kinda panicked, and acted defensively."

Me gorgeous? I gripped the phone tighter. "Flattery will get you nowhere, buster."

"Yeah, doll, I shoulda figured that. But I meant every word. You're really special, doll."

"So is Freni's bundt cake." I tried to think of food to keep from melting.

"You're one of a kind, doll. I should have realized that. So, what do you say, can we try again?"

"When?" I was fast becoming a slush pile.

"Tonight, doll. Same time, same place."

"Tonight? Tonight's Monday!"

"So it is, doll. That a problem for you?"

"No, no problem, Jim."

"See you then, doll."

The hand that hung up the phone was shaking. I could not believe what I had done, or not done. Perhaps I should have told Jumbo Jim to go take a drive, blindfolded, in reverse, on the autobahn. If only it had been one of those obnoxious salesmen. I would have told him I had a telephonically transmitted fatal disease for which there would never be a cure. And then, if he didn't get off the phone pronto, I would have screamed directly into the mouthpiece. Last time I did that to Melvin, he wore earmuffs for a week.

Twenty-two

HEATHER WAS NOT the one to take my troubles to. We stopped shooting for the day about five, but Heather and I remained in the corner of the barn that had been set up for use by the makeup crew. Although she generously agreed to touch up my hair, provided I give her a lift back to her motel in Bedford, we couldn't seem to click.

"You have to forgive me, Miss Yoder, if I seem down in the dumps. Today is Don's funeral, you know."

"You can call me Magdalena. And I'm sorry about your missing the funeral. I guess I should have talked to Arthur about giving you the time to fly out to the West Coast."

"It's not that. Don's married. I mean, he was. I mean, he was when he died. His wife will be at the funeral."

Well, call me old-fashioned, but even though I can overlook a lot of hanky-panky and carrying on, I simply

cannot abide adultery. "He got what he asked for, then,"
I said.

The furrows Heather dug in my scalp with her comb
were deep enough to plant corn—between them and my
wrinkles it would be a good harvest. I may have yelped
just a little. "Just what is that supposed to mean?"

"A married man should not fool around. Under any
circumstances."

Heather decided to go for a bumper corn crop. "What
if the wife is an unappreciative little bitch?"

"We don't swear here, Heather."

Instead of a part, Heather made a groove deep enough
for the transatlantic cable. "What would you know about
being married, *Miss* Yoder?"

I calmly pointed to her rather intrusive belly. "About as
much as you do, sweetie."

"Arrrgh," said Heather.

"That's much better than swearing, dear. I appreciate
your sensitivity, I really do."

"Brrrrgh-agh!"

"Keep up the good work, dear, but try to be a little
more creative." After all, when I was only seven, and Susannah not even born, I created a whole language of my
own. I even had my own alphabet, which I sometimes
confused with the one I had just learned at school.

"I'm not swearing, you dweeb!" screamed Heather. "I
think I'm in labor."

"Nonsense," I said stoically. "Your water hasn't even
broken yet." Not that I knew much about such things,
but I had heard a little. And I had helped deliver calves
several times.

"It has now," said Heather. She was beginning to
grunt and pant like a loose hog being chased from a corn
field.

"Are you sure, dear?"

"Aaaaaaagh!" screamed Heather, louder than any hog I'd ever heard.

I took a deep breath and told myself not to panic. I had been home alone with Mama when she'd gone into labor with Susannah, and even though Freni had arrived in time, and chased me from the room before I'd had a chance to see anything, I had learned two valuable lessons—having a baby takes a lot of time, and for some inexplicable reason, water has to be boiled. Of course it wasn't until years later that I figured out Mama's making me boil water and Freni's chasing me from the room were somehow connected with Susannah's untimely arrival. The connection I pieced together in retrospect. Sometime around my thirtieth birthday.

"Geeeeeeyah!"

"I'll go boil water," I said. In my shameful haste to retreat, I ran into, or nearly ran over, Jumbo Jim.

"Slow down, doll."

"Jim! What on earth are you doing here?"

Jim grinned up at me. "I had a feeling you might not show up at Ed's Steak House, so I thought I'd buzz by here and give you a little encouragement. Nobody answered up at the house, but I heard noises coming from here. Is it milking time?"

"More so than you think."

"Well, as soon as you're done, let's go, doll. You ready?"

"Ehrrrr-gaaaaahg!" bellowed Heather.

Jim jockeyed around me for a closer look at the cow. What he saw instead was Heather down on her knees, clasping her abdomen. "Hey, doll, you weren't fighting over me, were ya?"

"She's having a baby, Jim."

Jim stood stock still for a moment, and then sprang into action. "All right, doll, you run up to the house and call the paramedics. Forget about boiling water. And come back right away. Bring some clean towels and sheets with you."

"Yes, Jim." I bolted again for the door.

"And you," I heard him say to Heather, "you lie down with your head elevated, knees up—"

I dialed three times before I could get my fingers to cooperate enough to punch in the right numbers. Thank God Zelda answered the phone. She promised to relay my message to the paramedics in Bedford right away. Then I thrashed around the house looking for clean linens, but since it was Susannah's turn to do the laundry, there weren't any. In desperation, I tore the sheets off my bed, knowing they would be cleaner than Susannah's, and grabbed a couple of towels. Although at times it felt like I was moving in slow motion, I was gone only a couple of minutes.

"I made the call," I said between raw, heaving breaths.

Jumbo didn't as much as look up. "Better late than never, doll."

"What do you mean?"

"Unless the paramedics can fly like Superman, they won't make it in time."

I squatted down beside him for a closer look, but there was nothing to see. Something was wrong with this picture. Susannah tells me that in movies women are always having babies without having to take off their underpants or pantyhose first. In real life, however, shedding one's undergarments is probably advisable. "Shouldn't she at least take off her underpants?" I asked.

"Not in front of a man!" Heather gasped.

"You did once before," I reminded her sternly.

The next time Heather screamed, which was a second or two later, Jim and I pulled her wet underpants off. There was the baby's head.

"Push," said Jim.

Heather grunted. I said nothing.

"Push!" he commanded.

I shoved him uncertainly.

"Not you!" he shouted. "Her! Push, dammit!"

I forgave Jim his profanity and got into the act myself; exhorting a huffing, puffing, grunting, and screaming Heather to push. In no time at all the rest of the baby came into view.

"It's a boy!" said Jim with surprising joy.

"How can you tell?" I asked.

Jim cleared the baby's mouth with his finger, and, satisfied that he was breathing normally, laid him, still attached by the cord, on Heather's stomach. Then he covered him with a towel. Jim was still wiping his hands with another towel when the paramedics arrived.

"You did good, doll," Jim told me yet again over a cobbler and coffee. We were the only customers left in Ed's.

"Thanks, Jim, you weren't so bad yourself."

"So, do you think we could date, doll, or what?" We had talked about everything under the sun except our relationship.

"How can we date, Jim? I live up here, and you live down in Baltimore."

"I don't mind driving up, doll. And if that gets to be too much, you could spell me by driving down there. Where there's a will, there's a way, they say."

"*They* don't single-handedly operate one of the most popular inns in America," I retorted. Admittedly, there was pride in my voice. But there must have been something else too.

"It's the height thing, isn't it?"

"What height thing?"

Jim's diminutive right fist banged on the table with surprising force. "Dammit, doll, if there's one thing that pisses me off, it's you bleeding-heart liberals refusing to call a spade a spade."

"I don't know what you mean," I said quite honestly. Papa had once lectured at me at length on the difference between a spade and a shovel, but I still get the two confused.

"Cut the crap, doll. Cut to the chase. You don't want to go out with me because I'm short."

I was momentarily taken aback. I know that this might sound hard to believe, but while we'd been supping and engaged in general chitchat, I had ceased to pay attention to Jim's height. Of course he had been sitting on both the Bedford and Somerset county phone books. But still, I honestly had ceased to see him first and foremost as a short man, but rather just as a man. A man whom I admired but had decided I didn't quite like.

"Look, buster, it doesn't bother me that you are a little shorter than I am. Okay, make that a whole lot shorter. Even if you were a foot taller than me, Jim, I still don't think it would work out."

He stared, not believing me. "And why not, doll?"

I started to hem and haw, but Jumbo cut me off. "I said, cut the crap, doll. Give it to me straight."

I decided to do just that. "Because you're a boor, Jim."

"So, you don't like my stories?"

"You're definitely not a *bore*, Jim. What I meant is that you're—well, a little on the crude side. Rough around the edges."

"What are you, doll? Some kind of hifalutin snob?"

I considered that for a moment. "I am awfully picky, Jim, I'll grant you that. But I don't think I'm a snob. I just don't think you and I would work out as an item."

"An item, doll?"

"You know what I mean. Couldn't we just be friends,

Jim, and see each other occasionally? I mean, we don't
have to date to be friends, do we?"

"Ah, I see, I get it now," said Jim triumphantly.
"You're one of those!"

"Those what?"

"A lesbian, doll. I should have known."

"Good night, Jim. I've got to be going." I left without
saying anything to contradict him. And I'm sure Jim was
not the first one to suppose my sexual fantasies were
monomorphic. When you're forty-four and never been
married, tongues are bound to wag. Especially these days,
when all people can think about seems to be sex. Aunt
Sadie and her roommate, Mabel, never suffered such in-
dignities.

"You don't know what you're missing out on, doll,"
Jim shouted at my back. "They don't call me Jumbo for
nothing."

"Grow up," I said quietly.

Jim must have razor-sharp hearing. "What's that supposed to mean?"

"Take it any way you want," I said. Then I felt bad,
because I had stooped to his level, which is really pretty
low.

Just outside the front door of Ed's Steak House I ran into
Darla Strutt. "Darla!" I cried. I was actually glad to see
her.

Darla started to brush past me, but I accidentally
stepped on a yard or two of her flowing fabric. "As if that
wasn't enough!" she snapped.

"Come again?"

"I'll sue, Magdalena. Even if you are from Pittsburgh,
I'll sue." Of course she was carrying her dog, Fifi, and she
waved her in my face like a tempting morsel. But since I

had just eaten a steak bigger than the dog, I wasn't
tempted.

"I'm not from Pittsburgh, dear. But about your dress,
I'll pay to have it cleaned." I was assuming that clothes
like Darla's were not meant to be washed in old-fashioned
soap and water.

"Cleaning won't help!" Darla wailed. The woman was
so much like Susannah, I was going to have to do a more
thorough check of my family tree. It was beginning to
look as if there were a Strutt or two on one of the thinner
branches.

"Cheer up, dear. I'm sure it will be just fine. And if it
isn't, I'm sure my sister would be happy to lend you
hers."

Darla wailed like a banshee pup alone on the moors.
By the sound of it, Fifi was alone on the moors as well.
"Poor Fifi. My poor little baby! How could he do that to
her?"

I was as lost as Susannah in church. "I haven't a clue
what you're talking about, dear. Is this a Pittsburgh rid-
dle?"

"Fifiiiiii!" The banshee pup had lungs like a Great
Dane. Fifi's lungs were even louder.

I do my best to be a loving Christian from time to time.
I reached out, albeit gingerly, to give her a comforting
pat.

Darla attempted to jerk away from me. Unfortunately, I
was still standing on her clothes. Anything that rips that
easily should indeed be dry-cleaned.

"Try Quick-Clean. It's right up the street. They do
good mending too."

"You idiot! You blithering idiot!" Darla screamed. "I
don't give a flying fig about my clothes. It's Fifi, my dog,
that I'm talking about!" (Actually, those were not exactly

Darla's words, but Mama would spin into a blur if I as much as quoted them.)

I might have stared stupidly at her.

"Your sister's dog—Snickems—or whatever its name is, has gone and gotten my little Fifi pregnant."

I probably continued to stare. I was trying to imagine the two pint-size pooches in flagrante delicto. They must have looked like rats fighting. Why was it that not only the birds and the bees, but dogs as well, managed to do some things so naturally, while I, Magdalena Yoder, had yet to experience my first real kiss?

I was still closing the front door behind me when my personal phone started to ring. The number for my personal line is a secret I guard even more jealously than my weight—right up there with the secret ingredient in Mama's Peanut Butter Chiffon Pie. Even Freni doesn't know that. Freni does know my telephone number, but like any good Amishwoman, she does not have a phone of her own, and calls me only in emergencies, from a pay phone. Of course, Melvin Stoltzfus knew my number, thanks to Susannah, but I doubted even he would have the nerve to call me again so quickly. In tenth grade I had arm-wrestled Melvin and won. The match would have been over several seconds earlier if I hadn't had the flu.

I sprinted to get the phone. The odds were that it was Susannah, wanting me to come pick her up from a truck stop, but barring that, it could possibly be Freni, telling me she had just killed her daughter-in-law. "Hello?"

"Hi, Magdalena, it's me."

"You don't say. Well, this is me too. Of course that shouldn't be so surprising. Last I heard there were over eight billion me's on the earth. Now, which one might you be?"

"This is Martha, Mags. Martha Sims."

"Ah, *that* me. Well, Martha, you have exactly three seconds to explain how on earth you got my private number, and then three more seconds to apologize for having called it."

"Now, don't you be getting bent all out of shape, Mags. I simply wanted—"

"One—two—three, and my shape is just fine, thanks." I slammed the phone down.

The second time it rang I didn't pick it up until the tenth ring. "Well?"

"Susannah gave us your number, Mags. Back when she was dating that sweet young man who belonged to our church. If—"

Slam.

The third time Martha apologized right away, and profusely. Some people just need limits set for them.

"You already said you were sorry six times. Now, why is it you're calling?"

Having learned her lesson, Martha got straight to the point. "I heard about the hairdresser having her baby today. I'm calling to see if Mr. Lapata needs a replacement."

It would boggle your mind if I tried to explain to you how Martha Sims, the Presbyterian minister's wife, had already heard that a devil-worshipping hairdresser from out of state had given birth on a Mennonite farm only hours earlier, but that's Hernia for you.

"Why don't you ask him yourself," I said complacently.

"You mean he's there? Now?"

"It's twelve-thirty A.M., Martha. What kind of woman do you think I am?" Besides flattered, of course.

"Will he be there in the morning?"

"This is the morning, Martha."

She had the nerve to sigh impatiently. "I mean the real morning. Like ten or eleven. Like that."

"No, Martha, he'll be sailing a yacht from Fiji to Bora Bora. Of course he'll be here."

"Well!" said Martha, and she hung up the phone rudely.

I was too tired to be miffed anymore that night. I was just glad my day was finally over and Martha's call had not turned out to be one from Susannah, stuck at a truck stop. Even though Susannah doesn't have a car, she manages to find her way to various truck stops with some frequency. Needless to say, it's you truckers who transport her there. Next time you come across a thirty-four-year-old woman, five foot nine, about 135 pounds, medium-brown hair, blue eyes, and a lopsided chest, trailing enough yards of fabric to clothe a third-world country, who is looking for a ride, poke her in that lopsided chest and see if it yips. If it does, then that's Susannah, and you'd be well advised to leave her alone. If you don't, and she doesn't manage to make you totally miserable, I will. Fair warning.

Anyway, the last time that happened, I had to drive fifty miles to Shippensburg in the middle of a snowstorm to collect her. Lest you think me a fool and an enabler, I wouldn't have gone, except that Susannah had somehow managed to lose her shoes as well as her purse and coat. Although I was mighty tempted to let her hoof it on home, barefoot, in the snowstorm, thankfully it was the rational side of me that triumphed. With my luck, and Susannah's penchant for screwing up, the next call I received would have been from the North Pole, with an irate Santa accusing my sister of having molested three of his elves. She probably would have been guilty too.

Twenty-three

BRIGHT AND EARLY the next morning I headed out to
Miller's Feed Store to buy a new pitchfork. The prop department had somehow managed to come up with one
for the movie, but Mose would need one to toss hay come
winter. Besides which, I needed to plug in to the local
gossip circuit if I was going to find out who killed Don
Manley. Outside of Norah Hall and my weekly Women's
Prayer Circle meetings, Miller's Feed Store dishes up the
best gossip this side of Bedford.

Roy Miller is a triple fifth cousin of mine, but I certainly don't claim him. The official rumor has it that he
beats his wife, Elspeth. It is common knowledge, however,
that it is Elspeth Rhinehart Miller who beats up on Roy.
Elspeth is a German-German, not a Swiss-German like
most of the Mennonites and Amish in the Hernia area.
What's more, she was baptized a Lutheran—as an infant,
no less. No Mennonite or Amishman can comprehend

such a senseless act. Perhaps it was being splashed with all that water as a tiny baby that put Elspeth in such a foul mood.

One might have more respect for Roy if he didn't allow Elspeth to push him around. A man should listen to his wife (didn't Papa?), but he shouldn't put up with hitting. No one should—not even a true pacifist like Roy. Sadly, the long-sleeved shirts that Roy habitually wears, even on the hottest days, are not a sign of his Mennonite modesty. What makes the whole thing seem even sadder is that Elspeth is a little bitty thing with a beaked nose and horn-rimmed glasses that flare out like butterfly wings. She seems about as dangerous as Shnookums.

The store parking lot was already a sea of buggies by the time I arrived. Since Roy is a distant kinsman, and only sort of English, his store is the number one shopping spot for most of the plain folk in Bedford County. In addition to feed and pitchforks, you can buy bonnets and suspenders. Even wood-burning stoves. Even though she is Church Amish and not as strict as some of her brethren, Freni does almost all her shopping there. Compared to Miller's Feed Store, the Kmart in Bedford is a den of iniquity.

"Goot morgan," I said to all the Yoders, Hostetlers, Masts, and Millers I encountered on my way to the pitchfork display rack. The only person I didn't speak to was Agatha Yost. But since we hadn't been speaking since the fifth grade, when she purposely sat on my peanut butter sandwich, it made no difference.

When I was within feet of the pitchforks, with only a pile of milking pails between me and them, Elspeth swooped down like a great horned owl. "Why, Magdalena Yoder, whatever are you doing in my humble little establishment?"

I reminded myself that the good Lord died for all sin-

ners, including Elspeth, and forced a smile. "I'm here to
buy a pitchfork. Care to recommend one?"

Elspeth fluffed a few feathers and then cocked her
head, but she did not regard me wisely. "Tired of shopping at Sam's?"

"Sam Yoder's Corner Market does not carry
pitchforks," I reminded her patiently, "only groceries.
And anyway, Mose buys all our farm supplies here."

"Yes, so he does. But that's Mose. You, however, are a
different story. If you want to buy one of our pitchforks,
Magdalena Yoder, then you are going to have to sign a
special register."

"A what?" Because of all the background noise, I was
sure I was hearing things.

Elspeth scratched her beak officiously with a talon.
"You heard me, Magdalena. You want a pitchfork, you
sign a register."

"Do I need a permit as well?" I asked innocently
enough. With a Democrat in the White House, anything
was possible.

"I wish that were the case. Unfortunately, all I can do is
make you sign a register. And notify Chief Stoltzfus, of
course."

"Tell Mel and I'll—"

"You'll what? Kill me?" Beady eyes flashed accusingly
behind the flaring rims of her glasses.

I tried to swallow my anger. When dealing with Elspeth,
it doesn't take long to fill up. "I did not kill Don Manley!"

Elspeth arranged her face into what I supposed was a
smug smile. "You threatened him, didn't you? There
were witnesses, you know."

That did it. If the pot wants to call the kettle black,
that's one thing. But Elspeth is a virtual coal bin of ag-
gression. Everyone in Hernia has heard Elspeth threaten

Roy, and knows that she sometimes carries out those threats. Sometimes before their very eyes.

I struggled valiantly to temper my temper with Christian charity. "You two-bit hypocrite! How dare you accuse me of violence. Have you registered your fists in that precious register of yours?"

Beady eyes bulged behind the horn-rims. "You big damn bitch!" She took a step forward and prodded me, right on the breastbone, with one of her talons. "Get out of my store."

Undoubtedly, what I did next had both Mama and Menno Simons, the founder of my faith, rolling over in their respective graves. I prodded Elspeth right back. And since I am quite a bit bigger than she is, my prod might have been proportionately harder. Roy, why is it you don't stand up to your wife?

Elspeth flat out pushed me then. If it weren't for the pile of milking pails, I would have landed smack-dab against a pitchfork myself. Of course, this one was hanging from a wall display, but its tines were pointed outward, not toward the wall, as they should have been. The milking pails, which crashed around me like thunder, made me lose my balance, and I fell flat on the floor just inches from the deadly tines. Had the aisle been clear, I might well have been skewered like a frankfurter myself. Once she had me fastened to the wall, I'm sure Elspeth would have had no qualms about using my noggin as a bonnet display.

Fortunately the crashing buckets attracted more attention than our little quarrel had, and before I could properly compose myself, we were surrounded by a knot of curious onlookers.

"Avert your eyes this second!" I chided Jacob Beiler. As an Amishman, he should have been ashamed of himself for trying to peek up my skirt.

"Ach, it's only Magdalena Yoder." Rachel Krieder might have been Mama's double second cousin, but she would get no Christmas cake from me this year.

At least Elspeth acted in character. "Oh, how the mighty have fallen," she hooted.

"And the mighty will rise again to sue." I picked myself up with dignity. It is easy to act dignified when a million dollars has just been tossed in your lap. Along with a pail or two. I turned to my audience. "You all saw her push me, didn't you? You are all witnesses."

"I saw nothing," said Jacob. Not only did he have the nerve to turn and walk away, but he sounded disappointed to boot.

"I only heard you, I didn't see you, Magdalena." I made a mental note to ask Rachel to return the waffle iron she borrowed from Mama in 1963.

"Well, surely one of you saw it." I turned slowly around, so that each in turn could see the pain and anguish on the victim's visage. Apparently, they were not impressed. Each in turn turned and walked away, leaving me alone with the evil Elspeth.

"Hoo-ha!" she hooted. She flapped about noisily in her glee. "So you're not the big shot you think you are, are you? No, of course not! You're just a two-bit bed-and-breakfast owner who's gotten too big for her britches. Now, get out of my store before I give them all a chance to see nothing again."

I would have pondered longer what to do, but one of the pails had given me a pounding headache. I cannot be blamed, then, for appearing to leave at Elspeth's request. Needless to say, Miller's Feed Store would never have my business again. Neither would Freni or Mose ever darken that doorway, not if I could help it. Even if I had to drive all the way to Somerset to buy a bag of seed potatoes next spring, I determined never to let one more coin of mine clank into that cursed coffer.

I had just stepped outside into the warm, welcoming sunshine, when I nearly tripped again. This time it was not a pile of pails that impeded my progress, but my milk-livered cousin himself, Roy Miller.

"Pssst, Magdalena."

I caught my balance by clutching at the corner of a buggy parked too near the door. It must have been an old buggy, because a swatch of heavy black canvas tore off in my hand. Hopefully the buggy belonged to Jacob Beiler. I dropped the swatch and caught my breath. " 'Pssst' is something they say in books, Roy, not something real live folks say to one another."

"Pssst," he said again. He crooked and flexed his index finger several times, and then just as dramatically slipped out of sight around the side of the store.

Foolishly, I followed him. Roy Miller might not be able to stand up to his diminutive wife, but that didn't preclude any dangerous dementia on his part. He was, after all, my blood kin. Anyway, it was a bright, sunny day, and the birds in the overhead maples were singing their little heads off. Since we all have to check out sometime, it may as well be under these conditions.

I need not have worried. Roy wanted only to talk. "You won't sue us, will you, Magdalena?"

"I suppose not this time," I said reluctantly. I wasn't sure if one had to have witnesses to sue, and even if not, it really wasn't the Christian thing to do. My branch of the faith exhorts me to turn the other cheek when I am accosted.

Roy breathed a deep sigh of relief. "I'm awfully sorry about the fall you took. Really I am. If—"

"It wasn't a fall, Roy. I was pushed."

He blinked nervously. "Yeah, well, what I really wanted

to say is that the other day there was a man from that movie company looking at the pitchforks, and it must have been him who turned that fork around. I've been meaning to hang it back right, but I just haven't had time."

If I had kept my mouth open any longer, Sophie Shrock's bees could have built their hive inside it. "What man? What was his name?" I asked as soon as I regained the use of my most valuable asset.

"Don't remember exactly," said Roy, brightening, "but I think it had something to do with insects."

Melvin Stoltzfus flitted through my mind, but surely Melvin had no idea I thought of him as a praying mantis. "You mean like a bug? That kind of insect?"

"That's it! Bug Somebody. You know him? Is he famous?"

I hate it when I snort derisively. It is so unflattering, given my rather long teeth. "More like infamous, I'd say. And don't get your knickers in a knot, Roy, he is not an actor. Rumor has it he might have Mafia connections. Of course all this is hush-hush. You understand?"

Roy nodded happily. Spreading rumors was one thing he undoubtedly did better than his wife.

"Tell me, Roy, was Bugsy looking at the pitchfork before or after Don Manley was murdered?"

Roy's usually placid face contorted with concentration. "Well, let's see. I think it was just after Mabel Ediger bought the fifty-pound bag of pickling salt. Or was it paraffin? Yes, it had to be the paraffin, because Mabel didn't put in cucumbers this year."

"Praise God," I said in all sincerity. Mabel's homemade pickles would make a pig pucker, and she not only serves them at all the church suppers, but insists that everyone have a helping or two.

"And it was just before Martha Sims bought—"

"Was it before or after the murder, Roy?" I didn't really raise my voice that loud. It was mere coincidence that the birds stopped singing.

"Uh—uh, before, I think."

"Thanks, Roy."

I walked briskly to my car. I do not run in public. Just before I slammed the door, I could hear those foolish birds start singing again.

I found Steven in the barn, busily blocking out the morning's first scene. He was not at all happy to be interrogated. I'm sure he would have refused altogether, but I threatened to write his mother a detailed account of what Susannah had told me he'd done the night before in Bedford. Of course, I hadn't seen my sleepy-headed sister that morning, but with the Hollywood crowd, that sort of threat is a sure bet.

"This better be good," Steven snapped.

"I'll say, buster. You want to tell me just what in the world you were doing in Miller's Feed Store the other day?"

Bugsy brushed a fly from his cheek. "Buying a damn pitchfork, what else?"

I must confess to being a bit taken aback by Bugsy's honesty. I had expected him to deny even being there. "You mean you confess to everything? Just like that?"

"Confess to what?" Steven snarled.

"Everything!"

Steven squinted at me. It was clear he realized what I knew. "Okay, okay, I confess to everything. I did have them put the damn pitchfork on your account, but only because I had left my wallet back at the motel in Bedford."

"That's it? That's *everything*?"

Bugsy blushed. "You'll have to ask your sister if you want details. The bridle and reins were her idea."

I struggled to block out what Steven, alias Bugsy, had implied. It should have been Susannah my parents named Magdalena, not me. "You mean you really did buy a pitchfork for the movie?"

Steven smirked. "Bingo."

"So, I guess you bought this pitchfork *after* Don's murder?"

Bugsy bellowed something that isn't fit to print, and stalked rudely away. I decided to grill Susannah and write his mother after all.

Twenty-four

MY FIRST SCENE of the day wasn't scheduled until after lunch, and it was far too beautiful a day to spend the morning hanging around the set. Narrowly escaping the treacherous tines of a pitchfork is a tonic I can heartily recommend. Cheating the jaws of death had filled me with a strange elation. Therefore, I decided to take a walk. If that sounds indolent to some, so be it. I alone will have to answer to my Maker—and Mama—when I cross that Great Divide.

After lunch, there would be plenty of opportunity to put my nose back to the grindstone. In the meantime I just wanted to be me. To walk across Hertzler Lane, climb Aaron Miller's fence, and pick my barefoot way quite carefully through his cow pasture to the bank of his pond. Then I planned to dangle my feet and gaze up at yet another cloudless August sky.

I stopped at the house to shed my shoes and grab a banana.

"The kitchen is closed," Freni said crossly. "I can't for the life of me figure out this recipe I plan to make Arthur for lunch. Who ever heard of such a thing as a beef salad?"

"Speaking of lunch, I may skip it. I'm going to walk over to Aaron's pond. Care to join me?" It was a safe question. Freni walked to work from her farm every day. The last thing Freni wanted to do was to walk for fun.

Freni scowled and shook her finger at me, but it was all for show. "Don't eat the banana till you get there. Your body can't digest food while it's walking, Magdalena. You're either going to end up constipated, or with heart-burn."

"I'll take the constipation. Unless you want it again."

I waved at Mose, who was leading Bertha out of the milk shed. He waved me over.

"Magdalena, I'm afraid I have some bad news." For Mose, that was beating around the bush.

"Is Bertha sick?"

"Ach, no, she's fine. This is about that new pitchfork Mr. Freeman bought. He said I could use it when he wasn't filming. Now I can't find it."

My good mood could not be shaken. "I'm sure it will show up, Mose. Keep looking," I suggested kindly.

Mose grumbled something about Steven blaming him for the missing pitchfork, but I didn't stay to listen. The beauty of the morning was calling me.

I sang to myself as I climbed Aaron Miller's fence and traipsed across his field. Partly I sang out of joy, and partly to keep his cows at bay. Cows are curious creatures. They'll investigate anything unusual as long as they aren't intimidated by it. A barefoot woman in a blue dress is certainly worthy of investigation. Although normally quite docile, cows can do a lot of unintentional damage. An eight-hundred-pound cow accidentally stepping on my bare foot is not my idea of a good time. By singing I hoped to intimidate the cows just enough to keep them out of stepping range. Not that I'm such a bad singer, mind you, even though there was that anonymous petition passed around our church asking me to resign from the choir. That was before the reverend's wife lost her panties.

The cows left me alone, and I didn't step in any of their pies, so I was still in a good mood when I reached the pond. In my opinion, Miller's Pond deserves to be called a small lake, but no matter what you call it, it is just plain beautiful. I sat on the soft grass near the bank, and leaned back against a young pin oak with the morning sun, which was shining from across the pond, full in my face. I closed my eyes and soon slipped into a blissful state halfway between sleep and waking. So far it could not have been a more perfect day.

"Perfect day," someone said. Probably the beginning of a dream.

"You can say that again," I agreed heartily.

"Perfect day."

I opened my eyes, and then felt them with my hands to make sure I really was awake. As far as I could tell, I was. I could feel the rough bark of the pin oak against my back. I could feel the grass between my toes. I could see the sunlight dancing off the pond in front of me, and I could even hear the cows grazing somewhere to the left.

Having concluded that I was indeed awake, I gave myself a quick mental test to see if I was crazy. I passed it— with flying colors I might add—which meant I had to think of another explanation. Perhaps it had been God speaking to me. Such things happen, you know. If you doubt me, just read the story of Samuel in the Bible.

"Yes?" I asked tentatively.

"Yes, what?" Frankly, it didn't sound like God. This disembodied voice sounded a couple of thousand years younger than God, and a bit sexy to boot. God, I know, doesn't sound sexy.

"Yes, what is it you want? And who are you?"

"Ah, it's time for introductions, is it?" At that, the voice took shape by swinging down from the tree.

I hate to admit it, but I screamed. After all, wasn't that a serpent up in the tree who spoke to Eve in the Garden of Eden?

"Sorry about that," said the voice. It was by now wearing a drop-dead-handsome man's body. I know such things are subjective, but this body was about six foot two, lean but not skinny, and was topped with a strong-jawed head that sported two intensely blue eyes and a lot of very dark, almost black, curly hair. Who's going to argue with that?

I'm only slow, not impossible. By this time my brain had completed its processing and come up with the conclusion that this was a real live, flesh and blood man who deserved a real live, flesh and blood response. I gave him one that would have made all my pacifist ancestors disown me.

"Damn!" he said as he cautiously moved his arm away from his face. "You pack quite a punch there."

"That's what you deserve for sneaking up on me like that."

He laughed easily. "I didn't sneak up on you. I was already in the tree when you sat down."

"Well, you should have said something!"

"I think I did. That's why I frightened you."

If I weren't a pacifist, I would have punched him again.

"I wasn't frightened, only startled. And you should have said something immediately!"

"And that wouldn't have frightened you more?"

"Just go away and leave me alone," I said quite reasonably. "You're spoiling my quiet time."

"Ah, but I was here first, remember?"

I tried a new tactic. "Look, buster, if you don't beat it, I'll sic the owner on you." Fat chance of doing that. Unlike me, Aaron Miller was a Mennonite who lived by his pacifist faith. He was also about eighty years old, and had been bedridden ever since slipping on the ice back in March.

The handsome but loutish oaf in front of me had the temerity to grin. "So sic him," he said mockingly.

I faked it as best I could. "Aaron!" I called through cupped hands. "Aaron, you have a trespasser!" The Miller farmhouse wasn't even in sight, and I doubt my voice carried even halfway across the pond, but still, my ruse should have worked. I know I always get scared and run when I'm challenged. In a manner of speaking, that is.

"You called?" The grin had become a smile that displayed obscenely white teeth.

That did it. That made me madder than a wet hen. Even madder than a plucked goose. I lunged at the interloper, hoping to catch him off guard and push him into the pond. Unfortunately, he had great reflexes and sidestepped me as neatly as a matador does a bull. The result was that I ended up in the pond instead. When I finally quit sputtering, I shouted something shamefully wicked at him. Mercifully, I have since erased the exact words from my memory.

Rude and Handsome only laughed.

"You think that's so funny, do you?" I screamed. "Well, come on down here and fight like a man, then!"

He came down to the edge of the pond, but only to

offer an extended hand. "Here. Better get out of there. When I was a kid I stocked this pond with Mississippi River catfish. They get to be eight feet long sometimes, and have been known to nibble on fishermen. They're especially fond of bare toes."

I dug my toes safely down into the mud. "Who are you?"

The blue eyes danced, or maybe it was the sunlight reflecting off of the pond. "I'm Aaron. Aaron Miller, Jr. My pop owns this place. Now, who are you?"

"That's for me to know and you to find out."

Rude and Handsome laughed again. "I intend to find out. You know, in some places trespassers are shot."

"But I'm not a trespasser. I live—" My jaws clamped shut with more force than those of a Mississippi catfish. I couldn't believe how stupid I had almost been.

"Well, you do look familiar." He paused and stroked that sinfully handsome chin of his. "You wouldn't happen to be Susannah Yoder, from across the road?"

"That slut?" I shook my head in bewilderment. Anger and flattery are harder to mix than vinegar and water. Either those blue eyes were blind, or I was being toyed with. Susannah is ten years younger than I, and frankly, she looks it. Of course, Susannah spends a fortune on beauty routines, whereas the only mud pack I had ever worn, I was wearing right then.

"Susannah had a sister," he said, pretending to be thoughtful. "Now, what was her name. Matilda?"

"It was Jennifer," I said. "And she died. About four years ago, visiting her cousin in Nebraska. Got caught in a combine while helping with the wheat harvest. The combine sucked her in and she was never seen again. That is, until that woman up in Michigan found parts of her in a cereal box."

I must admit that young Aaron Miller had a sense of

humor. His laugh was actually quite pleasant once it was directed at something I said, rather than at me.

"I'm glad you find that so funny," I said, trying to sound as angry as I could. "It just so happens that Jennifer Yoder was my very best friend. And anyway, I don't think you are Aaron Miller, Jr. Little Aaron left Hernia after high school graduation, and was never seen again. I think he joined the army and was sent to Vietnam. It broke his father's heart to have him join up like that. Being a Mennonite, he could have gotten a deferment on religious grounds, but he didn't even try."

That face was just as handsome serious as it was smiling. "You're right. It did break Pop's heart. But that was then, and this is now. Fortunately Little Aaron is not the same person now that he was then. And I suppose that Jennifer has changed some too." There was an annoying hint of query to his voice.

"I am not Jennifer," I snapped. It was, after all, an honest response. "Anyway, I better get going. I have to get to work." I sloshed out of the pond, all ten toes still intact.

"Just what kind of work do you do?"

"I'm an actress," I blurted out stupidly. I mean, how dumb can you get? Hernia is not Hollywood. The only acting game in town was one pasture away. It wouldn't take Sherlock Holmes to track me down. Even Watson could then figure out that I really was Jennifer, so to speak, and that I hadn't ended up on a breakfast table after all. I suppose this shouldn't have mattered so much, but I didn't want Little Aaron, who was now anything but, to formally make my reacquaintance until I'd had time to wash the mud off my face. A lot of time.

"Well, see you around," said Aaron. He didn't sound like he cared one way or another.

"I doubt that. I'll be much too busy working to come back here," I said nonchalantly.

"All right, then. Bye."

I don't tolerate indifferent dismissals. When I was still in my twenties, when Mama and Papa were still alive, and the PennDutch not even a gleam in my eye, I once worked as a secretary in Bedford. Unfortunately I caught my boss, Mr. Oberlin, in a compromising position with Annette, another secretary. Thereafter Mr. Oberlin refused to speak to either Annette or me unless it was about official business. We may as well have been voice-activated office machines. But I didn't take it lying down like Annette did. I fixed his wagon good. I dissolved four of those chocolate-flavored laxative bars in his cup of hot chocolate an hour before a very important business meeting.

I didn't have a cup of hot chocolate to offer young Aaron Miller, but I did have a free right hand, which I extended. "Yeah, bye."

Foolishly, the man took it. The second we made contact, I squeezed hard and pulled. I teetered back a few steps myself, and nearly went back down the bank again, but nearly doesn't count. What does count is that Aaron Miller, Jr., was reunited with the Mississippi catfish he seemed so taken with.

I didn't even turn around, although I knew that I was being watched as I made my way back across the pasture, adroitly dodging cow pies. As I walked, I tried to concentrate on the beef salad Freni was going to make for lunch.

Twenty-five

FRENI HOSTETLER'S VERSION OF BEEF YUM YAI
(Thai cold beef salad)

Makes 6 servings

1 pound of thinly sliced roast beef
2 medium cucumbers
3 bunches green onions
Juice of three limes
1 tablespoon lemon zest
1 tablespoon fish sauce
$^{1}/_{2}$ teaspoon salt
Lettuce leaves

Cut the roast beef into half-inch-wide strips. Peel and slice the cucumbers, then cut cucumber slices in half. Chop the green onions. Assemble the first seven ingredients and mix well just before serving. Serve on a bed of lettuce leaves. (Freni served fresh hot loaves of homemade bread as the accompaniment.)

Twenty-six

MARTHA SIMS was hired as Heather's replacement, and I must confess that it was I who twisted Arthur's arm. Martha made a lousy hairdresser, but she was a font of information. While she fiddled and faddled with my damp mop, using the most foul-smelling of hair sprays, she babbled endlessly about everyone and everything. I would like to say that I am above such gossip, but after all, Martha is a minister's wife, and therefore privy to everything worth mentioning that goes on in Hernia.

"You're not having an affair with Doc Shafer?" I asked innocently. That would have explained the rapidity with which Doc got his news.

Martha tugged sadistically hard at a lock of my baby-fine hair. If I didn't learn to censure myself, and soon, I would be as bald as my great-uncle Ernie. Susannah used to check her makeup in the reflection of his dome. "No, I am not having an affair with that old geezer," snapped

Martha, "but I know who *is* having an affair." She paused needlessly to build the suspense.

"Do tell," I begged.

"You have to guess."

"Kay Weinstein?"

"Ha! Not even close. Guess again."

"Marietta Burgess?"

"That was last month. Guess again."

"Sharon Hadley?"

"Three years ago, and it was a pitiful excuse for an affair, if you ask me. Her husband didn't even threaten to leave her when he found out. Keep guessing."

"I can't guess," I wailed.

"I'll tell you, then," said Martha through a mouth full of hairpins. I knew that she would, but in her own good time. Either that or she'd self-combust. I am firmly convinced that all those stories of spontaneous combustion you read in the pulp magazines are true, just inaccurately reported. Behind every one of those gals going up in flames was a juicy bit of gossip that never found an audience.

Apparently Martha liked to live dangerously. Five minutes later she still hadn't told me. I was beginning to imagine that I smelled smoke. "I'm still waiting," I nudged.

"For what? I already sprayed the back once. Now I have to let it set for a few minutes."

"Not that. I'm waiting to find out who is having an affair. Of course, by now it could well be over."

"Oh, that," said Martha casually. "Well, if you simply must know, it's none other than that snooty priss, Norah Hall."

"Norah Hall? Is that all? I've known about her for ages." Okay, so it was only a few days, but sitting on that kind of information for a few days can seem like ages.

"You have? How?" She started spraying again, this time the front.

"I caught her in action, you might say."

"Magdalena Yoder, how you talk! But that means you know who the man is!"

"I don't have a clue." Trust me, it was a harmless lie. I don't believe in passing on gossip, although I am not above confirming things now and then. Had Martha asked me if Norah's paramour was named Garth, that would be a different story. But she hadn't, and anyway I didn't have a last name, did I?

Martha was disappointed enough in my answer to direct the hair spray perilously close to my eyes, but not so upset as to clam up altogether. "Well, she may not look it, but she's a dangerous woman," I thought I heard her say.

"What?"

"Norah Hall, that's what. I said she's a dangerous woman."

This interested me. "How so?"

Martha put the non-aerosol bottle down and leaned in closer. "She spent time in an insane asylum, you know."

"I didn't know. Are you sure?"

"Positive. And do you know what for?"

"No. What for?"

"Intense clinical depression. Something like that. Tried to murder her own baby."

"What baby?" To my knowledge, Norah had only the cone-bobbing Sherri.

"Sherri's not her first one. She had another baby before Sherri. And where is it now, I ask you?"

"Martha, are you sure you've got this right?"

Fortunately, the spray bottle was now empty and emitted only harmless puffs of air. "The woman was as crazy as a loon. I wouldn't be surprised if having her daughter fired from the movie has tipped her over the edge again."

"I see." Frankly, I didn't. Norah Hall was a pushy, and sometimes rude woman, but she didn't strike me as being crazy. Not any crazier than the rest of us, at any rate.

I felt a hand clamp down on my shoulder. Of course I jumped in my chair, banging into Martha, and causing the hair spray container to fly across the barn. While Martha went scrambling after it, I confronted the interloper.

"Sneak up on me again and die, buster."

Steven snickered with sadistic satisfaction. "The old man wants to see you in five. They're ready to shoot."

"So am I. Now, am-scray."

Steven sauntered off, full of himself, now that he was assistant director. As I watched him go, it suddenly occurred to me that it could well have been him, dressed as Susannah, whom Mose saw enter the barn on at least one of the three occasions. After all, they were about the same height and weight. And if it weren't for the bulk Shnookums provided, there would be very little difference in their shapes. Camouflage that tall, thin frame with enough cloth to dress a third-world country, and how was a seventy-four-year-old man to tell the difference from across a pasture? My new theory seemed worthy of serious investigation. I would talk to Doc about it first chance I got.

"Feeling all right?" Martha had returned with the hair spray, but instead of throwing it in the trash, she tucked it in her purse. I can't say I blamed her. When properly cleaned, they make excellent plant misters. In this troubled economy of ours, it pays to be frugal. Although the Presbyterians pay their minister more than we do ours, it can't be all that much.

"I'm feeling fine," I said. "In fact, you might say espe-

cially fine.'' Nailing Steven meant exonerating Susannah.
Blood is thicker than water, even bad blood.

"Feeling a little light-headed, then?"

"Unh.'' Susannah has taught me well the art of non-committal grunting. Between my luck and Martha's mouth, Steven could be halfway to Patagonia if I didn't put a lid on it.

That night had been designated party night, which, if you ask me, made it no different from any other night as far as the movie people were concerned. But anyway, according to Arthur, the shooting went extremely well that day, and so he wrapped up early—about five. An hour later the cast and crew left for Bedford, taking Susannah with them. Freni and Mose had already departed, having been told earlier that dinner was not necessary that evening. Presumably the Reels and Runs gang were planning to eat their supper at Ed's, but what they planned to do afterward, I didn't want to know, and probably wouldn't have been told if I'd asked. However, if Hernia were hit by an earthquake that night, I would know, beyond a shadow of a doubt, that it was Mama, spin-digging in her grave again. If Mama had had half as much exercise alive as she was getting dead, she wouldn't have left me that closet full of size twenty-four-and-a-half dresses.

I was just locking up the inn on my way over to see Doc when I got my second scare of the day. It was Aaron Miller who, despite the fact that the nearest tree was a good fifty feet away, managed to somehow pop up out of nowhere. This time he ducked.

"Lead with your right, but remember to keep that left up there to protect your face,'' he said smugly.

I prayed the blood would drain quickly from my face. "Polite people don't sneak up on you."

Aaron laughed too easily—his perfect white teeth were

always on display. "I didn't sneak up on you. I just hopped over the fence and walked up the drive. Anyway, I'm Aaron Miller, and I'm here to see Miss Yoder."

"I know who you are," I said recklessly. "Which Miss Yoder do you want to see?"

"Why, Susannah, of course."

I would have pushed him off the porch, but it was my property, and I didn't want to get sued. "Susannah Yoder is not home at the moment," I said evenly. "Would you like to leave a message?"

Aaron shook his handsome head. "Nope. In that case, I'd like to speak to her older sister. Jennifer, I think it is."

I would have pushed then, but he had grabbed the railing with his right hand. "Jennifer Yoder is dead," I said solemnly. "She was flailed to death by a combine and—"

"And made into breakfast cereal?"

I pushed anyway, but he pushed right back. He must have caught a fever from his dunk in the pond, because his hands, when they touched me, were burning hot. I let go, and stepped back to protect myself from disease.

"Don't stop now," he chortled. "That was rather fun."

"You are the rudest man I ever met," I calmly informed him.

His feelings didn't seem at all hurt. "Let's see, it's Magdalena, if I remember correctly."

"And what if it is?"

"Nothing much. I just thought I'd repay your visit. Us being neighbors and all."

"That's where you're mistaken. You and I aren't neighbors. It's your father who is my neighbor, and *he* is welcome anytime."

"But, of course, he can't come over because of his fractured hip."

"I visit him fairly regularly, if you must know. Although now I think I'll wait until you're gone."

"Suit yourself, but Pop won't like that, because I'm not going anywhere."

"What did you say?"

Aaron hoisted himself up on the guardrail and sat there, just as cocky as a teenage boy. I should have waited to push him. "I said that I'm not going anywhere. If I was to give you the lengthy version, I would say something about me moving back in with Pop on a permanent basis. No matter what the version though, we are neighbors now. You and I, Magdalena."

"Reels and Runs Productions did offer to buy the PennDutch," I said, thinking aloud. "Susannah and I could move to Lancaster County and open up a new place. Hey, why stop at owning an inn? Why not combine it with a theme park? We could call it Amishworld— or has that been done? Or maybe we should start on a smaller scale. Just a three-story cinema depicting Amish life. That's it! Yoderama. How does that strike you?"

That was when Aaron Miller, son of my dear, old, sweet neighbor, jumped off the railing, and before I could as much as protest, grabbed me and kissed me. On the mouth!

"Well, I never!" I gasped as I pulled away. Truer words were never spoken.

"I had to do something to make you shut up," said Aaron, who, despite his explanation, did not seem at all embarrassed by his actions. He had already jumped back on the railing and was grinning down at me like the Cheshire cat.

I preserved my dignity, or what I had left of it, by walking as quickly and sedately as I could to my car. It wasn't until I had turned the bend in the road that I allowed even my hands to shake—which they did, but just a little. Overall, I was really quite fine, I assure you. It was only my lips that gave me trouble. All the way to Doc's they burned just as surely as if I'd kissed a hot stove.

Twenty-seven

"ARE YOU SURE you don't want any more shepherd's pie?" asked Doc.

I shook my head. Doc is a thumbs-up cook, but I had hardly eaten a bite. Usually the two of us can pack away enough food to feed three third-world countries, or the frequenters of one average-size salad bar, take your pick. But I had a terrible lump or something in my stomach that night, and was already beginning to accept it as part of my future. With extreme good luck, the lump would turn out to be a benign tumor that would elicit a lot of sympathy and give me a good excuse to sequester myself for a very long time. If, on the other hand, it turned out to be malignant, and inoperable, I would die an agonizing death, which would still elicit sympathy, and ultimately offer privacy of its own sort. Only for a second did I entertain the thought that my abdominal discomfort was caused by a very sudden pregnancy. Despite what

Mama told me, I know now that one cannot get pregnant by kissing.

Doc was ever solicitous. "Are you sure I can't get you anything? Maybe a bicarbonate of soda?"

"What I need is an intimate," I wailed.

"I think there's a pair of ladies panties, size eight, in the top dresser drawer of the guest room. Just help yourself to them," he said generously.

I shook my head again. The lump had grown at an alarming rate, and was now occupying my throat as well. How could I explain to Doc that what I needed was a best girlfriend. Someone I could pour out my secret thoughts to. Everyone I knew had a best friend, except me. I mean, Doc had his—some old horseshoe-playing crony who was every bit as licentious as Doc, and whom I studiously avoided. Freni had her husband, Mose, and vice versa. As for Susannah—she had the Pennsylvania Turnpike. Well, the truckers, at least. Anyway, although Doc was always there for me, there were certain subjects I knew he didn't enjoy discussing. And men was at the top of the list.

"It isn't that gangster from Maryland again, is it?" asked Doc dutifully, proving that he is really a very good friend in his own way. "What was his name? Jumbo Jet?"

"Jumbo Jim. And no, it isn't him."

Doc slid the leftovers from my plate onto his. "Ah, some new guy, then, is it?"

I glared at Doc. A man doesn't have the right to be perceptive, especially when you're feeling vulnerable. "It isn't a man, Doc. So can we just drop the subject?"

Doc looked relieved. "Well, whatever it is, Magdalena, I'm your friend, remember?"

"I remember, Doc."

"Read any good books lately?" asked Doc in a valiant attempt to change the subject and make us both feel better.

In fact I had. I had just read Dorothy Cannell's latest, so I forced myself to tell Doc some of the high points.

"Sounds good," Doc agreed. "I haven't had much time to read lately. Got myself a new computer, and I've been having a ball teaching myself how to use it. Got a fax machine too. Want to see them?"

"Sure," I said listlessly. "Why do you need a fax machine, Doc?"

Doc glanced dramatically at the nearest window, so I wasn't sure if he was pulling my leg or not. "To play the horses," he whispered.

"Do tell, Doc." I didn't expect it to help a whole lot, but surely hearing about Doc's vices would at least take the edge off the pain in my gut.

"It's all very simple," Doc started to explain, "I've got this buddy, Garth, down in Hialeah, who—"

"Speaking of Garths, Doc," I interrupted, "you did know that Norah Hall was seeing someone by that name?" Perhaps I was rude, but when old Doc starts talking about his buddies, you either cut him off or plan on taking a nice nap.

"Yeah, I know," said Doc, only mildly irritated. "What about it?"

"Just that it's an unusual name." Then I thought of something I really did want to ask Doc. "You pretty much have your finger on the pulse around here, don't you, Doc?"

Doc looked pleased with himself. "You might say that. Everyone talks to their vet, you know. You see, they can talk to their pets and their pets don't rat on them, so they figure they can talk to me as well. Some sort of transference thing, I guess. Whatever it is, I hear it all."

"I figured it was something like that. Anyway, Doc, I was wondering if you ever heard anything about Norah Hall losing it and ending up in a loony bin?"

"Losing what?"

"Her marbles, of course. Come to think of it, a baby too. Rumor is she killed it."

Doc had definitely forgotten Garth and his new fax machine. "Who on earth told you something like that, Magdalena?"

I debated confidentiality for all of three seconds. "Martha Sims."

Doc laughed while he cut into the freshly baked chocolate crazy cake in front of us. "And I thought Norah Hall was our most inventive gossip."

"Then it isn't true?"

Doc slid a slice of still-warm cake in front of me. I didn't resist. During our idle chitchat my appetite had slowly started to return. After all, I was eating for two, wasn't I? I mean, the lump did count for something.

"Look," said Doc, "that Norah Hall might be a first-class bitch, but she's always been one of the sanest, most calculating women around. To my knowledge, Norah has never been away from Hernia longer than it takes to fly down to Jamaica to renew her tan."

"Then Sherri really is her only child?" I'd known Norah all her life, and I sure couldn't remember her being pregnant more than once. That one time I had no trouble remembering. Norah is one of those women who opts for full-blown maternity clothes the moment following conception. When she was pregnant with Sherri, Norah wore maternity clothes for such a long time that some of the elderly ladies in Hernia chalked her up for two pregnancies. Perhaps that was the origin of Martha's rumor.

Doc cut himself a piece of cake twice the size of mine. "I am not Norah's obstetrician, although I have delivered puppies for her three times. Still, I'd have to say that little Sherri is, and has always been, Norah's only child. Poor thing."

"At least she has a child." I hoped I didn't sound bitter.

"I meant the child, not Norah."

I felt better for the rest of the evening, at least until I pulled into my own driveway and was faced with the front porch again. I did suffer a momentary relapse when I laid eyes on the rail upon which that arrogant Aaron had perched. Angrily, I ran my fingers along the length of the thick wooden rail. It is one thing to be mocked by virtual strangers when one is out in the world, but to have one's emotions assaulted on one's home ground is a terrible ordeal I wouldn't even wish on Melvin Stoltzfus. In a way I almost felt violated. Now I could never enjoy my front porch again without seeing Aaron Miller's mocking face, or feeling the heat of his lips as they pressed against mine. Then suddenly, and shamefully, I was aware that my fingers had slowed in their angry race across the smooth, worn wood, and were almost caressing it. Horrified, I jerked them away. But it was too late. The cool wood had somehow managed to scorch my fingertips just as surely as if I had touched hot coals. Despite the pain, I felt a strange sense of exhilaration. For the first time in my life, I, Magdalena Augusta Yoder, was playing with fire.

Mama was right. I am a shameless hussy. No doubt about it. I was in the shower, trying to cool off, when I heard a knock on the door. Quite wittingly, I grabbed my summer robe and practically flew to answer it. Of course I put the robe on first, and I did cinch it tight at the waist, but I will confess that I did not clasp it tightly shut at the collar as I might have in the past.

"Yes?" I said in a naturally but appropriately breathy voice. The wet hair in my eyes prevented me from seeing clearly.

"You were expecting someone else maybe?"

"Melvin Stoltzfus!"

"In the flesh. Oh, you might want to dry off, Mags. You're dripping water all over your nice hardwood floor."

"And you'll be dripping blood, Melvin, unless you vacate my property in the next three seconds."

"No can do, Mags. I'm here on official police business." He patted a tawny-colored leather briefcase, undoubtedly made from the skin of one of his victims.

"What's the business?

"You sure you don't want to get dressed first?" I could feel at least one of Melvin's eyes staring at my robe. It is, I'll have you know, a modest terry robe that comes well below my knees.

"State your business, Melvin. In ten words or less."

"You can't rush me when I'm on official police business, Magdalena. I have to say what I have to say in as many words as it takes to say it."

I changed first. My hair would be dry and my floor probably moldy before Melvin got through with his badgering. I've known cheese to age in less time than it takes Melvin to get to the point.

"Yes, what is it?" I asked again a few minutes later. This time I was wearing a calf-length dress that buttoned up to the chin. There are advantages to being too lazy to store away one's winter things. Let Melvin's eyes rove. They would tire well before they alighted on anything of interest.

"Sit down," said Melvin peremptorily.

"Give you an inch, and you'll take a mile," I said. "This is my house, Melvin, remember? I sit or stand only when I want to." So saying, I scooted to claim my favorite rocking chair.

Melvin sat on a hard, high-backed antique thing that

had once belonged to Grandma Yoder. I blessed the
woman inwardly for her austere taste. Not even a cushion
can remain long on that chair without squirming.

"Well, spit it out," I said. "I don't have all night."

"I'm afraid your gig is up, Magdalena. It would be easier for you if you just came clean and confessed."

I complied. "I confess that I loathe you, Melvin Stoltzfus. There, will that do? Will you please leave now?"

Melvin looked rather comfortable in Grandma's chair.
Perhaps he was considering spinning a cocoon there, or
whatever it is that praying mantises lay their young in.
"Joke all you want to, Magdalena, but the last joke's on
you. This evening I got an anonymous call telling me that
a pitchfork had been found in the woods behind your
barn. Zelda and I checked it out, and sure enough, we
found it, all right. It was pretty stupid of you to leave it
right out in a clearing, if you ask me."

I willed my hands to maintain their grip on the arms of
my favorite rocker. Melvin's neck was probably a fragile
and unrepairable thing. "So, you found a pitchfork, what
of it? It just so happens that I'm missing two pitchforks.
The one used to kill Don Manley, and the one Steven
bought to replace it. That one has been missing as well.
Ask Mose about it. He was complaining earlier. He'll tell
you."

"I bet he will. So, in other words, Magdalena, you are
confirming that the pitchfork we found in the woods belongs to you?"

I rolled my eyes like Susannah does when she's exas-
perated.

"Oh, no, you don't," Melvin practically screamed.
"Don't you go having an epileptic seizure on my time!"

I rolled them spitefully again. "Get a grip on it, Melvin.
You're the one who's having fits." I paused until he had
calmed down enough to, at least theoretically, hear what I

was saying. "Just because you found a pitchfork in my woods doesn't mean it belongs to me, and even if it does belong to me, it could well be the replacement pitchfork. Did the one you and Zelda find have any blood or other body tissue on it?"

"You could have wiped it off."

"I'm not that bright, Melvin. Besides which, a good forensics lab can easily find traces of blood that can't be seen by the naked eye." Although maybe that wasn't true in Melvin's case. He looked like he had 360-degree peripheral vision. Who knew what those eyes could see.

"Ha! I'm one step ahead of you, Yoder. I'm taking the pitchfork into Harrisburg myself tomorrow. And I'm going to camp outside on the lab steps, if I have to, until I get that report."

"Good for you, Melvin. It warms the heart to see a lawman doing his job. But you keep forgetting one thing. Even if that is the same fork that killed Don Manley, it doesn't prove I did it."

The hoods on Melvin's eyes came down like miniature barbecue covers. "Prints, Yoder, prints."

"Prints shmints!" I said loudly (I do not scream, regardless of what Susannah says). "What would my fingerprints prove? It was my pitchfork, and of course I used it! I don't wear gloves when I pitch hay, Melvin."

Melvin rolled back the hood on one of his eyes and regarded me balefully. "I can produce fifty witnesses who will each swear that you threatened them with a pitchfork on the day Reels and Runs Productions held their first casting session."

I put my mind in fast-reverse. Even then it took me a couple of seconds to figure out what Melvin was talking about. I guess it is simply a matter of perspective, something of which I admittedly always seem to be in short supply. But from my point of view, brandishing a pitchfork (quite harmlessly) to maintain an orderly presence on one's property is hardly the same thing as threatening someone. This I hopelessly tried to explain to Melvin.

"Look, Yoder, it's as simple as this. You can give me your thumbs here, or I can haul you down to my office. Take your pick."

"You brought your own screws with you?" I eyed the tawny briefcase nervously.

Melvin's laugh was typically invertebrate; his mandibles moved, but little or no sound was emitted. "You're a laugh riot, Yoder. Now, look, you want me to do the printing here, or not?"

I gave Melvin the finger he was asking for.

Twenty-eight

"THERE IS NO JUSTICE when it comes to paychecks," Papa used to say. He was right. If there were justice, ditchdiggers would be millionaires, and ballplayers would be half a paycheck above the poverty level. I guess the same holds true for movie stars, although I would give them that extra half paycheck as compensation for all the waiting around they have to do.

I didn't know, and didn't want to know, what went on at those motels in Bedford every night, but from what I could tell about life on the set, movie stars lead very boring lives. Even a pill bug in a pot of dead petunias is bound to have more fun. For every minute of film one sees on the big screen, there's an hour of sitting around and waiting while camera angles are changed, lights and sound equipment adjusted, and the director and his subordinates gab endlessly. While all this is tediously transpiring, the actors sit around perspiring, presumably counting the money they're getting in return. Ballplayers have downtime too, but they at least spit, grab their crotches, and if they find nothing there worth grabbing, pat each other's fannies.

"You have got to be bored to tears," I said to Darla Strutt. Perhaps if I showed some understanding, so would she. I did not fancy being sued because of Shnookums's sex life.

"One million three hundred and fifty thousand, seven hundred and ninety-six dollars and thirteen cents," she said, proving my assumption.

"You want to play a game of cards?" I meant ROOK, of course. We Mennonites don't generally play with face cards.

"Piss off, Magdalena."

I forced a smile. What's a little pain if it's for a good cause? "Darla, one of my best friends is a vet. He can take care of Fifi's—uh—problem, if you want. It'll be on me."

Darla stared hard at me. Perhaps she was sizing me up for a coffin. "I wouldn't even speak to you at all, Magdalena, if it weren't for the fact that we're almost family."

That was news to me. "We're definitely not kissing cousins," I hastened to say.

"Don't get me wrong, Magdalena. I still might sue you —for emotional damage—however, I have decided to let my precious Fifi have her pups."

"Why, I'll be a monkey's uncle," I said with relief. "Actually, I'll be a dog's aunt. No, make that great-aunt to an entire litter. I'm sure I don't deserve such an honor."

"Just because we're related doesn't mean I have to be nice to you. I still might sue, you know."

"I know."

"Good, just keep that in mind. Now, what is it you wanted in the first place?"

"I thought we might have a little chat."

"What about? I already spilled my guts to the tabloids."

I smiled patiently. "Guts aren't measured by cup size, dear. Anyway, I don't want to talk about your personal scandals, interesting as they might be. I thought maybe you'd enjoy dishing a little dirt on other people for a change. You know, be on the giving, rather than the receiving end."

Boy, did I feel awful saying that. I really don't approve of gossip, unless, of course, the gossipee is especially deserving—like Tracy Ediger, who ran off to Maryland with Pete Flanagen, our postman, leaving behind a grand total of three spouses (Pete was a Morman), eleven children, seven dogs, four cats, and a badly leaking aquarium. Even then I wouldn't have gossiped about it, except that Tracy had the nerve to come back only a month later and try out for a spot in the choir at the Beechy Grove Mennonite Church. Even then I would have held my tongue and kept one ear covered, but when Tracy started making eyes at Reverend Gingerich, I'd had enough. After all, Tracy is a Methodist. If anyone is going to have an affair with Reverend Gingerich, it should be a Mennonite.

"Well, who do you want to talk about?" asked Darla generously. "I'm one of the few people who know Zsa Zsa's correct age, and I did get a chance to count Jane Fonda's ribs in a locker room one day."

I smiled my appreciation. I even went so far as to pat that little ratty dog of hers. Carefully, of course, given its delicate condition. "Wouldn't it be more fun to talk about people we both know?"

Darla has a heart of gold. "Well, Kitty in makeup had her thighs liposuctioned in May. Apparently it was a botched job, which is why Kitty walks that way."

"I wondered about that."

"And Bruce, the lighting technician, lights up more

than cigarettes on his off hours. Those sunglasses he wears are not job-related."

"Very interesting. But you know, one of the most enigmatic people around here seems to be Steven Freeman. What can you tell me about him?" I asked casually.

Darla blew a bubble the size of Uranus. Somehow she managed to talk without popping it. "Steven's a washout, if you ask me. He comes on big in his Bugsy persona, but there isn't anything there to speak of, if you know what I mean."

I made a mental note to give her Jumbo's number. "But what kind of person is he? Inside?"

The bubble popped, and Darla staggered back from the force, but she was otherwise undaunted. "You're asking about his mob connections, aren't you?" She started to laugh, and loudly, before I could even begin to answer. Of course that ratty mutt of hers had to contribute to the fracas as well. Had I only had a pitchfork, Freni could have added shish kebab to the lunch menu.

When you've lost face, you might as well face off. What have you got to lose? "Okay, so that's my question. What about it? Does Bugsy, I mean Steven, have mob connections?"

At least Darla stopped laughing long before her dog did. "Yeah, Steven has mob connections, but only in a very roundabout way. Before he started doing behind-the-camera stuff, he worked as an extra back in Hollywood. *Godfather Four* was his biggest triumph."

"Is that a movie?" I asked innocently.

Strutt and mutt howled again, and when, after a few minutes, they showed no sign of letting up, I simply walked away. It's bad enough that Susannah attacks my morals, but I won't tolerate that kind of criticism from a bitch. Or Darla either.

———————

Doc called while we were eating lunch. "What's it today?" he asked politely.

"Oh, some kind of Thai food again. This time it's got squid and eggplants the size of marbles. Frankly, I can't wait until Freni makes up with Barbara. This morning she gave Art a pair of John's suspenders as a present. If this feud keeps up much longer, Freni's liable to adopt Art and return with him to Hollywood. Who will cook for me then?"

"I will." Doc sounded like he meant it. "Speaking of food, you're welcome to join me for lunch."

"Thanks, Doc, but if I duck out now, Freni will blow a gasket. She's threatened second helpings of squid to anyone who doesn't finish their first."

"Can you drop by after lunch, then?"

"As tough as this squid is, Doc, lunch could be an all-day affair. Besides, I have a big scene to shoot this afternoon."

"Tonight, then? There's something important I need to talk to you about."

"Can't we talk about it now?"

"Uhn-uhn," grunted Doc. He sounded like he was losing his patience with me.

"Okay, tonight. Supper?" I asked hopefully.

"Pot roast with carrots, onions, celery, and new potatoes. Three-bean salad. Homemade chunky applesauce. Pineapple upside-down cake."

I told Doc I'd see him with bells on.

The afternoon's shoot went even better than that of the day before. Despite the makeshift script, or maybe because of it, our scenes seemed to flow rather naturally. Art Lapata not only permits ad-libbing, he promotes it, and this method of acting seemed particularly well suited to our little group. It was only on those few occasions when Darla blew a bubble or Rip swore that we had to do retakes. And those were all at my insistence.

Apparently Bedford was not a half-bad place for partying, because the minute Art yelled "that's a wrap" for the last time, the whole shebang packed up and hit the road north. There was only the briefest of delays when a fistfight broke out over who would be the lucky crew member to have Susannah sit on his lap for the twenty-mile ride. The winner drove an otherwise empty van with my slut-puppy of a sister perched between him and the steering wheel. According to what Susannah told me later, her weight, which is not all that much, left the poor guy stuck in neutral all night. If I knew what she meant, she added. I did not.

After Freni and Mose left—she, eager to snub her daughter-in-law, and he, willing to try to patch things up —I had the place deliciously to myself. When I got out of the tub an hour and three water changes later, I could have been a spokeswoman for the California Prune Board. But I had plumped up enough to look presentable by the time I pulled into Doc's.

"You didn't take enough potatoes," said Doc as he spooned some carrots onto my plate.

It was time to give my fork a brief rest. "Okay, Doc, out with it. Something's been bugging you all evening. Whatever it is, you can tell me. I'm your friend, remember?"

Doc sighed. Suddenly he looked his eighty-four years. "It's because we're such good friends, and I"—he paused, swallowed and then chickened out—"am so fond of you, that I'm worried."

"Spit it out, Doc!" I hate it when people build things up just for the sake of drama. Of course, on the plus side, things are seldom as bad as they want us to think, and so there is that wonderful sense of relief when they do finally tell you the scoop.

"Well, Mags, the thing is, I've been toying around with my new fax machine, and—"

"And you found out that Also Ran is a washout for the Kentucky Derby?"

"Dammit, Mags! Don't you ever quit? What I'm trying to say is that I faxed a letter to a buddy of mine, who shall remain nameless, who has a practice over in Pittsburgh. Not a vet practice, for your information, but a psychiatric practice. As it so happens, he's on staff at the Roselund Clinic. Of course patient confidentially has to be respected, it's the law. But there are ways of flexing the law just a little bit, for the greater good, you understand?"

"Completely. So what did you learn?"

"That there was a young woman admitted as a patient thirteen years ago, and the facts pretty much line up with the ones in Martha Sims's story."

I inhaled hard enough to extinguish one of the candles Doc had so thoughtfully lit before dinner. "You mean Martha was telling the truth? Norah did have a complete breakdown?"

Doc shook his head. "No, not Norah. It was Martha who came unglued."

Of course, the news chilled me to the bone, and Doc and I hashed it over for at least an hour before we figured out what to do. Finally we agreed that in the morning we would go together to see Reverend Sims at his office at the church. In the meantime, there was nothing else to do but to polish off the pineapple upside-down cake. Fortunately Doc was still a little off his feed, so I got the lion's share. Why is it that standard cake pans don't come any larger than nine by thirteen?

Twenty-nine

THE NIGHT was still young. After the cake was gone, and after trying to dodge Doc, who is not at all as doddery as he should be, I was faced with one of those agonizing decisions that almost make you wish you were living under a strict totalitarian regime where everything is decided for you. It wasn't until I hit Main Street in downtown Hernia that I decided not to go into Bedford that evening to visit Heather and her new baby. After all, I hadn't had time to make a decent gift, and I didn't want to insult either of them with something store-bought. Plus there is the safety factor, you know. Bedford might not be the Sodom and Gomorrah Mama always said it was, but there are a few undesirable elements living in town. By that I mean strangers; people who might foolishly try to take advantage of me in darkened parking lots, forcing me to rake them across the eyes with a fistful of keys.

In Hernia, on the other hand, I feel perfectly safe. No

one has bothered me since that night almost ten years ago when Jimmy Harshman, wearing a ski mask, tried to snatch my purse outside Sam Yoder's grocery store. Jimmy now lives in Coos Bay, Oregon, and reportedly sings high tenor in his church choir.

Having made up my mind not to go into Bedford made it easier for me to live happily with choice number two. Not that I should have felt guilty in the first place. How often does a back-to-back marathon of *Green Acres* reruns occur on noncable television? I know, three or four hours of such fare might be considered decadent by some, but I don't smoke or drink, engage only in the safest sex there is, and tithe religiously to my church. Still, Mama would never have approved of such idle, self-indulgent behavior. For my own peace of mind, I stopped impulsively at Yoder's Market and bought the largest bag of Cheese Crunchies I could find. Hopefully, the noise would drown out the sounds of Mama turning rhythmically in her grave.

I was letting myself in by the back door, when I heard the door on the six-seater slam. It was a still, cloudless night in August, the kind with fireflies and crickets, and the distant sound of whippoorwills. There simply wasn't enough breeze to ruffle a cobweb. Besides which, the door to the six-seater was locked, its hasp securely jammed into place with a piece of maple branch. But raccoons have remarkably agile hands, and are forever removing the lids of my garbage cans and scattering trash from here to kingdom come. The last thing I wanted was a clan of furry bandits taking up residence in the six-seater, just yards from the garbage-can corral.

"Shoo! Scram! Beat it!" I yelled angrily. "Head for the woods while you still have four good paws to run on!" I don't wear fur coats, but I'm not above raising my voice at those who do. Just because their fur is not easily de-

tachable doesn't mean they should get special treatment.

But no coon clan was forthcoming. In exasperation I
grabbed the sidewalk broom from the back steps and
headed for the six-seater. If war was what the coons
wanted, war was what they'd get. Unless one or more of
the masked marauders had rabies, they'd soon be running with their tails between their legs. I may be a pacifist
by breeding, but when provoked enough, I can be just as
ferocious as the English. While I have yet to actually bite a
living animal, I do own a strong, healthy set of nails.

When I slammed the six-seater door open again, I fully
expected to be greeted by the smug smiles of a coon
platoon. But there was nothing. Just six empty wooden
stalls. It took me only a few seconds to scan them all and
determine that those cagey coons had outfoxed me once
again. I bolted for the exit just as the door slammed one
last time—almost in my face.

"I'll get you yet, you lily-livered vermin," I yelled.

I shoved hard at the door, but it didn't budge. Now,
some of the coons we have around Hernia are so big you
wouldn't want them stepping on your feet, but none of
them is big enough to blockade a door. And besides,
from the way the door gave a little at both the top and
bottom, it was pretty clear someone, not something, was
behind these shenanigans, and the maple stick had been
jammed back into the hasp. At first it was irritation, not
fear that followed the realization that someone was playing a practical joke.

"Give it up, Susannah," I growled.

Susannah didn't answer, which was no surprise. My sister has the memory of a politician. Sometimes she forgets
things even as she's doing them.

I tried the door again. Still, it did not budge. "Okay,
okay. It's a very funny joke, and it was very clever of you

to think of it, but enough is enough. You've had your fun. Now, open the door and let me out before I forget that you're my sister." All this was said in a voice loud enough to wake the dead—including Mama, who was always a little hard of hearing—just in case Susannah had indeed forgotten and wandered off someplace.

The door remained unmovable. "I give!" I shouted. "I surrender. Uncle!"

My answer was the slosh of gasoline against the outside wooden planks. Suddenly my predicament became eminently clear. I was as vulnerable as a trussed turkey on the fourth Wednesday of November. "Who are you, and what is it you want?" I asked, hoping that my voice reflected respect and not fear.

My answer was the whoosh of flames and an immediate rise in the temperature of my confined space. Like the Thanksgiving turkey, I was going to have my goose thoroughly cooked unless I came up with an escape plan. Fortunately, I have more brains than your average turkey. Knowing that Great-Grandpa Yoder had been a carpenter of some accomplishment, I didn't waste even a precious moment trying to break through the roof. Instead, I set my sights quite a bit lower.

Great-Grandma Yoder had been a woman of considerable girth. It always surprised, and even amused guests that one of the six seats was a lot larger than the rest. I'm sure Great-Grandma never dreamed that the size of her caboose would someday save the life of one of her descendants, but had she known, I'm sure it would have made carrying all that weight around worthwhile.

Without a second thought I lifted the sturdy wooden seat and lowered myself into the dark, cool pit. It was a drop of about ten feet, but my adrenaline, fueled by the crackling flames above, prevented me from feeling any discomfort when I hit the ground. At first I thought it was also adrenaline that prevented me from smelling, or feeling, anything unmentionable, but I was wrong. Great-Grandpa's outhouse had not been used in thirty years. Anything unpleasant had long since returned to dust, and I found myself standing in a dry, cool pit, not unlike a small cave.

"Thank you, Lord," I prayed. I must confess, though, that I also prayed whoever had done this to me would suffer from a terrible and incurable case of eczema. I'm sure that God in his mercy took into account the stress I was under.

Although the air in the pit was originally cool and completely breathable, as the structure topside continued to burn, conditions began to change. Since there was no one around to see me anyway, I removed my half slip and wrapped it around my face like a scarf. I also decided to seek refuge in one of the corners of the pit, against that time when the row of seats, which had just began to burn, collapsed and sent down a shower of flames. It was as I was making my way through the half dark to the nearest corner that I stumbled across something painfully sharp.

"Ow!" I screamed. Given that I was the only one present in the pit, with a burning outhouse to shield me from the disapproving eyes of the world, I may even have cursed. But a fairly benign curse, mind you.

Reaching down, I felt around cautiously. When my fingers gently made contact with the offending object, it took my brain what seemed to be several seconds before it could, or would, process the information. What had jabbed my leg, and now my fingertips caressed, was nothing other than a pitchfork. Perhaps even *the* pitchfork. It took my stubborn and reluctant brain another second or two to send me a message that, though it remained un-spoken, was deafening. Whoever it was who had locked me in the outhouse and started the fire was also undoubt-edly Don Manley's murderer. And he or she meant busi-ness this time as well.

Thirty

FRENI HOSTETLER'S RENDITION OF TOM YAM GOONK

Makes four servings.

3 cups chicken broth
1 cup coconut milk
1 can straw mushrooms, drained
Juice of two limes
1 bunch scallions, chopped
1 stalk fresh lemongrass, sliced, or zest of $1/2$ lemon
1 tablespoon fish sauce
$1/4$ teaspoon salt
$1/4$ teaspoon galanga powder (if available)
1 hot green chili pepper, chopped (optional)
$3/4$ pound peeled and deveined raw shrimp

Bring all ingredients but the shrimp to a boil. Add the shrimp and cook at reduced heat for another three minutes, or until the shrimp are done. Serve piping hot in bowls, with white rice on the side.

Thirty-one

I THOUGHT it was only moments, but it was actually eleven hours later when I woke up in the Bedford County Memorial Hospital. The last thing I could remember was a shower of sparks and burning wood as the outhouse collapsed on itself, plunging the row of potty seats down into the pit. Apparently it was a loose lid that hit me on the head.

"Where am I?" I asked Nurse Dudley. Of course I knew where I was. Any conscious idiot, no matter how badly concussed, can tell by the white uniforms and characteristic smells that they're in a hospital. But certain questions are expected at times like this, and one is likely to gain more cooperation by going along with the plan.

"You're in the hospital," said Nurse Dudley delightedly. "And I'm a nurse."

"Mama, is that you?"

Nurse Dudley patted me joyfully. Her work was cut out

for her. "No, dear, I am your *nurse.*" Even Cousin Agnes
Yoder, at age ninety-three, isn't deaf enough to warrant
that many decibels.

I smiled, a slow-spreading smile of recognition. "Hospital? Nurse?"

"That's right, dear. Now, you just lie right there while I
go and get the doctor. I'll be right back."

What did she think I was going to do, skip down to the
gift shop and buy a magazine? The woman deserved to
have her chain yanked a little. "Doctor?" I asked.
"You're a doctor?"

Nurse Dudley smiled appreciatively. My delirium had
quadrupled her salary and given her a modicum of respect. "Now, you be a good girl and just lie there. I'll be
right back."

While she was gone, I picked up the TV remote control
from my bedside table and flicked through the channels.
The *Green Acres* marathon had ended, and all I could find
were three talk shows. The first show had on some politician so slippery they almost had to tie him in the chair.
The second one featured an evangelist turned actor who
was talking about how God had told him to steal from the
offering plate to cap his teeth. The third was at least a
little interesting. It featured lesbian nuns of Spanish origin who were starting up a gladiola farm just outside Tel
Aviv. One of the nuns even sang on the show; a snappy
hymn done to the tune of an Elvis Presley song. Frankly, I
would have watched more of that show, but when I heard
footsteps coming down the hall, I switched off the set and
prudently resumed my delirium.

"Mama, is that you?"

Dr. Rosenkrantz was not amused. "Can the dramatics,
Yoder, and just tell me how you feel."

I remembered I'd met him before. He'd been Susannah's doctor the time she was whacked on the head with a bottle of beer in some honky-tonk down in Maryland. The hospital there was even smaller than the one in Bedford. "Moving up in the world, are we?" I asked.

Dr. Rosenkrantz made a few hen scratches on my chart. "She'll be fine," he said to Nurse Dudley, not me. "I'll keep her in for observation another twenty-four hours, then she's free to go. Oh, one word of advice. Don't go running yourself ragged on her account. The woman's got more tricks up her sleeve than an octopus magician."

I graciously accepted the compliment by turning the TV back on. The nuns had somehow talked the host of the show, a man, into donning one of their habits, and one of the nuns was futilely trying to teach the dullard a few words of her newly acquired Hebrew. Surely this was American entertainment at its best. I watched nervously, aware that I was being seduced by a force more powerful than drugs or alcohol. As I watched, I began to appreciate that it was for good reason I had heretofore limited myself to one quality show. Television is definitely addictive.

"Get behind me, Satan," I said as I clicked off the set only moments into the next show. It was another talk show, this one featuring the obese children of one-legged accountants, and even though I failed to see the connection, I was mesmerized. Had it not been for the power of prayer, and a sudden urge for a candy bar, I would still have been watching TV when my visitor arrived.

I might have expected Susannah to show up, or even Freni, if given a lift, but Aaron Miller's was the last face I expected to see looming over my bed. I must have been dozing when he came in, because one minute I was alone, and the next thing I knew there was Aaron, twice as big as life and three times as handsome. Suddenly the room felt very hot.

"How are you today?" Aaron asked kindly, if not stupidly.

"Hot," I said. "Would you mind turning up the a.c. please?"

Aaron fiddled with some buttons. Then he had the audacity to come over and place his hand on my bare arm. His hand was as hot as a branding iron. "Well, I bet you don't feel as hot as you did last night."

"You lose. Anyway, how would you know how hot I felt last night?"

Aaron's smile revealed flawless teeth. "I felt you then. I mean, I was the one who carried you out of the pit."

"You?"

The sinfully blue eyes twinkled shamelessly. "Yeah, me. Hernia has only a volunteer fire department, and I live right across the road, remember?"

"Actually, no. The doctor says I may suffer from amnesia for some time to come."

Aaron shook his head. "That's too bad. The children want to visit you too, but now I guess they should wait until their mother remembers them. Otherwise it could be traumatic for them, don't you agree?"

"Very." I tried not to smile. "Is little Miriam remembering to brush her teeth?"

Aaron had the nerve to sit on the foot of my bed, even though there was a perfectly good chair in the room. "I couldn't help noticing the fire. At first I thought it was a bonfire and you were throwing a party without inviting me."

"Oh! I plum forgot to mail the invitations." Aaron's left hand was resting disturbingly close to my toes, and seemed to be inching closer and closer. If he so much as touched me, I would scream my head off, although I wouldn't necessarily verbalize the sounds.

"But all's well that ends well," said Aaron airily. "Pop

put in a call to Melvin, and by the time I got there, half a dozen cars were pulling up. We got the fire out in minutes. You know, one of the things I'd forgotten about Hernia was that everybody pulls together here. There's a real sense of teamwork, you know."

Since I had nothing to lend, I decided to borrow some trouble. "Since there was a team of you there, why was it you who got me out of the pit?"

Those blue eyes twinkled infuriatingly. "It was the team's consensus, Magdalena, that I was the only one strong enough."

I threw my plastic pitcher of water at him. Unfortunately the water missed him, but hit my feet.

"That's one way to cool yourself off," said Aaron arrogantly.

I tried glaring at him. It was like trying to glare at a cloud-streaked sunset or a bouquet of daylilies. "For all I know, you were the one who locked me in there and set it on fire."

Aaron flashed me the kind of smile that would have made my knees buckle had I not been lying down. "Why on earth would I do such a thing? That old place had special memories for me. When we were little kids, maybe five or so, we sneaked in there when the grown-ups weren't looking and—"

"I remember no such thing," I said. Okay, so Aaron and I did play together sometimes as children, but there is no point in remembering all the embarrassing details. Anyway, Mama washed my mouth out with soap the next day after I'd confessed what we did on that one occasion. That should have been the end of it.

Aaron was easily amused. "You're blushing! Ah-ha! So you do remember."

I willed the excess blood to drain from my face. "I have more important things to think about now than our childhood shenanigans. Like who it was who tried to kill me, for starters.''

The blue eyes took on a serious but still handsome look. ''Do you have any ideas at all? Any clues to who it might have been?''

I shook my head, and shaking your head is not the same as lying. After all, what was the use of sharing my suspicions until I had something a little more concrete to go on? It would just worry people, and undoubtedly make me look silly in the bargain. For the moment, I was quite safe where I was. A hospital is about as public a place as one can hope to find.

''As usual, you're being honest to the core,'' said Aaron accusingly.

''I do my best.''

''In that case, I'll have to do my own investigative work.''

''Good luck,'' I said. I had tried to sound irritated, but of course I was flattered. And worried too. Aaron knew virtually none of the players. Although some of them seemed more pathetic than dangerous, there was obviously at least one very dangerous soul out there. Hopefully Aaron would not tangle with that individual until I came up with the evidence I needed.

The foot of my bed was still wet when Freni Hostetler sat down on it. *''Ach Du Aimer!''* she squawked. ''Why, Magdalena, you should have asked the nurse for help.''

''It's only the water I threw at Aaron Miller.''

''Aaron Miller was here?'' Susannah was practically panting like a dog. A big dog, not the pint-sized Shnookums she had so brazenly sneaked into the hospital in her bra.

''Yes. He was, until I made him leave. And why on earth would that interest you?''

Susannah took Shnookums out of the nether reaches of her bosom and plopped him down on the bed near my pillow. "I ran into him at Yoder's Market yesterday afternoon. What a hunk, Mags. He's absolutely gorgeous!"

"Down!" I snapped. I meant Susannah, not the dog.

"Ask me what's new," said Freni, beaming.

I refused to bite. "Tell Art I'm sorry about holding up the shooting schedule, but the doctor says I can go home tomorrow."

"Art shmart," said Freni tartly, "who cares about the English and their films?"

"I do. That film is currently my bread and butter."

"You always did have expensive tastes," Susannah had the nerve to say.

"Forget about bread and forget about Art," Freni said. "The big news is that Barbara is taking a trip."

"You were finally able to book her on the space shuttle?" I asked.

Freni smiled. She could obviously afford to be magnanimous. "Barbara's going back home to visit her parents. For two months!"

"Who is going to help with the corn harvest?"

Freni shrugged. "God will provide. My John will have all the help he needs. Maybe I can cut back my hours at the PennDutch and give him a hand. And Mose can too."

"In a pig's ear," I said.

Freni made some clucking noises that indicated I would have a fight on my hands if I wanted to keep the best cook east of Pittsburgh. Of course I was mildly irritated by this turn of events, but I didn't mind as much as I would have just twenty-four hours earlier. A near-death experience, while not something I would recommend, can do a lot to provide perspective. Then, too, I was feeling unusually optimistic for some reason. Something I couldn't quite define was working on my psyche. Despite a lump on my head, and a wet bed, I was feeling strangely happy. Maybe even happier than I had ever felt before. You might even say I was feeling goofy.

Thirty-two

I WAS STILL feeling goofy when Nurse Dudley brought in my lunch tray. "Since you weren't a patient yesterday morning when it was time to order today's meals, it's potluck for you today," she informed me smugly.

"That will be fine."

"And if you don't eat well, I'm going to write it down on your chart."

"There's a pen in my purse," I said pleasantly. "It's in that little, tiny, minuscle closet over there."

Nurse Dudley glowered at me. "A poor appetite may be a sign of complications. If you don't eat, the doctor might keep you here longer than you want."

Her threat rolled off me like rain off a duck. "It's actually a very nice room. Will they let me get new curtains?"

Nurse Dudley stamped a white-shoed foot and charged from the room, leaving me alone with the controversial lunch. I lifted the hard plastic cover and peeked gingerly inside. It looked like a hodgepodge of tapioca, mashed potatoes, and creamed onions. I tasted it. It was ambrosia. Maybe I could hire the hospital chef if and when Freni quit on me.

As I was licking my spoon for the last time, Steven "Bugsy" Figaretti slithered into my room. "Hey, Yoder," said Bugsy blithely, "how's it going?"

I pulled my covers up around my chin. Reptiles of any kind make me nervous. "That depends. You wouldn't mind terribly if I smelled your hands, would you?"

Steven smiled obscenely. "I've got to admit, that's a new one."

"I'd be sniffing for gas." Okay, so I may have tipped my hand, but my reputation will follow me to my grave, and if Steven was going to finish the job, I might as well set him straight.

"Sniff away," said Steven smugly, "but I have an airtight alibi. If you have any doubts, ask Melody, the day clerk at my motel. *She* knows how to make a visitor feel welcome. I rang her chimes three times."

"Ah, yes, Melody, formerly known as Marvin Brubaker."

Bugsy blanched. "Anyway, Art sent me to convey his best wishes for a speedy recovery, and to tell you to take all the time you need to mend. He has to fly back to L.A. this afternoon anyway. He'll be gone a couple of days."

"Had to see his therapist, did he?"

"Yeah," Steven smirked. "How did you know?"

"His mother substitute was just in here."

"You mean Susannah?"

Clearly, Hollywood families were different from those in Hernia. I told Steven to run along and play, but to be just as careful in Bedford as he would be back home. He probably thought I was warning him about AIDS, which can happen in Bedford, and even in Hernia, but I was not. If Marvin Brubaker, Melody's husband, caught up with him, Steven wouldn't live long enough to know he had a disease. Marvin Brubaker had been a national weightlifting champion until steroids made him so mean, he was jailed for biting a pit bull.

Having discovered the seductiveness of television, and promising myself it was only a temporary aberration that would cease the moment I stepped out of the hospital, I allowed myself to watch, for the very first time, one of those daytime dramas the English call soap operas. They are very aptly named, you know. Mama would have washed my mouth out with soap, and my eyes too, if she had caught me so much as glancing at such filth. Still, they are entertaining. In the one I watched, the siren (who had apparently been married six times and was currently dating her step-grandson) was having a catfight with her rival (a frisky vixen who had a habit of marrying the siren's rejects). Much to my surprise, I found myself identifying with the frisky vixen, even though I have never been married, and would most certainly never even date someone Susannah had looked at twice.

The siren and the vixen were rolling around on the floor, pulling each other's hair and just generally slapping each other around, when Melvin Stoltzfus and his sidekick, Zelda, walked in.

I zapped off the TV. "How nice to see you," I trilled. If Reverend Gingerich found out about my lapse in judgment, I might be the *ex*-Sunday–school teacher at the Beechy Grove Mennonite Church.

Thankfully, Melvin and Zelda were so engrossed in their conversation that for a few seconds they didn't even notice me. "She has a right to know," Zelda was saying. "Even a chicken knows it's going to be killed when you tie it up by its feet."

"But she isn't a chicken," countered Melvin. "And let's leave her feet out of this. Even if she washed them, she'd still have to go."

I glanced surreptitiously under the covers. Nurse Dudley hadn't said anything about my using the shower, although having been pulled from a cesspit the day before, I suppose it did make sense.

"But she's your mother," said Zelda emphatically.

I breathed a deep sigh of relief. Melvin Stoltzfus had been threatening to send his mother to a nursing home for the past six years. Everyone in Hernia knew about it except the old lady herself. Fortunately everyone in Hernia understood there was nothing to be gained by enlightening Mrs. Stoltzfus. Since Melvin lacked the cartilage to move out of his mother's house in the first place, it followed that he lacked what it took to ship her off to the Bedford County Home for the Mennonite Aged. If Zelda wasn't so enamored of the man, she would have seen that he was a spineless arthropod.

"Yoder," said Melvin warmly when he came to his senses and realized where he was and that I was looking at him.

"That's my name, Melvin. Don't wear it out."

Melvin strained to focus both eyes on me. "Proud of playing the heroine, are we?"

I considered fixing Melvin up with Nurse Dudley, but then dropped the idea like a hot potato. On the off chance that the two of them hit it off and produced children, my name would live on in the infamous annals of history along with Hitler, Stalin, and Idi Amin. "Melvin dear," I said sweetly, "whatever do you mean?"

Melvin's mandibles mashed futilely a couple of times before he produced a word. "Next time, leave the detective work up to professionals, Yoder. Apparently the killer almost roasted you alive."

"Ah, so you've removed me from your short little list of suspects?"

Melvin looked at Zelda and me simultaneously. "I never officially accused you, Yoder. And you must admit that I had a good enough reason anyway."

"I'll admit to no such thing. Now, what is it you want with me, Melvin?"

"Magdalena, did you hear or see anything suspicious last night before the fire?" asked Zelda quickly.

"Was Jacob Amman Swiss?" I asked. That is the Hernia equivalent of asking if the Pope is Catholic.

"Just give me the details," urged Zelda, who had one eye on Melvin, who had at least one eye on me.

I told Zelda everything, which wasn't much. An outhouse door that refused to stay closed wasn't much of a clue. And gasoline and matches could be purchased by anyone in Hernia. "But, of course, there might be prints on the pitchfork," I concluded.

Zelda and Melvin exchanged glances, and I knew it was still up to me to find out who had forked Don and tried to barbecue me to cover their tracks.

Thirty-three

IT WASN'T Nurse Dudley who brought in my supper tray, but Martha Sims.

"Hello, Magdalena dear," she bubbled. "The nurse had her hands full with a cranky patient two doors down, so I volunteered to lend her a hand. Guess which hand?"

I simply stared at her. What is there to say when a grown woman acts like a fool to try and cheer you up? Some people shout at foreigners to make themselves understood, and others act like idiots in a hospital for much the same reason.

"Ooh, looky, what have we here?" said Martha unabashedly. She'd lifted the lid off my entree and was sniffing at it like a hound dog on a fresh scent.

I simply can't abide people sniffing my food. Great-Uncle Harry used to sniff everything at Thanksgiving dinner, and he once sat through an entire meal with whipped cranberry chiffon clinging to his nose hairs because no one had the nerve to say anything. Even though Martha's schnoz was not as hirsute as Great-Uncle Harry's, I felt compelled to speak up.

"You breathe on it, you eat it," I informed her politely.

Martha immediately decided that being nosy wasn't worth lima beans and chipped beef in white sauce. "So, how are you feeling, Magdalena?"

"Like a million bucks after seven-digit inflation has set in. Why?" I hardly considered Martha a friend. To be honest, I wouldn't have visited her in a hospital.

"Well, you look good," said Martha generously, "considering all you've been through."

I would have smiled my appreciation, but Mama always said it was rude to show your food.

"Would you like me to pour your chocolate milk for you, Magdalena?"

I shook my head no.

"It's no trouble at all," said Martha breezily. She reached for the carton, but I snatched it away just in time. I didn't want anyone else's thumb poking into the cardboard spout of my carton.

"Hey, this crummy thing's already been opened," I said. Truly, it disgusted me. And as for those people who take swigs out of bottles and cartons and then put them back in the fridge, they should have their lips sewn together and cauterized.

Martha smiled proudly. "Oh, that was me. I shook it and opened it for you before I brought it in. I know how it is. When one feels bad, one appreciates having the little extras done for one."

"Done for one?" I said perhaps a bit caustically, but then quickly changed my tune. Martha was a far cry from Mother Teresa, but she was making an effort to accommodate, which counted for something. "Well, in that case, would you mind terribly feeding me? I seem to be having trouble lifting this fork.''

Martha beamed her appreciation at being allowed to serve. What a shining example she was of Christian charity. Surely this was a woman from whom I could learn a lesson or two. Without so much as a wince, she picked up my fork and shoveled some chipped beef onto it. "Are you sure you don't want me to pour your milk?''

My mouth was already open like a baby bird waiting to be fed, but I quickly rearranged it for speech. "Positive. What you can do, though, is hop out there into the hall and see if you can chase down the dinner cart. They might have some extra milks you can snag.''

Martha put the laden fork down, which in some courts might be construed as cruel and unusual punishment. "I'm afraid it's too late for that, Magdalena. This was the last of the chocolates.''

"White will do, then," I said. "I'm not prejudiced.''

"I didn't see any more of those either," said Martha smoothly. "Tell you what, I'd be happy to fetch you a glass of water.''

"Water is for livestock," I said stupidly. I drink water all the time, but Martha wasn't playing straight with me, and I aimed to find out why. Had she done the unforgivable and sneaked a sip from my carton?

"Oh, don't be so fussy, Magdalena," said Martha as if reading my mind. "I simply opened your milk for you. I didn't poison it.''

"Ha-ha," I said obligingly. "Actually, I'm not that thirsty after all. Why don't you drink the milk while I eat my supper? If these lima beans get any colder, we can use them to seed clouds.''

Martha seemed agitated by my remark. Perhaps she was fond of cold lima beans. "But you must drink your milk,

Magdalena. It has calcium in it. A woman in your condition needs her calcium.''

I almost choked on an ice cold bean. I pushed the lethal legumes aside. "Martha dear, I am *not* pregnant, contrary to any rumors that might be circulating around Hernia at the moment.''

"Oh, I believe you,'' Martha hastened to assure me. "Besides, I refuse to listen to those nasty rumors. What I meant was that your body needs extra calcium now because of your fall into the pit. You know, your bones were all jarred up. That sort of thing.''

It was becoming clear just how much of a basket case Martha really was. "My bones are not all jarred up,'' I explained patiently. "I didn't fall into the pit, Martha, I climbed down into it.''

Martha looked strangely disappointed. "Well, anyway, women our age should drink as much milk as they can, while they can. Osteoporosis is just around the corner.''

That did it. Mama may have gotten away with making me drink my milk, but Martha Sims was not my mama. Like the defiant little girl I wish I'd been, I picked up the open carton and started to dribble it over my lima beans.

You would have thought I'd threatened Martha's very life. The next thing I knew, she reached into her purse and whipped out a gun. A tiny gun, smaller than most toy pistols, granted, but a real gun nonetheless. "Drink it!'' she ordered.

Mama had never needed to go that far. "Okay, okay,'' I said. "I'll drink the stuff. But only if you join me. You can even have first sip.'' I may be slow, but something was definitely rotten in Denmark, and at the moment Martha looked Danish to me.

"Drink it now!''

I slowly raised the carton to my lips. But before partaking of the much-discussed liquid, I stalled one last time.

"Have you ever considered taking up a hobby, Martha? I hear ceramics is fun. Or how about volunteer work?" God forbid she should volunteer as a candy-striper.

Martha was not amused. "Drink!"

I pretended to drink, just as I had with Mama. Of course, sooner or later Mama always caught on, as would Martha. Sipping and swallowing is easy to fake, but an empty milk carton is not. Still, I was at least postponing the inevitable.

"It's your fault, Magdalena." Martha sounded close to tears.

I pretended to swallow a gulp, and even wiped my mouth on my sleeve. "How is that?"

"If it weren't for you, the movie company wouldn't have come to town. That's where it all started."

I tried to look sympathetic. "They are a horrible bunch, aren't they?"

Martha shook her head, which made the diminutive pistol shake even more. "You still don't understand, do you? My whole life I wanted to be somebody."

"You *are* somebody, dear. You are a very special person." Prudently, I omitted the word "loon" from my sentence.

Martha wanted more from me. "No, no, you don't understand. I didn't want to be just *anybody*. I wanted to be an actress, like my grandmother."

"*The* Cassandra Hicks?" Thank the good Lord for an ironclad memory.

"Exactly. But I couldn't, you see. Not after I married Orlando. And especially not after we moved to Hernia. Ministers' wives in Hernia do not pursue acting careers."

"But you are a Presbyterian," I pointed out. I was no expert on Presbyterians, but I did know they were permitted to do gobs of things we Mennonites hadn't even heard of.

"But I'm still a minister's wife!" Martha practically shrieked. "I have to set an example."

I mimed another sip. "You're a snappy dresser," I said quite honestly. "Your shoes and purse always match beautifully."

Martha was not appeased. "That isn't the point, you idiot. The point is that I had managed to put aside my dreams, hard as it was, and then you had to go and open Pandora's box by inviting that movie company to town."

If loose lips sink ships, then mine could sink a navy. "I didn't invite them. They came on their own. I simply gave them permission to film at the PennDutch."

"And they made *you* the star!" There was genuine pain in her voice, and surprisingly, I could understand it. In eighth grade Mrs. Oberlin ran a writing contest, with first prize being a trip to Pittsburgh to meet a real live, professional writer. I had wanted to win that contest more than anything in my life, before or since. And I had written a good story, I knew it. It may even have been a great story. But it was Billy Pascoe who won first place with a story he wrote about baseball. Baseball! And instead of taking him to meet the writer, Miss Oberlin took him to a Pirates game! That was my first real taste of just how unfair life can be.

"I understand," I said.

"Understand!" Martha shrieked. "You understand? How can you understand? I had a part at first, you know. It wasn't much of a part, but it was a part. And it wasn't that bad a part. I mean, I could have done it, and Orlando could have kept his job. But then that Don Manley, that slimy, evil snake from hell, ruined it all for me."

"He was an awful man," I agreed tactfully.

"He was the devil incarnate! You won't believe what he asked me to do in that movie."

"I believe it," I said quickly. If it was too much for a Presbyterian to take, I surely didn't want to hear it.

"He deserved to die, Magdalena. God wanted him to die. So it wasn't my fault, you know."

"We all have to die sometime," I offered.

"But why does mankind sometimes interfere with what God ordains?" The arm holding the gun began to sag encouragingly.

"Beats me."

The arm snapped back into position. "But it was you, Magdalena, who interfered."

"Me?"

"It was you who snooped and probed, and then eventually found the instrument of divine justice."

"Me?" I think I said again, although that might have been just an echo. Stress was beginning to alter reality, even for me.

"Don't play dumb, Magdalena. You came out to my house with all your questions. You knew what had happened, but you tried to play games with me."

"I knew nothing," I said honestly.

"Of course it didn't take a genius to figure it out, since Susannah and that Darla woman share my build. But dressing up like them that morning was pretty clever, if I may say so myself."

"You certainly may," I said encouragingly.

Martha smiled, revealing white, even teeth. She might have made a pretty actress at that. "I took advantage of the remnant sale at Fabric World in Bedford. And I didn't even have to sew a stitch, not with the way those two dress. Like mummies coming unraveled."

"Absolutely disgraceful," I agreed.

"I had Mose fooled, I can tell you that."

"Mose maybe, but not Matilda," I said foolishly.

"What?"

"Nothing, dear. You were telling me about your clever masquerade."

"Yes, I was. Tell me, Magdalena, how did you figure out I was hiding in your henhouse that day?"

It was definitely time for me to change the bulb in my brain. So it had been Martha's grocery list I'd found! "Sam's parsley is the pits," I informed her. "If you want fresh parsley, we have oodles out by the back door."

Martha didn't seem grateful for my offer. "You have something of the devil in you too, don't you, Magdalena? That lunch I made for you should have made you very sick. Sick enough to give up acting, at any rate, and give me the break I deserve."

I swallowed reflexively. Fortunately my mouth was empty. "Your lunch was delicious, Martha."

"So you kept your acting job, Magdalena, but you weren't content with that. Oh, no, you had to go looking for the pitchfork. What were you trying to do, Magdalena, destroy me altogether?"

I shook my head. I wasn't about to say anything further, on the grounds it would incriminate me.

"I certainly threw Melvin off by hiding the second pitchfork in the woods, Magdalena. That should have thrown you off too."

Martha was definitely off. So far off that she must have left the deep end behind years ago. Perhaps it was a case of the bends that was affecting her brain. Wisely, I said nothing.

My silence did nothing to placate her. "But now it is my turn to destroy you, Magdalena. Say good-bye, Magdalena. Then say hello to the devil and Don Manley. Or is it the same thing?" She laughed maniacally.

I tried to act calm, like that time the year before when a man named Billy Dee held a knife to my throat. "You don't want to kill me, Martha. You don't want to kill me

because you'll never get away with it. Someone will hear
the gun, and even if they don't, Nurse Dudley knew you
were coming in here. Getting shot with a gun in a hospital is not a natural way to die. They'll put two and two
together, Martha."

Martha had the nerve to smile. "You always did talk too
much, Magdalena. But it's time to stop talking now.
Which side of the head do you prefer?"

"What?"

"Or would you rather it was between the eyes?"

"You're crazy!" I know that was a stupid thing to say,
but I couldn't help myself.

"You can comb your hair first if you like, but make it
snappy. Orlando expects his dinner on the table at six."

Martha was acting like the photographer at Kmart, only
it wasn't photos she was planning to shoot. It was all so
bizarre that it was laughable. I mean, literally. I laughed.
If one is going to die, one may as well die laughing.

"So what's so funny in here?" The door to my room
had swung open and Heather was standing in the doorway in her gown and robe. I'd quite forgotten that she
had had a baby.

"Shut it!" hissed Martha. Presumably she meant the
door.

But Martha's back was to Heather, and Heather could
neither hear her nor see the tiny gun. She advanced nonchalantly toward us. "You guys hear the one about the
priest, the rabbi, and the minister who get stuck together
in an elevator for three days?"

"Do tell," I said.

Martha, as crazy as she was, had no choice but to slip
the pistol back into her purse. She even cooperated by
turning halfway around, so she could keep an eye on
Heather as well.

"Well, the three of them get stuck, you see," said Heather happily, "without any food or water, and—"

As Heather told the joke, I slipped my hand over the side of the bed and pressed the call button. Given Nurse Dudley's temperament, help would be forthcoming in an hour or two. Just to be on the safe side, I grabbed the pitcher of water beside my bed and swung it upside Martha's head. It connected, and Martha, who hadn't even had a chance to comb her hair first, fell backward into my supper tray, spilling lima beans all over the bed and floor. Regrettably, I never did hear the punch line to Heather's joke.

Thirty-four

"ALL'S WELL that ends well," said Doc Shafer, glaring at Aaron Miller.

"Some things are far from over," said Aaron, winking at me.

Doc drew himself up to his full height, which, at age eighty-three, was undoubtedly a good six inches shorter than it once was. "Some things are best left to the experts, son."

Aaron stretched, just enough to flatten his tummy and extend his chest an inch or two. "A wise man knows when it's time to retire, my pop always says."

"Care for a celery stick stuffed with cream cheese?" I shoved the plate under both their noses, but I may as well have been invisible at that point. Strangely, the object of their desire was no longer central to their argument.

"Retire?" bellowed Doc. "I could whip your butt any day!"

"Care to step outside, old man?" Aaron was grinning, and I'm sure he didn't mean it. Still, it was rude of him to egg Doc on that way.

"Think I'm bluffing, do you?" Doc had begun to jump around like a barefoot kid on a hot pavement, and was swinging his arms in tight little circles.

"Say, what's going on here anyway?" demanded Susannah. She had just come on the scene and the yards of fabric she trailed had yet to settle into swirls.

"I think these two are fighting over me," I said in all humility.

"Dream on, Sis," laughed Susannah.

" 'Fraid she's right," panted Doc.

Turning her back on old Doc, Susannah started batting her false eyelashes at Aaron Miller. "Now, what's really going on?"

Aaron didn't even look at her.

"Care to walk me over to the food table?" my sister persisted shamelessly.

Aaron continued to ignore her, but apparently she had given him an idea. "Magdalena, can I bring you a plate?"

"Not so fast, you snot-nosed sidewinder," snarled Doc. "The lady is with me."

"Maybe she is, and maybe she isn't. How about it, Magdalena, who is your date for the evening?" The twinkling blue eyes challenged me to choose him.

I could feel myself blushing. This was supposed to be a cast and crew party for Reels and Runs Productions, not a stag fight. How Doc and Aaron managed to wrangle invitations was beyond me. But probably not beyond Freni. That woman is controlling enough to be a Democrat, but at the same time as devious as any Republican you could hope to meet. It was now September, but still very hot. Perhaps it was all the heat collecting under her bonnet, but that brain of hers had cooked up what looked to me like a matchmaking scheme. The trouble was, I just wasn't in the mood to be matched.

I hate to say it, but it was a relief when Steven sidled over and cheekily slipped an arm around my shoulders. "You're quite a hero, Yoder."

"Bug off, Bugsy," I said. It was nice, though, to know that my efforts in apprehending Don Manley's killer were appreciated.

"Art called from L.A. this morning. He's started the editing, and he says it looks great already. He thinks it stands a chance of being nominated for an Academy Award."

"For best supporting actress?" I asked sincerely.

Steven smiled, but deflected. "And Art says he's finally come up with a title."

"Yes?"

"*The Sins of Freni Hostetler.* What do you think of that?"

"I think it's a good thing Art's in California, and that it's against Freni's principles to fly."

Steven stifled a yawn. "Oh, and Art said to tell you he'd like you to read for a part in his next film."

"Is Mel Gibson going to be in that one?" I'd seen a commercial for one following a *Green Acres* episode the night before. I am ashamed to say this, but Mel Gibson is capable of making me think impure thoughts.

"Sorry, no. But Tom Cruise is," soothed Steven.

"Forget it, then."

"Why can't I read for a part," whined Susannah.

Steven squeezed me good-bye before slipping his arm around Susannah's shoulders and squiring her off to talk business.

Left alone with the two battling titans, I glanced wildly about for an excuse to flee, and found one in the half-empty cut glass punch bowl across the room. "See you later, fellows, I've got work to do," I said as I skedaddled. No telling if they heard me or not.

In front of the punch table I ran into the Reverend Orlando Sims. I mean literally.

"I'm very sorry, Miss Yoder," he said.

"No problemo," I said magnanimously. "An ice pack, three aspirin, and a good night's sleep, and this goose egg on my forehead will only look like a hen's egg."

"Sorry about that too. But that's not what I meant."

"What did you mean, Reverend Sims, and what are you doing here? This is supposed to be a party for the cast and crew of *The Sins of Freni Hostetler.* You were neither cast nor crew, Reverend Sims."

"Yes, I know. But I'm not here for the party. I came to tell you how sorry I am about the things Martha did, and tried to do."

Only fools and masochists hang on to grudges, Mama used to say. Since I was only one, but not both, I decided to give forgiveness a shot. "No sweat," I said, mimicking Susannah's slang. "You want to chill out here for a while?"

Reverend Sims looked vastly relieved. "Thanks, but no thanks. I've got to get home and finish up my sermon for tomorrow morning. It's all about forgiving. I'd like to use you as a shining example, if you don't mind?"

"Use away." Mama, did you hear that? That should cancel out a couple of your spins, shouldn't it?

"Maybe you'd like to stop by our church tomorrow and hear the sermon yourself. Who knows, you might even like it so much that you'll consider switching denominations."

The nerve of some people! Even if he was joking, it was in unforgivably bad taste. Especially with Susannah present as a reminder. The man deserved to be defrocked and deflocked. "That will be $26.95," I said with admirable restraint."

Reverend Sims blinked his noncomprehension. "What for?"

"For a new pitchfork, that's what."

I cleaned up after the party by myself. One of Mama's rules, which I will always buy into, is that one should never go to bed or take a trip when one's house is messy. Although Mama's primary concern was that unexpected company (i.e. burglars) should be spared having to view our untidiness, I think there really is an underpinning of wisdom to this dictum. Dirty dishes left overnight, or longer, are all that much harder to clean. And isn't it so much nicer to come home from a journey and not face a mountain of work? Besides which, it is much easier to tell if you've been robbed when your house was in order to begin with.

It was almost two A.M. when I staggered outside to catch a few breaths of night air before going to bed. In my right hand I carried half a peanut butter apple cake, and in my left hand a quart of milk. I am a firm believer in never going to bed hungry. To do so only insures that one will be ravenous the next morning and start the day off by overeating. Even wild animals know that, which is why they always nap after eating. And how many fat wild animals do you know?

Just as I was bringing the first loaded forkful to my mouth, I heard a sound on the porch behind me. Honestly, I wasn't frightened. I immediately thought of raccoons. Hernia and environs is a very safe place to live as long as you keep your mouth shut and mind your own business. So what did I have to worry about?

"Scared you, didn't I?"

I whirled to face the speaker, taking care not to spill my

milk or drop the cake from my fork. Even in the shadows I could see Aaron's blue eyes twinkling. "What are you, a spy?"

He laughed. "Nope. Spies sneak around. I'm not sneaking anywhere. As a matter of fact, I haven't even left yet."

"The last guest left over an hour ago," I reminded him. "And, as I recall, you left before that."

"Nope. I got as far as this porch and decided it was as far as I was going to go until I had a chance to speak to you."

"Then why didn't you knock or ring the bell? I've been up the whole time—putting things away and washing dishes."

"And singing."

My face stung, just as surely as if I'd been slapped. Singing is an intensely personal activity for me. Even God has agreed not to listen. "Aaron Miller, you are the rudest man I've ever met," I said, perhaps raising my voice just a little. I would have thrown the milk at him, but it was all I had, and it went so well with the cake.

Aaron had the audacity to laugh again.

"Just go home!" I ordered.

"Don't you even want to know what it is I wanted to talk to you about?"

"Absolutely not. I'm not in the least bit curious." Okay, so it was a white lie. But it was two in the morning, and my usual bedtime is ten.

Aaron approached until he was scarcely an arm's length away. "Well, I'll tell you anyway, Magdalena. I wanted to ask you out on a date."

When your mouth hangs open at night, it is mosquitoes you catch, not flies. "A date?"

"Yeah, a real date. Like in high school. Well, like dates were back when we were in high school, anyway."

I set the cake and milk carefully down on the porch railing. When your hands are empty, the shaking is less noticeable. "Well, it is an interesting idea, Aaron. But why didn't you ask me out when we were in high school?"

For just a second or two the blue eyes stopped twinkling. "Because I was a fool, I guess."

"You got that right."

The blue eyes started to dance again. "So, now that we at least agree on something, what do you say about accepting my invitation?"

I pretended to think about it. After what I hoped seemed like an interminable length of time, I gave him my answer. Then I generously shared my milk and cake. Again we both agreed on something. The peanut butter apple cake was the best we'd ever eaten.

Oh, for the record, the answer was yes.

Thirty-five

MY OWN VERSION
OF PEANUT BUTTER APPLE CAKE

Makes 8 servings

$^1/_4$ cup softened butter
1 cup brown sugar
$^3/_4$ cup chunky peanut butter
1 egg
1 cup chunk style applesauce
$1^1/_2$ cups sifted flour
1 teaspoon baking powder
1 teaspoon salt
1 teaspoon cinnamon
$^1/_2$ teaspoon nutmeg
$^1/_4$ teaspoon ground cloves

CREAM TOGETHER the butter, sugar, and peanut butter. Beat in the egg. Stir in the applesauce. Sift the remaining dry ingredients together and slowly stir them into the batter. Mix well. Liberally grease and flour an eight-inch-square pan. Pour the batter into the pan and bake at 350 degrees until done (about 40 to 45 minutes). The cake is done when a toothpick inserted in the center comes out clean. Cool before attempting to remove from the pan.

Even better when eaten with someone you love.